TURTLE BEACH

BLANCHE D'ALPUGET

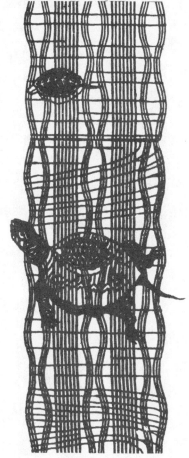

SIMON AND SCHUSTER
NEW YORK

Published by Simon and Schuster
A Division of Simon & Schuster, Inc.
Simon & Schuster Building
Rockefeller Center
1230 Avenue of the Americas
New York, New York 10020
SIMON AND SCHUSTER and colophon
are registered trademarks of Simon & Schuster, Inc.
Manufactured in the United States of America

10 9 8 7 6 5 4 3 2

Library of Congress Cataloging in Publication Data

D'Alpuget, Blanche, date.
    Turtle beach.

    I. Title.
PR9619.3.D24T8   1983   823   83-9907
ISBN 0-671-49241-1

For
Mike Epstein,
with love

AUTHOR'S NOTE

I wish to express my heartfelt thanks to the Literature Board of the Australia Council. The Board's grant of a one-year Senior Fellowship enabled me to research and write this book.

Again, my thanks to Tess.

B. d'A.
September 1980

PART ONE

MALAYSIA

1

At midnight the sky had a sunrise glow that came not from the east but from the centre, near Chinatown, as people still called it. 'Chinatown', in a city of Chinese. The colonial habits of expression, colonial assumptions, had resisted change.

In the days of the Raj – a time so different that it seemed unreal now, and ridiculous – an Englishman had noted that a Malay would kill a Chinaman with as little conscience as he would kill a tiger that trespassed on his village. For were not all Chinese cunning trespassers in this country, and predators on the Malays? The red-orange midnight was no trick of atmospherics but a new illustration of the old grudge. The Malays had fired Batu Road. They were heading now for Chinatown.

The whole city had been turned into a hunting park.

Men with white headbands, white for death, and flat-bladed parangs or sharpened bamboos had gathered in swarms, as many as five hundred at a time, buzzing like enraged bees. They cried 'Kill the Pigs!' and did it in the name of Allah, roaming the streets murdering the eaters of pig flesh. The Chinese – who had brought this calamity upon themselves, people said, by supporting radical-left candidates in the elections, by marching in demonstrations, by throwing pork at Malay crowds – were retaliating with hand guns and meat cleavers. And they also lit fires, in the Malay kampongs.

After four days the riots were over. The city smelt bad from the burnt-out buildings and the bus and car tyres that smouldered in the streets. People wept for their destroyed property and their dead relations and because they hàd awoken from a protective dream. Their leaders had insisted that modern Malaysia was unique, that its races could co-exist in harmony. Their leaders had lied.

Judith Wilkes had been married five days when her editor tracked her down in Singapore and told her to fly to Kuala Lumpur to cover the riots.

'I don't suppose it's even occurred to you that I'm on my honeymoon,' she had shouted over the crackling line.

'I'm sorry about that, dear,' had been the answer. 'It's a good story and you're the nearest to it. You're lucky to be asked.' At twenty-three, she was.

Richard, her husband, had butted in then, and when he had understood what was going on, had urged, 'Take it, take it.'

Afterwards he had said, 'You can't ignore the chance of a lifetime. This could make you.' Richard had strong notions about the importance of work and success.

By the end of that week Judith was a celebrity. Breathless with fright and excitement, she had been interviewed on television and for a while became a night-time darling in suburban living rooms. Her jerky prose filled the front pages of her newspaper under the by-line Judith O'Donahue, because the sub-editors forgot she was married now to the lawyer-boyfriend from the Attorney-General's Department and had changed her name. Her stories were syndicated and widely published.

She returned, bruised and enervated, to Singapore and found Richard indulgent with pride. 'My brilliant wife,' he said.

He was five years older than she; Judith felt protected

4

by his age, his size, his suntanned arms with their black floss of hairs, and his tone of wry patronage. Still, she was now depressed and easily unnerved; the mayhem in Kuala Lumpur was to blame, Richard said.

By the time they reached London, Richard, by a process neither understood, had taken over her anecdotes. He could hold a pub audience – 'A mob of about a hundred Malays set fire to a car. When the Chinese inside it leapt out they flung him back into the flames, yelling "roast pork"' – while Judith nodded, satisfied by the impressed glances people snatched from Richard to bestow, fleetingly, on her.

Home again, they were known at first as a handsome couple and, later, as a perfect couple. They were joined in common speech as Judith-and-Richard and in people's minds they grew into a double-headed creature.

But Judith's life had been irrevocably pulled off its course during one night in Kuala Lumpur. She had seen a youth break from the swarm and hack down a pedestrian with a two-handed swing of his sword, a boy who would melt back into his kampong and who would go for the rest of his days unaccused and unpunished for that moment of gory ballet. Like him, she felt, she would have to live with a crime she herself had committed in Kuala Lumpur, during what people later called The Incident of 13 May 1969.

PART TWO

AUSTRALIA

2

When colleagues said that Hobday, that is, Sir Adrian Hobday, Australian Ambassador and Plenipotentiary (Taipei,
Paris, twice to Saigon), had gone mad, they blamed the Vietnam war. Or rather, the indignities he had suffered because
of his role as architect of the Australian involvement in it.
He had been harassed over the telephone and his border
collie had been poisoned. In 1971 at Sydney airport a
woman had thrown blood, aiming at the visiting US and
Vietnamese officials. Hobday, his hand still clasping the
American general's, had stepped back suddenly, turned . . .
'He's been shot!' people shouted, seeing it happen on television. A great red-black stain appeared, from Hobday's
neck to his belly.

He had touched himself with trepidation, then shrugged.

Five years later he was knighted in the Birthday Honours,
for his handling of the evacuation of Australian nationals
from Saigon in April 75. Some said it was this experience
of defeat and flight that was to blame for his outbreak, or
breakdown, whatever you chose to call it.

Though when it became clear after a few months that
Sir Adrian was not - not mad, exactly, but dangerously
wrong-headed - colleagues forgot their earlier theory and
looked for other reasons for his behaviour. There he was,
senior diplomat, senior public servant who for thirty-odd
years had carried out government policy without quibble,

who listed his recreations in *Who's Who* as reading and gardening. And now, at fifty-five, he was creating a scandal.

'I guarantee it's nothing more than a bad case of male menopause,' Richard Wilkes remarked to Judith when she rang him to say she had been delayed by a Press conference – could he do something about dinner? – and, to take his mind off her request, passed on the gossip about Sir Adrian.

Still, the Hobday Affair was kept quiet, so much so that the Governor-General did not find out for several months: the vice-regal lists reported that Sir Adrian and Lady Hobday had been invited to luncheons and dinners at Yarralumla. And for form's sake Hilary – Lady Hobday – had gone with him to all the functions. 'Looking haggard,' as people later recalled. Like Hobday she was tall and handsome. She had borne him four tall, not-so-handsome children, but they were all married and had moved away from Canberra and so were spared the worst of it – the thing that happened afterwards, to Hilary.

By then everyone knew about Adrian's folly.

'Adrian Hobday's finally done himself in,' Richard announced one mid-winter morning. He lowered the newspaper leisurely. Across the breakfast table Judith was still wearing her 'dressing gown', a duffle coat which years ago had been navy blue. She had not yet combed her hair, Richard noted.

'Listen to this,' he said. 'The headline is "Secret Wedding",' and he read aloud the item, just one paragraph, about Sir Adrian's marriage the day before.

In a more urbane tone – 'Richard's Young-Labor-Minister-To-Be voice', Judith called it to herself – he added, 'Of course, the Department will screw the old sod for this, for doing what they'd all like to do. Run off with an Asian dolly! He won't be ambassador to Washington now. They'll shove him out to some deadly hole.'

10

Richard was near enough to the mark to be smug when, a few weeks later, Hobday was appointed High Commissioner to Malaysia. At dinner parties Richard went around asking, 'How do you think our new High Commissioner will make out with the Malaysian nobility, with a former Saigon bar-girl as his consort? Hmm?'

In some quarters bets were laid on the possibility of scandal hounding Sir Adrian out of Kuala Lumpur and on to some even more obscure posting. But within days of his arrival in Kuala Lumpur Hobday had an unexpected piece of good luck.

International events had changed. China, having accused Vietnam of persecuting residents of Chinese origin, sealed her border to refugees from Vietnam. There were rumours of war between Vietnam and China, and the Chinese in Vietnam panicked. Tens of thousands of them began fleeing in small boats. Those from the south sailed across the Gulf of Thailand and two or three days later landed on the beaches of Malaysia. Malaysia was, abruptly, an interesting country for a diplomat, a country with a problem.

The problem enlarged as the year wore on.

'The old fox,' wiseacres said, recalling now that Hobday had negotiated stubbornly, inexplicably, for Kuala Lumpur when the Department had been prepared to be magnanimous and had offered him first Geneva, then The Hague. 'I want somewhere close to home,' he'd said wistfully, somehow convincing the Secretary of the Department of Foreign Affairs that Malaysia was a retirement village and thus appropriate for a weary, discarded man.

And then in January 1979, when the foreign news sections of the Australian papers were beginning to refer to a 'refugee crisis' in South-East Asia and Hobday was once again one of the country's most important envoys, sending cables every few days and even advising the Prime Minister direct, Hilary Hobday burnt herself to death.

11

It had been a frighteningly hot summer in Canberra, arriving late, in the New Year. Then for days there had been a heatwave worse than any in recent memory. The summer grasses had been bleached to straw, the purple mountains that ring the city had seemed to move closer in the harsh light; the inland sky had been smudged brown with the smoke of bushfires, some of them so near to town that householders could hear trees exploding and found terrified, hungry wallabies and snakes in their gardens.

The only fire in the suburbs, however, had been the one that destroyed the Hobday family home in Red Hill. And it had started at night. Neighbours had been able to stop it spreading but there had never been any hope of saving Hilary: her remains were not dug out of the ruins of the garage until the next morning. She had been smoking and drinking heavily since the divorce, friends now admitted. On the day of the fire she had been seen standing for a long time at the window that overlooked the street, staring into space.

Two days after the fire the heatwave ended with a cold change and rain sweeping up from the south.

3

'Sir Adrian flew in this morning for the funeral. I think I'll go,' Judith told Richard, telephoning him at the Attorney-General's Department. 'I want to have another look at him before I leave for Kuala Lumpur next month.'

Richard smiled into the handpiece. 'Lady journalist crashes distinguished gathering of mourners to interview senior envoy.'

'Come off it,' she broke in. 'There'll be a lot of Foreign Affairs people there. I might pick something up about how well Hobday's handling the refugee problem.'

Richard sighed, indulgent. 'I am merely drafting legislation for . . . Oh, what does my work matter? I suppose you want me to get dinner?'

'Yes,' Judith said. 'Thanks, darling. There's that chicken I bought on Monday. We should eat it tonight.'

She rang her editor in Sydney, told him she wanted to cover Lady Hobday's funeral that afternoon and asked, 'Is there any special angle you want, Bill?'

Bill said, 'Why ask me? You know my views on this Malaysia caper of yours, dear. You're a Canberra correspondent, not a bloody refugee-chaser.'

She sat biting her lip when she rang off.

At three o'clock as she was leaving her office for the funeral a colleague joined her in the corridor and trudged beside Judith down from the cubby-hole maze of the Press gallery

13

to the tarmac in front of Parliament House. She panted and squinted up at Judith through the fumes of a cigarette in the corner of her mouth.

'Well, Jude, I hope Hobday's satisfied, the self-indulgent swine,' she said. 'He doesn't even have to pay Hilary's maintenance now. The great survivor, eh?' She screwed up her shrewd old eyes as if the taste and smell of cigarettes – she was never without one stuck in her face – had abruptly become disgusting. 'Like you and me, eh girlie? *We're* survivors.'

Judith shrugged.

'No. I'm serious,' the woman persisted. 'You've got it made. You pull off this Malaysian job and you can name your own terms. Don't let Bill make you nervous.'

'I guess so,' Judith replied, and jerked away: she had been elbowed in the ribs.

'You guess so! You and that . . . ' there was a hesitation, 'that good-looking husband of yours, you've got the killer instinct, you two kids.'

Judith laughed and gave her a shove.

There was a light drizzle that turned the dust and splattered insect bodies into thin yellow mud on her car windows as Judith drove to St Luke's. She grimaced at the tiny creatures being emulsified by the windscreen wipers as she mulled over Hilary's death. Everyone knew that there was insufficient evidence for suicide and that the coroner would call it an accident.

By the time she reached the church the rain had stopped. She sat in her car for a few minutes, observing the mourners. They stood straight in their dark clothing with set, disapproving faces. Even the lavishness of the wreaths laid out on the lawn seemed more a protest than a mark of sympathy.

Judith joined the murmuring crowd and with nothing better to do – it was not yet the moment for buttonholing

14

anyone – counted the wreaths and jotted the number in her notebook.

A young man in a well-cut suit saw her do it. He looked her over – shaggy yellow hair, giant sunglasses, heels so high that she looked too tall – and muttered 'Press' to his woman companion. The brim of the woman's beautiful black straw hat, symmetrical as a flower, rose as she lifted her chin to stare, then she turned and passed into the church. Judith glared at her back.

A few moments later when she glanced down at her brown velvet blazer she noticed that she had forgotten to take the ABORTION ON DEMAND button off her lapel. She unpinned it and was still grinning as she walked towards the church porch. Ushers in tail coats had just given out the last of the hymnals.

There were three rows of empty pews at the back of the church. Outside the church was orange brick; inside it was lined with cream-painted gyprock and had metal girders, painted mauve, holding up its ceiling. Judith glanced around, with the sense of sacrilege she always felt in Protestant churches, and caught sight of the empty cross up on the north wall: it was three pieces of jarrah two-by-two. Some other people, perhaps those from Sydney where the Anglican establishments were older and more luxurious, were looking about in a helpless way, as if wondering whether they had come to the right place.

But when Sir Gregory Clark of the Public Service Board, large and bad-tempered, stamped down the aisle looking at his watch, the restless heads grew still. His impatience, it seemed, summarized for the gathering the attitude they should take: this ceremony was a licentious waste of time, as the events that had led up to it were a licentious waste of good reputation. It was to be endured as a tribulation; and a warning.

The organ quavered into something that might be Bach

15

and the vicar moved into view. At the same time Hobday came up the aisle, erect, clear-eyed, suntanned, forbiddingly grand himself in his dark pin-stripe suit and black tie and armband. He looked straight ahead as he walked, apparently unaware of the hostile eyes upon him. His and Hilary's tribe followed: plain daughters and plain sons and a straggle of other near relations. A pace or two back another figure wandered forward; his clothes had the stained, tramp-like look that seems natural to very old men. But the shape of his head and nose were so similar to those of the published photographs of Hilary Hobday that Judith guessed he was her father. There was something else, a numb confusion in the way he gazed around, questioning, that made her think with a sudden, cold ill feeling, that he still knew his daughter as a lively child. She saw his bewilderment: 'How is it possible that she is dead, so young? And I am still alive?' He paused as he came abreast of Judith's pew and looked at her, then shook his head and slowly walked on.

The burping of the organ sank and a light tapping of heels was heard from the church porch. For seconds the congregation waited, staring ahead at the icing of lilies that concealed the shape of the coffin, with its unthinkable contents. Then necks twisted.

Hurrying forward, hatless, with a streak of black hair lashed across her cheek, was an unfamiliar but instantly recognizable young woman – the second Lady Hobday. She was wearing a white summer dress.

The wife of a first assistant secretary, standing in front of Judith, muttered, 'NO! I don't believe it!' Her husband concentrated on his hymn-book. She turned and stared into his ear as if looking through his head at the mourners opposite. 'Murderess,' she said clearly.

An atmosphere of melancholy outrage settled over the pews when the vicar took the pulpit to speak of Hilary: good wife, good mother, gracious hostess, a homemaker in all parts

16

of the world, unstintingly giving her time in her country's interest. The wives of other ambassadors began to cry.

Afterwards Sir Adrian stood at the church door shaking hands with the men and touching the women's cheeks with his lips. Now and then he gave a faint smile. 'The famous Hobday smile,' somebody had once remarked to Judith. 'It's so rare that when it occurs it's like an eclipse, and you feel privileged to have seen it.'

Judith had seen it once, years ago, at a Press conference. Hobday had just returned from defeated South Vietnam and was facing thirty feverish reporters. 'Our policies were correct at the time,' he'd insisted and, when pressed, had added, 'Australia – no more than America – cannot be held responsible for the collapse of the government and armed forces of South Vietnam.' A journalist had shouted from the back of the room, 'But, sir, what do we owe our former allies, the people of South . . .?' Hobday, rising to go, had heard the question but had not answered. He had smiled and was still smiling when he reached the door, where photographers had captured his tender grimace.

The day grew colder as the mourners gathered outside on the lawns, subdued and dishevelled by the blustery wind. Grey cloud battalions manoeuvred over their heads. Judith stood by herself. She had been mistaken in thinking she could join a group as one can at cocktail parties, and pick up an introduction to the star guest. Death had united them; this middle-aged elite had no time for outsiders.

She noticed that the man in the expensive suit and his companion were also standing apart, and moved towards them. His expression had taken on a look of weakly amused contempt – Richard said that Treasury and Foreign Affairs cadets were drilled in that expression in their training year.

'Her name is Minou – that's what the French call to their pussies. Hits the spot, don't you think?' he was saying to Black Hat. His gaze, over Judith's shoulder, was at the living

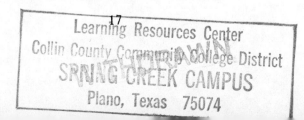

Lady Hobday who was standing some way off. 'She's got good legs – for a Chink,' he added amiably.

Judith moved past them briskly. She was about to step on to the roadway where her VW was queued between the Mercedes and Volvos, when a bony hand restrained her. It emerged from a padded, navy silk jacket that had recently been cried up in *Vogue*.

'Judith!'

'Sancha!'

They took in the effect of seventeen years on each other's faces. Sancha had fared worse than she had, Judith saw. She was intimidatingly well-groomed, but she looked even more tense, more horrified by life, than she had all those years ago standing up on the stage of the school assembly hall and flapping, like a broken-winged crane, speechless. She had burst into tears afterwards, saying, 'I'm too *skinny* to be Cleopatra.'

She had been weeping again today. She sniffed, sawing a finger across her nostrils, and said, 'God, no tissues.'

Judith recovered first. 'What are you doing here? Did you know Hilary Hobday?'

Sancha blinked. Judith's voice! It was as gentle and persuasive as it had been when she'd read her essays and poems to the class while Reverend Mother smiled and nodded at her. But something was different now: the voice didn't fit her expression. There was something brazen about her.

'Not her. *Him*,' Sancha said. 'He's Ralph's boss in Kuala Lumpur. Ralph is – Oh, God, I'm married to a man called Ralph Hamilton. He's head of immigration in KL. The schools there are terrible – no sport – and I've come down to book our eldest into Geelong.' She blinked again, her pale eyes asking for approval.

'We'll starve, of course,' she added.

The complaint struck a chime in Judith's memory – Sancha, eager with sincerity, saying 'You're lucky you don't

18

have a pony. The *grooming*!' Distrustfully, they had allowed her to disarm them of envy, to ingratiate herself. But once, after summer holidays, Sancha had said, 'Europe was ghastly – those Italian churches. Erk,' and Judith, whose big day had been to go to the test cricket with her Dad, had felt a dull bafflement which she had realized later was pain. It echoed faintly in her now.

She said, 'Immigration ought to be an important job up there, these days,' thinking Bull's-eye! The head of immigration would be even more useful than the High Commissioner.

'Yes,' Sancha said. 'The boat people. Ralph's worried to death about them.' Her thin face worked. 'He's had a bit of gut trouble – mixing with them so much in the camps. It's the dirty food. Asians never wash their hands.'

Suddenly her mouth hitched into a smile of well-bred apology. 'But tell me about *you*' and was amazed that she had spent years seeing articles by Judith Wilkes and had not realized.

'When I got married I took Richard's name. Everybody did then,' Judith said. She pulled a face. 'Now it's an established by-line I can't change back to O'Donahue.'

'I see,' Sancha said. There was the silence of people discovering they have violently opposed views.

'Do you enjoy it up there?' Judith enquired. A couple of weeks earlier she'd been briefed by a Foreign Affairs man, a suave fellow, silver as a Persian cat, with greedy cat's eyes. 'Malaysia is a country without a heart,' he'd said. 'It seems like Paradise. The Chinese are allowed to make as much money as they like; the Malays are allowed as many privileges as they like, and the Indians . . .' he had flicked them away.

'It's heavenly having servants,' Sancha said.

'And how's the communal problem in KL these days?'

'Oh, desperate. But the country is so rich now that it's

19

all sort of underneath the surface. You don't really notice it.' Sancha hesitated. 'How did you know about the communal problem?' she asked.

'I covered the '69 riots for my paper.'

Sancha looked – and felt – blank. She could not imagine how Reverend Mother's pet – it really had been the limit, the way Judith won prizes for everything – had got herself mixed up in the bloodshed that people in KL still talked about with horror. She glossed over the awkwardness with another smile. 'So, you'll be coming our way for a few weeks? God, your Richard must be an angel to let you go off, leaving him and the children!'

'He's liberated,' Judith replied lightly and thought, We hunt as a pair, Richard and I. She gave a quick, uncomfortable gasp of laughter.

Sancha stared at her for a moment. 'Ralph's not liberated,' she said. Her note of chagrin was so artless that Judith took off her sunglasses and for the first time looked into Sancha's polite blue eyes with her own bold hazel ones. They had sniffed each other over; they were friends.

I will loathe Ralph Hamilton, Judith thought as she accepted Sancha's invitation to stay with them in KL.

In the driveway Hobday was shepherding his group into black limousines. The incipient stoop of a spine decalcifying with age was just visible now, when he was no longer bracing himself against animosity, but was standing, head bent, among his taller sons. He looked vaguely forlorn. The hearse was moving off. The attitude of the groups watching him had softened, now that it really was the end. For the first time, there was sympathy in the air.

'Everyone seems to have forgiven him,' Judith said. 'I don't know about *her*.'

'Well! Coming to the funeral wasn't exactly in the best of taste, was it?' Sancha said. Then, seeing by Judith's expression that she probably did not agree, added hastily,

'God, look how everyone's ignoring her! Now *she's* the one who can get you into the refugee camps.'

'Let's go over,' Judith said. 'I want to meet her.'

The new Lady Hobday, thin and straight as a sheet of plywood, was standing alone close to the church wall. Someone had lent her a man's raincoat, a fawn Burberry, which drooped almost to the ground. She could have been pathetic but for the sexual vitality that radiated from her. She was gazing, as if unaware of any of them, at the departing limousine that held her husband. Her face had the gravity, the appearance of having lived through many lifetimes, that Asian features can suggest. As Judith and Sancha came towards her she gave no sign that she understood they were rescuing her. Judith thought, I've met my match in this one.

Minou said formally, 'How do you do?' and 'Thank you for coming, Sancha'. She spoke with a light American drawl.

Sancha began explaining that Judith would soon be in Malaysia, to write about the boat people. That would interest Minou, wouldn't it?

Minou said, 'Yes. As you know, I'm president of the International Women's Refugee Relief Committee.' She sounded bored. Her eyes, which were large and rounded, like Caucasian eyes, but padded tightly with Mongoloid fat, dwelt on Sancha's face for a moment. Sancha hitched up her nervous smile and said, 'I really must do more to help.'

Minou shifted her attention to Judith. 'You shouldn't be here and I shouldn't be here. At home in Cholon it would be the right thing for me to come to the funeral.' She paused and looked steadily at Judith. 'His children insisted that I could not go to the grave. They all hate me. Everyone here hates me.'

Sancha made tactful noises.

'*I* don't hate you,' Judith said, so assertively that she startled herself.

21

Hostility like a blade flicked from Minou's eyes. 'You don't even remember meeting me before.' She turned away to look at the dissolving groups of mourners.

'I think that perhaps we . . .' Sancha began.

'Yes, of course. I'll see you soon in KL, Sancha?' Minou held out her long smooth fingers and squeezed Judith's hand lightly. 'And you, too, Brenda Starr?'

Sancha was astonished to see Judith blush.

As they walked away Sancha began to worry about Ralph's reaction when she told him she had invited Judith to stay with them. At school she had been so popular, very bright – and not nearly so blonde as now. A bursary girl. Her father, who had been a policeman invalided out of the force, ran a little shop or newsagency, or something like that. Anyway, they were desperately poor, Sancha recalled. Judith used to say, 'I'm going to have seven children, like Mum.' Yet she'd only had two and – from what she'd said about taking only a couple of months off work when they were born – didn't appear to regard motherhood seriously. She had developed a sharp, career woman's manner of the kind Ralph detested. It made Sancha feel nervous and out-of-touch with things.

As they walked to their cars she noticed that Judith was wearing a skirt with its hem at the back held up with pins. Sancha suppressed a smile. How typical of Judith O'Donahue that was.

They had reached the kerb. 'Jude, let's go to Manuka for coffee?' she said.

Judith gave an involuntary jump. 'Oh, sorry. O.K. Have you got transport?'

Sancha pointed to a red Mini. 'All I could afford to hire.'

Judith was still tingling with shock from Minou's parting words as she stood beside Sancha's car, watching her put on her seatbelt. Sancha's face, as she peered anxiously through the car window, suddenly reminded Judith of a young nun whose disappearance from the staff had been bundled up in ominous silence; Sancha's mane of silver-streaked and lacquered hair aside, she and that wretched young woman had the same wrinkled brow, same round, puzzled, inane eyes, same unbearable vulnerability.

'I've forgotten my way around Canberra. Can I follow you?' Sancha asked.

It was only a three-minute drive to the coffee lounge. Judith, keeping her eye on the rear-vision mirror, was able to push Minou out of her mind. But as soon as they were seated and had ordered their *cappuccinos*, Sancha brought her up again.

'It's hell for us wives in KL, Jude. We've got to seem loyal to Minou. She's our boss, more or less. The most senior wife. A lot of people would never dare call her anything but Lady Hobday. I don't, of course. God, how old is she? Twenty-five? Twenty-six? Anyway, she does *dreadful* things at parties – turns up half-naked for national day receptions. Very smart clothes, of course – she has a Shanghai tailor who costs the earth – and she's got the figure. But after three glasses of champagne! I heard her introduce the head of Agfa, a Baron, as "This is the man whose company manufactured poison gas during the first World War". To the French Ambassador! Everyone nearly died. Whenever a European forgets where they've met before she says, "Never mind, la. All us gooks look the same, don't we?" And if any attractive woman dares talk to Sir Adrian for more than five minutes ... He's got an eye for the girls, these days, I can tell you, though people say he used to be incredibly aloof before Madam came along. Now, if a woman talks to him, Minou just saunters up and stares straight at her. Actually, Jude, I was wondering what you'd heard about her. People say she was a good-time girl in Saigon, and that she's illegitimate. Because she's half-French.'

Judith made a face. 'The gossip here is that she used to

23

be a bar-girl in Cholon, but that's the sort of thing people do say about flash-looking Asian women, isn't it?' She stirred her coffee gloomily, wanting to get closer to Sancha but unable to break through the anger and humiliation that Minou had recreated. It had produced a feeling of isolation that was almost palpable, as if she were inside a perspex box. With an effort she added, 'There are stories that she got out of Saigon the day before it fell. They say she claims she would have been shot, or re-educated or sent off to the labour camps. Probably bullshit. She and Hobday got married about six months ago, in Yass, to avoid being snubbed by the Canberra Establishment. There were a lot of hard feelings.'

She stared into the invalid's swill she had made by stirring the froth into her coffee, unable to think of anything else to say.

Sancha had been brought up to believe that any lapse in conversation was anathema. 'When *did* you meet her before, Jude?' she asked brightly.

Judith gestured vaguely. 'A couple of years ago. In Sydney.'

The restrained hurt of Sancha's nod, hoping for more information, made Judith add, 'At a dance. It was a radical women's thing. We only exchanged a couple of words.' She smiled limply.

After a moment Sancha rallied, but the effort showed. A few threads still held them together, and they beaded them with talk about what had happened to this former school friend and that. They parted with cries of 'See you in KL'.

Judith drove towards home barely seeing the looming purple mountains or the flocks of galahs that had gathered on every open patch of grass, jumping and tottering in pursuit of the bounty the rain had brought. As cars approached the birds would explode into the air like a firework display of pink stars, then drift down to a safer spot.

24

The motorcyclist ripped in front of her, as they do, out of nowhere. She braked and saw the speedometer drop to 60 mph.

The cop was waving her to stop up ahead on a gravel siding. She sat lumpishly, waiting for him to stroll back to her. 'I'm sorry, officer. My mind was elsewhere.'

He grunted and handed her the speeding ticket. The speedometer needle trembled at 35 mph for the rest of her trip, and after a while she was able to think more calmly about her first encounter with Minou.

It had been in mid-summer, too, but in Sydney the heat was stupefyingly sticky, with a north-easter flicking city grit against your shins and tossing bits of dirty newspaper up from the pavement outside the Glebe town hall into your face.

Judith hadn't had time to change before catching the plane from Canberra and that morning she'd interviewed the mining lobbyists, so she was still dressed up. When she walked into the hall she could feel the hostility like a firing-squad. All the women were in overalls, and most were drinking beer out of cans, tipping it down their gullets like wharfies. There were strobe lights. A sign on a wall said 'No Grass or Hash, please', and scribbled underneath 'Coke is O.K. The Pigs Can't Smell It'. A few of the less serious types were sitting around, snorting. Judith found an organizer, told her she wanted background for a story on the difficulties of the women's movement and mentioned that she was a member of the Canberra Women's Electoral Lobby. The organiser, 'WEL. Well, fuck me. Wanda dance?' When Judith said 'No', she replied, 'I don't suppose you could, in *those* shoes.' Somebody else said, 'They make her bum stick out; that's the important thing for her.' Then a dark girl came up wearing a battle jacket and a peculiar cap, black with large green Hermes wings over the ears. 'Write about my hat,' she said. 'It's the latest. That's all your readers want

25

to know about – the latest gear.' Bill was delighted with the story she'd written. He said, 'Only a woman can be as nasty as this about the sisterhood. Great work, dear.' It was almost a year before some people, people Judith liked, spoke to her again. That was the unbearable part. Richard had said she was imagining it. But she hadn't imagined the letters and telephone calls. One caller said, 'I'm one of your mindless militants from Sydney, one of what you called The Feminist Thought Police . . .' When Judith asked, 'What do you want?' the caller had laughed and drawled out, 'Don't you remember me, Brenda Starr? The gook with the terrific green hat?'

4

There was no argument about the better-looking half of Judith-and-Richard. It was Richard. He stood 1.8 metres tall, had dark wavy hair brushed to the side and a commanding, straight nose. His eyes, however, were disproportionately small – like brown pig's eyes, Judith had once thought, when she was angry with him.

Richard's father was a successful surgeon and had given all his children expensive educations – the daughters at the Rose Bay Convent, the sons at Riverview and St John's. Richard looked expensive. He was glossily groomed and carried himself with the aplomb of a tall man conscious of his importance to society. At parties guests would navigate a room to introduce themselves to the political journalist Judith Wilkes and would end up listening to Richard. Of recent years, however, since Judith had regularly appeared as guest commentator on radio and TV, people had pointedly asked for *her* views. Nowadays Richard stood by with his head lowered, silent. She would watch him from the corner of her eye and say things like, 'You should be asking Richard, not me. He really understands the Constitution.'

He was in the living-room listening to Mozart on the FM, when she nudged the front door open with her elbow. He breathed in, murmured 'Divine' to the sound system, and rose. He was still wearing his running shorts and Adidas joggers and he had forgotten, Judith could smell, to put the chicken in the oven.

As he relieved her of some of the shopping he said, 'How intelligent of you to bring my beer ration. I forgot,' and patted her bum. 'Nice funeral?'

'Dreadful,' she said. 'Where are the children?'

'Where do you think they might be at 6.30?'

'They watch too much bloody television,' she muttered and went through to what her brothers and their wives called the family room and she called the kitchen.

He followed her and sat at the breakfast bar to drink his beer. 'This should be Dom Perignon,' he remarked.

She glanced up from the leftover casserole which she had taken from the refrigerator and was suspiciously sniffing. 'Is that so?' she asked.

Richard made a humming noise and closed his smallish eyes. 'Yes. I've got the numbers for pre-selection. I have to pick up eleven more votes from the Tuggeranong Branch tonight – a formality – and then, my darling . . .'

Judith's rush unbalanced him on his stool. He fended her off gently. 'Will you enjoy floating around as the wife of the Member for Canberra?'

She stepped back. 'You're not suggesting I give up my job?'

Richard shrugged. 'Well, when I'm a Minister, it would hardly be appropriate.'

'When! You mean, if. Anyway, Labor's got no show of winning in 1980. You're looking at 1983 *and* you'll have to beat all the other smart young oncers who'll be in Caucus.' She had moved away again, towards the wall oven.

'We do know it all, don't we? Us political scribes, I mean.'

Judith spun around. 'Why didn't you cook the chicken?' she demanded. As she planted her feet for battle she skidded and almost fell on some squashed, wet thing on the floor. The floor was always covered with little traps the night before the cleaning woman came, and as it never occurred to Richard to sweep it, Judith would not either, on principle.

Richard expanded his rugby-player's chest. 'I thought, naively, that we were discussing the 1980 elections.' He added, 'You really should buy some sensible shoes. You'll break your leg one day.'

She threw an oven glove on the floor and began to cry.

Richard sighed and placed his beer can carefully on the bench. His face had an expression of sorely tried but unshakeable patience. After a while he coaxed, 'Come on, silly one. Tell me what's gone wrong.'

Judith skipped some details, but even so it took time. She had been sneered at by a Foreign Affairs chap and the hem of her skirt was down, while Sancha looked a million dollars; Lady Hobday, whose co-operation would be essential for the boat people story, was an old enemy; the remembered humiliation of that dance in Sydney, and ratting on the women's movement; the speeding fine ... and the chicken would go rotten if it weren't cooked tonight.

'Oh dear, oh dear,' Richard said. 'The problems of a modern pluralistic society.'

'I'm sorry for what I said about Labor's chances, and yours,' she said, sincerely. 'With your background in the Party, of course you'll make the Ministry.'

Richard smiled comfortably.

'Especially if I write your speeches,' she added, more defiantly.

He strolled over and kissed her forehead. 'That's my girl.'

The rainclouds had cleared, leaving a summer evening sky the colour of goldfish skin against which the mountains stood detached, spiky and black. They sat outside at the terrace table to eat the warmed-up casserole and a salad Richard made, then shooed the children away to watch the Thursday night variety show. It was perfectly quiet. From where they sat no other house was visible, only open

29

paddocks and black mountains backlighted by orange sky. When Judith's brothers had come to stay for the first time they had looked around them and one had remarked, 'Not bad, for a couple of socialists. You'd have to pay more than a hundred thou for this, in Sydney.' They were proud of her, although they teased her about being a women's libber and for having only two children.

'Don't you let him near you?' Pat, her favourite brother, had asked her one day, grinning.

She was thinking about that when she realized that Richard was watching her, his eyebrows raised.

'How would you like to start helping me now?' he asked.

His challenging tone, his look of restrained eagerness, alerted her. 'M-m?' She was wary.

'This boat people story . . . There's a lot of double-think in the electorate about them. Guilt, resentment . . .'

Judith nodded.

'The wind is blowing against them'.

Her interruption was furious. 'Blowing! It's a force eight gale. The Department of Immigration is getting hundreds of letters a week objecting to our taking *any* of them. And, for Christsake, *that* after we've bombed their country flat, defoliated it, panicked everyone in the South by telling them for years that the Northerners will murder them, cut off aid, encouraged China to attack them'.

Abruptly, she closed her lips. Richard was looking bored.

At length he said, 'I was thinking of the difficulties the ALP is having in forming a policy on Indo-Chinese refugees that will get across to the Party faithful *and* to the Australian electorate. Our Party' (Judith mentally corrected this to 'Your Party' – she had never joined the ALP) 'stands for succour and strength. But it's as shot through with envy as the rest of Australian society. When everyone had jobs, well, that was different. But now the envy is oozing out. That's what the "dole bludger" campaign is all about, isn't it? And the tax swindling scandals. You know who rats on doctors with good accountants? Other doctors who can't get a piece of the action. We're living in mean-spirited times, Judith.'

'So what do you want me to do about it?'

Richard shrugged. 'I thought that would be obvious. Write up the boat people in a way that won't cause bleeding hearts for them here. That'll make it a lot easier for the Party to come out against our taking too many of them. And *that* policy is necessary – I shouldn't have thought I'd need to explain this – because the unspoken grudge issue at the next elections will be jobs for all, and Aussies *first!*'

Having come out with it he flung himself back on the red cedar chair, smiling naughtily. He knew as well as she did that she must not slant her copy – unless directed by Bill, anyway.

'Think about it, darling. It's amazing what can be achieved in the name of objectivity.'

Later, as he was dressing for the Tuggeranong Branch meeting he called out, 'Look, if they've been able to escape they've got money and they'll want to make more. What are we going to do with a bunch of Asian entrepreneurs? We've got no entrepreneurial skills, in their terms. They're the most daring businessmen in the world, and the most clannish. If you want to get into the camps to talk to them, I suggest you get right on side with the dusky Lady H, somehow. Get everything tied up here, before you leave.'

Judith clasped her hands over her ears. It was always like this. He leapt from asking a favour to the certainty that she would give it. Almost always, she did. She supposed that was the basis of a partnership. But she marvelled once more at her stupidity in bullying and cajoling Bill for months to be sent to Malaysia to do a story on the boat people.

Nothing had been said, but she and Richard had, ever since that first time, avoided Asia on their holidays abroad. These days she could barely remember Kuala Lumpur. If she tried to picture it she had only an impression of heat and darkness. When she had first told Richard she would like to go there during the slack time when Parliament was in recess he had lifted an eyebrow and said, 'If you think that's wise'. And Bill, when she'd flown to Sydney to nag him, had objected, 'It's too expensive. Talk to the refugees who get to Darwin.' Finally, he'd wrapped his arms over his head in mock fright, shouting, 'I give in! I never argue with a woman who's made up her mind.' When he was signing the approvals for her airfares and expenses he'd looked at her straight and said, 'You'd better bloody well get into the camps, dear. It's the only angle I can see.' She'd eyed him off coolly, saying 'I will.'

She thought now, What am I doing? She felt as if something had pressed on her temples causing oblivion, the way an angel, in Jewish myth, touches the forehead of a new-born baby, making it forget the trauma of its birth.

'Hell!' she said aloud. Her thoughts had shambled to a standstill.

From a metre away David, her eight-year-old, was observing her with grave blue-and-white porcelain eyes. He came forward and made a shy feint with his hand towards her shoulder – he often proffered these small gestures of affection to her when Richard was not around. When he was, both David and the young one, Sebastian, patronized her, calling her 'silly one'. His eyes were large with inquiry.

'Work is driving me mad, that's all,' she said to him.

Richard got home after midnight from his meeting, smelling of beer. He threw some papers on the bedroom chair. Judith was half asleep. 'How'd it go?' she mumbled.

'Bastards!' he said. 'Six closet coms have promised to vote for that great intellect from the Miscellaneous Workers' Union, John Land. John Land! Mother of God! I've got to pick up the numbers somewhere else, before March.'

'Make a list of whom you need. We'll have a barbecue.'
She was washed back into sleep before she had finished the
sentence.

The animals were there. They'd been waiting all night
to reveal themselves and they sprang out now, so clearly that
she could see individual hairs on their coats and the blank
ferocity in their eyes. Then a siren blared. But the beasts,
not alarmed by it, continued to tear at each other. Judith
was gasping. She forced her eyes open and knew then that
the bedroom-extension telephone was ringing and that it was
daylight. She was shaking as she picked up the receiver.

A friendly voice said, 'Hi. Sorry to ring so early.'

'Who is it?' Judith said.

'Ooooh, la! You've forgotten me again. It's Minou Hobday. Good morning, Miz Wilkes.'

Her mind winced to attention. She took a deep breath
and replied in kind. 'Hi. Thanks for ringing. Where are you
staying?'

There was a giggle. 'The honeymoon suite at the
Lakeside.' There was no honeymoon suite at the Lakeside.
'What a dump,' Minou added. 'Why don't you come over
for lunch and a chat about the boat people?' They agreed
to meet in the foyer at noon.

Judith was still grinning to herself when she noticed that
Richard had rolled over and was staring at her. He must
have been very drunk the night before, she thought, seeing
his solemn, vacant eyes, and the idea made her irritable. He
was a supercilious drunk; he would have played into the
Land faction's hands.

'Lady Hobday has summoned me. I've been forgiven.'

His vocal chords were not yet working. He patted at her
dumbly and this diminution of his powers made her want
to cherish him.

'I'll nail her,' she said. 'She'll get me into the Malaysian
camps. Don't worry.'

33

By nine o'clock the mountains were a soft lilac; the huge inland sky stretched above looking as frail as pale-blue tissue paper. Judith dropped the boys off at their holiday activities centre then sang as she drove on to work.

When she brightened at the sight of a frisky dog or a garden full of roses Richard would explain, to nobody in particular, 'My wife has simple reactions'. It made her seem, she thought sometimes, as mindless as an anemone stretching or shrinking from the organisms around it. But it was true, in a way. She would rave at the children for pulling the legs off grasshoppers and cried when the cat killed an owl which on long, silent wings had visited the terrace pergola each evening and had stared at her – as remote and intense as The Lord in Judgment, he'd looked. Only the family knew of these outbursts of distress, which her colleagues would not have suspected in her. Around the Press gallery her nickname was Eyeball-to-Eyeball because of her habit of bailing up honourable gentlemen and asking them questions which they did not like.

At the office today she spent most of the morning reading through the Australian and foreign papers for news on the Vietnamese refugees, swearing when she could find only one small item. The panic flight of late last year – after the rupture with China, the floods that had ruined Vietnam's rice crop, the increased pressure on city dwellers to take up work in the 'new economic zones' – had eased off.

'They're just not leaving,' Judith said to her room mate, Barney. 'There hasn't been a boat reported for four days. Last October, when I decided to go, there were hundreds of them.'

Barney said after a while, 'You're in a real sweat about this trip, aren't you?' He was a small morose man who spent hours planning revenge on people for slights upon him of which they were unaware. On Monday mornings he would dump on Judith's desk handfuls of zucchini and cherry tomatoes grown in his garden.

34

'You've been there before. You know your way round.'
He watched the discontent in her face. 'It's still a good story,
if you can talk to them in the camps. What's the trouble?'

'Richard is pushing me on the angle I should take.'

Barney heaved in his chair and turned away from her.
'That figures,' he muttered.

'It's not really Richard,' she said quickly. 'I had a bad
dream last night and I'm still a bit . . . fazed.'

Judith arrived at the Lakeside at noon.

A banner across the front of the hotel said 'Welcome To
The Atlanta Lions Club'. Lions in sports jackets were gathered
in a pride on the foyer's red armchairs while others wandered
to and fro across the blue-green carpet to the gift shop,
buying toy koalas and boomerangs. All Canberra's hotels
were decorated in a way that suggested the furnishings had
been ordered by catalogue, unseen, and that the wrong
colours had turned up.

Minou was not in sight.

After ten minutes she went to the desk and asked for Lady
Hobday's room number. The clerk hesitated.

'What's the problem?' Judith asked.

He became prim. 'Security,' he said. 'Lady Hobday has
had calls from certain ladies she does not wish to see.' His
expression indicated that nobody would wish to see such
ladies, and he gave a sharp glance at Judith's uncombed
hair. 'You may ring from there.' He pointed at the house
telephone.

Minou's voice was languid. 'Please come up. I've been
busy this morning.' She sounded reproachful, as if it were
Judith's fault.

A young Asian man let Judith in, then went back to what
looked like a furtive attempt to disguise events of a recent
and unusual wantonness. Judith had a glimpse of Lady
Hobday herself, wearing a bathtowel.

'Take a pew!' she called, waving, then disappeared back through the bathroom door.

Judith picked her way between the litter – there were clothes, newspapers, room-service trays and a silver flute in an open velvet-lined case – lying on the suite's sitting-room floor, and sat down on the one uncluttered chair. The man continued his tidying up without looking at her, then scuttled through an adjoining door. Splashings from a shower were mixed with boisterous singing in what Judith took to be Vietnamese. From somewhere beyond – the bedroom? – the man began singing the same song.

She waited several minutes, then assumed an expression of irritable boredom which she had to maintain until twelve-thirty, when Minou reappeared.

This was a different Minou. Her face, without cosmetics, was barely pretty and her hair fell in straight, wet strips. She was wearing black trousers and a crumpled white shirt. She looked, more than anything, like a young market coolie.

One arm was stretched behind her back. She whipped it round and held in front of Judith the forage cap with green wings. Then she pulled it over her dripping hair and began to kick at the debris left on the floor, adroitly jerking some underwear and a blue sequinned evening dress into the air, catching the bundle and tossing it through the bedroom door.

'No amahs,' she explained. She gave a larrikin grin.

A coffee-table-sized book had been lying on the carpet, under the evening dress. Minou picked the book up and riffled through its pages. 'I liberated this, in Bangkok,' she said. She smiled reflectively at a coloured photograph. 'Do you steal things? Ever?'

'No,' Judith said. 'Never.'

'I bet you'd steal this,' Minou said. '*Regardes*, la.'

Judith took the book, printed in some Asian script – Japanese? – aware that Minou was observing her closely. Somehow she kept her voice steady.

36

'Very impressive. The colours are nice.' She could not think of anything else to say.

Minou was smirking. 'Don't you want to look at the other pictures? There are more interesting ones.'

Carefully, as if it might break, Judith handed the book back. 'Pornography isn't my bag,' she said.

'Ooooh. Sorry.'

Her tone suddenly made Judith irate. 'I suppose you were in Bangkok after you escaped from Saigon, were you?' she asked. 'That's where all the smart people first landed. The ones who fought their way on board the American military transports.'

The gibe hurt, or at least startled into life some secret memory of Minou's. The hostile amusement in her eyes drained inwards, leaving them shuttered. For a moment, Judith saw, Minou was not lounging like a young thug in a suite at the Lakeside, but was elsewhere, and different. Then suddenly she smiled.

'Yes, la. That is when I was in Bangkok.' She dropped the book back on the carpet and poked at it with her bare big toe. 'Do you think I wouldn't have stayed, if I'd had the option? What do you think they'd do to women who'd been friendly . . .' she shrugged, ' . . . with the enemy?'

Judith felt the foolishness that follows the ebbing of sudden rage. 'Yes. It must have been frightful for you,' she murmured.

Minou continued in her American drawl, 'I saw what happened to my mama, after Dien Bien Phu. People spat at you, in the street. Nowadays, things are better organized – they have re-education camps and new economic zones. But the truth is,' she sounded offhand now, as if bored with the subject, 'because I was born in Vietnam, and so was mama and grandmama and great-grandmama, and everybody, I wish sometimes I was still there. It's not good to be ripped away from your family and your customs, la, all the things

37

you like. All the people who've looked after you since childhood. What's the West got for me?' She retracted one nostril
in an exaggerated sniff of distaste.

'Comfort?' Judith asked dryly.

For a moment Minou appeared not to have heard her.
But she had, for she went on, irritably, 'Comfort. A comfort-
able existence.' She fell silent, then said in a low voice, 'I'm
Asian. I feel *déracinée* here.'

It was pretty rich, Judith thought, coming from someone
who was half-French, spoke English like a Long Island debu-
tante and enjoyed to the full the privileges of being married
to a member of the Australian Establishment.

'Anyway, let's have lunch,' Minou added, in a different
tone.

She dialled the telephone but instead of speaking to room
service began giggling into the receiver. Her voice had
become childish. 'Judith and I are going to have lunch up
here in the suite. What will we eat, Papa?' She giggled during
his reply, then asked, 'What wine will I get?'

Judith stared out the window at the splendid view of the
southern mountains – 'groaning purple', they'd been called
in a poem. She tried hard not to notice that Minou was
telling Hobday, 'Judith is lovely, Papa. With bi-i-i-g boobs.
Boobs like *pamplemousse*. The sort you like.' She broke into
French.

Judith could feel through her back that Minou was glancing at her, watching her for a reaction. There was a click,
the telephone was dialled again, and Minou was saying in
her cool American voice, 'Two fish-of-the-day. That's O.K.
with you, Judith? *Pommes frites* and side salads. O.K., Judith?
And a bottle of Leasingham Riesling. Immediately, please.
We're running late.' To Judith she called, 'One moment'
and vanished into the bedroom, pinching at the wet strips
of hair that escaped under the green wings of her cap.

She came back thirty-five minutes later, transmuted into

38

a cosmetics-advertisement beauty and wearing a cobalt-blue silk kimono dress.

While a waiter, an Australian, was murmuring, 'Yes, Lady Hobday. Thank you, Lady Hobday', palming Minou's tip, she waved him off. Then she arranged herself in one of the dining chairs he had drawn up for them and crossed her mannequin's legs one way, then another, as if she could see herself in a glass. It was already a quarter to two. Judith noticed, with resignation, that Minou in the interim had varnished not only her fingernails but also her toenails. She was determined now not to get angry with Minou again.

'Well, about the Malaysian camps,' she said cheerfully.

Minou stuffed a piece of fish in her mouth and slopped out the wine as if there were plenty more where that came from. Between bites she mumbled, 'Eat. Drink.'

From time to time Judith told herself to stop drinking so quickly and laughing so loudly – Minou was a born mimic and her imitations of the diplomatic wives in Kuala Lumpur were maliciously accurate. She also knew several silly 'Irish' jokes and to illustrate one she snatched up the silver flute and played 'God Save the Queen'. Later, to give the punch line for her riddle, 'Why aren't women allowed into the same part of the mosque as men?' she got down on the floor and made improper movements and noises.

They ordered another bottle of riesling, then coffee and cognac, then more cognac, and had to go often to have a pee. Once Judith looked out the picture window and the mountains seemed black. She felt panic-stricken as she said, 'I must go', but Minou insisted so sweetly that she stayed on.

Later, as she was going down in the lift, Judith repeated to herself, 'She's a monster. She's a lunatic. Hobday must be out of his mind to have married her.' It was small excuse for what they'd done together that afternoon.

5

Judith stalked briskly out through the hotel foyer, hoping none of the staff would recognize her as a party to the incident there with members of the Atlanta Lions Club. There had been a look of horrified bewilderment on the face of the red-skinned man, a bank manager perhaps, whom Minou had picked as their butt. He had stepped back as if to defend himself from a blow, his blood-spotted eyes bulging with incomprehension.

Judith had burned with resentment against Minou for talking her into helping play the practical joke, and with shame for agreeing.

Afterwards Minou had said, 'You live in such a safe world. That's why you're so squeamish, la! You just talk, and risk nothing.' The old memories this remark had stirred up had worsened Judith's sense of moral emptiness. Minou had sneered, 'I remember you at the dance in Glebe. What a Queen Bee! We all said "Here comes a Queen Bee".' Judith had slanged back, 'You should talk! In your Jourdan sandals and your Zampatti dress! You're just a dyke ripping off a middle-aged lecher.' It had all been ridiculous and demeaning.

She had driven home from the Lakeside in the late, golden afternoon feeling nothing for the beautiful landscape and its barricade of ancient mountains.

'Enter the thunder cloud!' Richard had said when she

walked into the living-room at half-past six. 'We're not entirely sober, I see. Another speeding fine?' he added, and put on a look of sham astonishment when she did not answer. When she walked past him into the bedroom he followed and said, 'You're pissed. What's going on?'

'I've got to ring Sancha,' Judith said. 'I've just had a row with Minou Hobday and I've got to find out how much damage it's likely to do me.'

It was easy for Richard to manhandle her, as he did now, propelling her from the bedroom to the living-room, where he pushed her on to the Bamboli four-seater.

'I'll make you a pot of tea so you can sober up and tell me what you've done. Then we'll decide if you're going to ring Sandra.' Judith thought, You lawyers get people's names wrong on purpose, as an intimidation technique.

She looked around the large white-and-silver room, with its tropical palms in pots and the imported Italian furniture that the children were not allowed to touch. We've got everything, she thought. Two of everything. Forty-five thousand a year and no debts. Neither of them drank spirits or smoked. Neither had the nerve to suggest they should risk the envy of their friends on lower incomes, or the disfavour of the Party, by getting more household help. 'I can't afford a live-in au pair,' she'd lied to Sancha yesterday. Only with skiing holidays and Richard's investments in Georgian silver flatware – kept hidden at the bottom of the dirty clothes basket – could they get rid of the money.

Judith's head began to thump.

When Richard came back with the tea she told him how a chance remark of hers had incited Minou to say how much she despised the Atlanta Lions, who were staying in the Lakeside. Somehow they had egged each other on, and before Judith could get out of it, they'd gone down to the foyer and had begun flirting with the men. One man, believing in his luck, had accepted Minou's invitation to her room.

41

At the lifts she had bent over, coughed, and juggled a handful of plastic vomit from the kimono sleeve of her dress, dropping it on the carpet at his feet. He had not seen her sleight-of-hand. She and Judith, half collapsing with laughter, had slid into the lift. As the doors closed Judith had caught the man's expression.

But when Minou had realized that Judith felt ashamed, she'd become abusive. There in the lift they'd had the first round; then, back in the suite, Minou had suddenly and irrelevantly demanded if Judith found Hobday attractive. A moment before replying Judith had known that any answer would be the wrong one, but she was too emotionally exhausted to care.

'Yes, I do,' she had said.

'Get out of my suite! Get out and leave my man alone!' Minou had shouted at her, and Judith had gone. She had spent fifteen minutes skulking on the mezzanine floor before getting up the courage to pass through the foyer.

She said to Richard, 'Minou lost a lot of her family in the war. Her father disappeared before she was born. Hobday's all she's got here.' It astonished her to hear herself defending Minou, but Richard had just called Lady Hobday a string of copulative names.

'So Sir Adrian is her daddy now,' he said. The story had shocked him out of his irritation with her, but it was returning, Judith realized. He added tightly, 'It is a peculiarity of your trade to consider that getting drunk is not only a permissible but also a useful method for pursuing facts. Could I put it to you that sobriety is a more useful one?'

'You sound like a bloody lawyer,' Judith said.

'That's a remarkable statement.'

'I'm sorry,' she murmured.

His chest deflated. 'Well, ask Sandra if there's any way you can still get into the camps without this strumpet's help. Or should we say, in the teeth of her opposition?'

Richard had fed and bathed the children and put together a creditable niçoise salad by the time she had finished talking to Sancha. When the boys hung around the terrace table and Sebastian wanted to sit on her knee Richard said, 'Go away. Your mother has got herself into trouble again and I want to talk to her in peace.'

Judith put her elbows on the table and slumped her chin into her hands. 'I may as well cancel my ticket tomorrow. Minou is the only interpreter I'm likely to be able to get. Through the UN High Commissoner for Refugees – a Frenchman who Sancha says thinks Minou is God's gift – she can stop me getting into the camps. She's done that already to a television team from West Germany. They wasted ten days there, trying to talk their way in, and got nowhere, thanks to Lady Hobday's influence.'

Richard sat silent, studying her. He was wearing the green-and-white PVC apron that said 'I AM A HUMOURLESS FEMINIST'. It had seemed more amusing on him in the photograph that had gone with a magazine article, 'Husbands Who Are Liberated And In The Kitchen'. He was sulking. Judith noticed how heavy his jowls were going to be in a few years, even if he did keep up his jogging.

She said to him with her eyes, Give me sympathy.

'You've buggered things up, haven't you?' he said at last. 'You were determined not to do a critical piece on the refugees, and now you've found an excuse for not doing the job at all. They'll send somebody else, I suppose? Barney?'

'They will bloody not!' The heat of her reaction surprised her. 'You spiteful bastard!' she called at Richard as she rushed off to the bedroom. She heard him saying later to the boys, 'You mother's a proper harridan when she's upset,' and grinned evilly to herself when David asked, 'What's a harridine, Daddy?'

At 9.30 pm the telephone rang. Judith answered it and

as she did, heard the click of the other receiver, in the study. She thought, He monitors my phone calls now.

'Yes?' she said briskly. There was no immediate answer. Then, 'Oooh, la! Still cross with me, Miz Wilkes?'

Minou talked for an hour, dropping the wheedling little-girl voice after a few minutes for a tone of authority. By the time Judith rang off, telling Minou that she would indeed be delighted to stay in the Kuala Lumpur Residence, she had covered pages of her notebook with information. It included important statistics and the names and telephone numbers of officials in Malaysia.

Richard came into the bedroom a few moments later and kissed her forehead. 'My apologies,' he said. 'Your Lady Hobday is all and more than I had imagined. A neurotic, an obvious liar, a creature of charm and cunning. That story she just told you about begging on her knees for a seat on the plane out of Saigon!' He looked put out. 'I was quite moved. Were you?'

Judith nodded.

'You've had a tiring day,' Richard said as he unzipped his fly. He made this excuse on her behalf often; she never offered it herself, these days. She wondered sometimes what happened in other marriages where there were the same difficulties. Once he had asked her to go to a doctor about it and she had cried for hours, reduced to childishness and with a child's instinct to grab at excuses, snivelling, 'It's not my fault. It was the way they told us things at school.' They had not referred to the matter again. She *was* always tired at night: she worked so hard, and they entertained and went out so much, and there were the children to cope with on weekends. She and Richard had found, if not peace of mind, a truce in these evasions. He had, she knew, his little diversions. What else could she expect?

It only took a few minutes, and she kept her eyes closed. In the days when, for his sake, she'd pretended to enjoy it she'd watched his face a couple of times and seen in his eyes a different kingdom. Now that she had trained herself to reduce sex to mere physical assault she could remain tranquil, and slipped easily into sleep when Richard rolled off her.

The beasts were waiting, wrestling with each other playfully in the long, bleached grass. Then they set out to hunt, padding through the stretched shadows of forest twilight. The creature they felled was only half-grown; they had just captured it when it vanished. In rage at being cheated they turned away from the empty patch of grass, and the larger tiger – who with dreaming eyes had groomed his mate with his tongue, cuffing her lightly for attention – reared up and leapt towards her. She cringed back from him and suddenly was inside a cage. People were shouting abuse and glaring at her.

Judith opened her eyes. They had left the bedroom curtains drawn back and outside the terrace was washed with moonlight, its blond slate paving still barred with the shadows cast by the pergola, as it had been when they had gone to bed. She wanted to believe that the pattern of shadows had suggested the cage. But the dream that had happened two nights running now was an ancient one, forgotten, as an injury can be for years until one day, running to greet a friend, a leg collapses and you cry out in astonishment. And afterwards live with an unvoiced dismay.

She woke fresh and cheerful in the morning and gave Richard his breakfast in bed.

'I slept like a log,' she said, and looked puzzled. 'I think I had a dream. Oh, well, I can't remember it now.'

PART THREE

MALAYSIA

6

Her anger dissipated at Sydney airport as the herd instinct took hold of her. Judith shuffled along in line with the three hundred others and submitted to a stewardess who took her beach hat, rolled it out of shape and threw it in an overhead locker. This is how you get people to walk into gas chambers, she thought. They'll do anything they are told, as long as they are all together and one will lead the way.

Her low frame of mind did not improve when she found herself imprisoned in the centre seat of the jumbo's central block; four metres away some people could see out a window, she supposed. It was as much like travelling as a caesarian section was like giving birth: a painless blank with efficient life-support systems. No conscious terror; no joy, either.

After a while melancholy gave way to resentment again and she began to brood over the words she and Richard had had on the way to Canberra airport. The row had been evolving through snaps and snarls ever since she had first mentioned that she would return to Kuala Lumpur. And then that morning, like an egg cracking open to reveal the slimed limb of a hatchling monster, it had broken: Richard had come into the bedroom where she was packing, holding her diaphragm between his thumb and forefinger.

'You have forgotten this,' he said.

She had chosen to pretend he was joking. 'I won't be needing it.' His expression had made her add, 'Don't be stupid'.

With distant disgust, as if the thing were infected, he had dropped it into the suitcase, on top of her portable typewriter, and had walked out. Judith had picked it out and thrown it on the floor. When he came home later to drive her to the airport she had said, 'I've been faithful to you for ten years, and you know it.'

He had replied, 'If fidelity could be described as lying flat on your back, composing shopping lists in your head. Kindly remember that I've foregone my run around the lake so as to get you to the plane. I'm in no mood for an argument as well.'

They had driven in silence until the Fyshwick turn-off and there, while they were held up by the traffic, Judith had said, 'Because I don't enjoy screwing you've bullied and humiliated me for a decade', and he had grinned.

'You did enjoy it, once. Perhaps you will again.'

'I resent you!' she'd shouted. 'I resent everything about you. You patronizing, pompous, boring, macho – *phony* macho . . .'

She had felt sick with rage from Fyshwick to Sydney, not least because they had stopped short, as they always did, of the truth – and so, left unspoken, the truth remained a looming shadow in their minds. Now the recollection of the scene and her return to anger exhausted her. She was too fretful to sleep and too distracted to concentrate on reading, so she watched the in-flight movie, a silly comedy, and made frequent trips to the back of the plane. From a window there she gazed out at the washing-blue sky and down at the desert, its red ripples as orderly as the grooves on the roof of a mouth. The plane's reflection, down there, cruised steadily; the desert's vastness and the constant pattern of the plane moving above it created a hypnotic effect. After a while Judith admitted to herself, I'm running away from him. The confession made her feel calmer and she was able to sleep for almost an hour when at last, their chase after the sun failed, night embraced them and the lights were turned down.

The order to fasten safety belts and extinguish cigarettes wakened her and told her that they were over Singapore. Not long after, on the platform of the stairway leading to alien ground she jerked back from the hot, wet air, then clattered down the stairs.

I've escaped! she thought.

The tropical night drew images out from oblivion. The airport here was like a partly lit theatre, as visually dramatic with its caverns of darkness and stages of orange light as Kuala Lumpur had been during the nights of riot and arson. There was the same madly exciting smell of kerosene in the air . . . and there were the sulphur-and-blue painted Neoplan buses. In KL the mobs had flung themselves on buses, howling as they rocked them . . .

Judith had met Ben, the Reuters man, that morning at the hospital where they were both after information on the number of casualties. Ben was KL-based, had a car and a curfew sticker for it.

Standing there in the hospital where people lay on the floor in their own blood, I felt in danger of spilling, like a brimming glass, and he'd said, 'You'd better stick with me, kiddo. You're too young to be out on your own in this town.'

He had food in his flat, he said, but his amah had disappeared and he couldn't cook. So I fried some eggs for our lunch. He fixed up the spelling on my copy and argued on the telephone with the tele-communications staff to get me time on the wire to Sydney. Then it was night again. We were driving back from a tour of the burnt-out Chinese shophouses. Round a corner we ran into one of the street gangs which the police were not even pretending to control, despite the curfew. There were about thirty Malay boys on the roadway, shouting the slogan of the day, which had been made up after yesterday's big mass-acre of the Chinese. They were laughing and yelling, as if they were off on holiday. 'We've got the pigs! Now for the cows!' Further down

51

the road Ben's headlights lit up two tall figures – a couple of Indians who must have risked curfew-breaking to check their shop. Suddenly one of the boys from the gang began to run and I saw, as we overtook him, that he held a parang above his head and was rising on his toes. He was flying. The blade swept down and across in one movement and the incredible thing was that the Indian remained standing for a fraction of a second, without his head. 'A cow! We've killed a cow!' they were yelling. I screamed when the second Indian's shoulder crashed into mine. Ben had dragged him into the car and he was lying across both of us, blocking the steering. The Malays were whooping at us; they'd almost caught up with the car. I felt suddenly as though I'd lifted out of my body and was flying, too. The Indian was big and fat but there was lightning in my arms; I just picked him up as if he were a parcel and threw him over into the backseat. Ben said, 'Jesus!' and then 'We're safe, now'. The back window of the car was shattered, where the boys had struck it with their parangs, and the Indian's turban was covered in glass. He'd pissed himself and I got pee all over my skirt later when I was picking the glass off him. He kept on crying and kissing my hands, saying, 'Madam, God put strength into your arms' and then wailing because his father or uncle or somebody was dead, back there. We got rid of him as soon as we could, dumped him outside a police station and drove off. We couldn't wait. It was if the universe would stop if we didn't get to Ben's flat and on to his bed. I don't think we even spoke until the third or fourth time. Then Ben hugged me round the waist, with his face pressed into my belly and said, 'Jesus, we're alive. You saved our lives, kiddo, with that weight-lifting act,' and we started to laugh. I said, 'I feel as if I've known you for ever,' and he said, 'Yeah. Mr Singh' (he meant the Indian) 'would say that we'd once played together in Paradise.'

Judith had returned to Richard with a badly bruised shoulder and excuses of being tired. In London she realized she was pregnant and knew – as certainly as she knew that Richard's embrace, joyfully anticipated all the years they had been engaged, was now unbearable for her – that the child was Ben's.

The ground hostess in a snappy batik uniform who had herded them on to the bus leaned down to Judith. 'Are you feeling unwell, Madam?' she asked.

Judith swallowed. 'I'm fine,' she croaked, and managed a smile to confirm it.

She got out of the Neoplan bus and walked into the huge, bright and very clean transit lounge where small, bright and very clean Singaporeans handed out passes and snapped out directions to the shopping arcade. These people were the new Asians, the economic miracle-workers. A perfectly painted doll jabbed a pass into Judith's hand; she felt her hackles rising. Deep down, I'm a racist, she thought. We all are. In an accessories shop where every article bore the label of Christian Dior or of Pierre Cardin a Dutchman who had been on the plane said, 'This is not Dior. It is all made in Hong Kong, with fake labels.' The shopgirl snatched the bag from his hands saying, 'It is Dior, la! You look!' and pulled crumpled tissue paper out of the bag to display the 'Made in France' sign. 'Not fake, la!' she shrilled at him.

Judith walked away as the girl tried to draw her into the argument; she felt too raw-edged to become involved. She thought, I'm surrounded by aggression. The bright lights of the terminal, the sharp, assertive colours of the tarmac buses, the monosyllabic jabbering of the shopgirls . . . I'm panicking, she thought.

She got out of the shop. A fear had arisen and would not abate, that something horrible must befall her again, that the exorcism she was seeking would be as painful as the sum of all her guilts for sins against Richard, against Judith-and-Richard, against David – yearning, she'd been, for the courage to get rid of that nodule of flesh. She had never asked advice from friends or relations. It had remained her secret, the amorphous shadow between her and Richard. But one day, she now recalled, she had tried to do something about it. Richard had complained that she no longer treated him 'like a wife' – they'd become so delicate, so oblique with each other – and on impulse a few weeks later she had gone to confession. She'd been in Melbourne, reporting on a conference, and had walked in off the street, hatless.

The priest was very old, she could tell from his faint, old man's voice and his slow wheezy breathing. In the calm of heavy curtains with the smell of candles and incense she had quietly told him everything. It took a long time. He had not replied for a bit and she'd wondered if he had gone to sleep. Then he said, 'Child, you have sinned and for that God will forgive you as soon as you ask Him to. But you must also forgive yourself, d'you understand? Your sexual feelings you have as the bounty of God and if you go on abusing this gift, which is also the gift for a woman's love of man, hating it because you once misused it, you're sinning against y'self. D'you understand what I'm saying? The sin against oneself brings nothing but sorrows and more sins. D'you get my meaning, child? That you must make atonement with yourself? Atonement. At-one-ment, people used to call it.'

'Yes, Father,' she'd replied demurely. That evening in the pub, she'd made everyone roar with laughter, describing the dust motes that exploded from the curtains and imitating the priest's quavery voice: 'Say forty-nine Hail Marys and three hundred and six Our Fathers and give ten dollars to the poor.' Someone unexpected – a fashion writer – had said, 'These days, for people like us, things have to pass the intellectual test. If they can't be intellectually accepted they can't be emotionally reassuring. That's the problem for religions, these days.'

Judith sighed at a windowful of French wines and forced her concentration back to the earlier thought – how horrible this trip would be. But I can bear it, she thought. I can bear anything, these days. As she approached the transit lounge the panic was all but gone.

She found a seat among the crowd of grey-faced people

54

from Europe who clung to plastic carry-bags of duty-free liquor and cigarettes. They were stunned with fatigue and gave off an air of wretched patience. 'I've been here four hours,' a woman said. 'There's a strike in Kuala Lumpur and all the baggage has got mixed up.' Judith tried to look sympathetic. 'You wouldn't think they'd have strikes in these parts, would you?' the woman added reproachfully, as if strikes were a unique privilege, reserved for Caucasians.

A group of men, two foreigners and a Malay, strode down the stairs, laughing and talking loudly. One was telling a story, obviously funny. Judith recognized him as the local ABC representative. She watched him for a while, then decided to introduce herself.

'I've come for the boat people story,' she explained. The other men were from Reuters and Antara.

Her announcement brought a fresh shout of laughter. 'Haven't we all?'

The Malay, who turned out to be Indonesian, giggled so much he had to be hit on the back by the Reuters man. When he recovered he asked, 'Where is the President of the International Women's Refugee Relief Committee? Ha!'

Judith looked from one to another of them. 'I've been out of touch for twelve hours. What's up?'

The Indonesian bent towards her and whispered, 'Disappeared. Lady Hobday has vanished. Whoosh. Gone with the wind.'

The Reuters man was swaying around, holding an invisible microphone to his mouth. 'Good evening,' he rumbled. 'And here is the news: the beautiful, young – blah-blah – has vanished on the east coast of – blah-blah – while trying to make contact with Vietnamese blah-blah . . .' The Indonesian grabbed the microphone from him. 'Where has she gone? people are asking. And why?' He paused for effect. 'Special Branch knows. Kuan Yew knows. But these bloody Singaporeans . . .'

'Shut up, Moh,' the ABC man said. 'You've got the whole bloody transit lounge listening.'

Moh swayed slightly and wagged a finger at Judith. 'A good Muslim like me can hold a ton of piss,' he said and sat down abruptly.

The ABC man pulled his concerned, serious television face out of the air and put it on. 'That's the story,' he said to Judith. 'Jack', jerking his head at the Reuters man, 'got a phone call six hours ago from his local man in KL who'd picked it up from a Special Branch contact. Lady Hobday and her chauffeur have been missing since the day before yesterday, somewhere on the East Coast. They're searching Kuala Trengganu for her. The villagers there aren't exactly enamoured of the boat people. They might have ...' He ran his forefinger across his throat. 'And she's one of them, you know – she's half-Chink.'

Judith said stupidly, 'I thought she was Vietnamese' and did not bother to glance at Moh when he put in, 'No, bloody Chinese. Cunning bloody ...'

'What have you sent?' she asked the other two.

They exchanged glances. 'Nobody has sent anything. It's been officially denied in KL and here, and embargoed by both governments, no doubt at the request of the Australian High Commission.'

'Press freedom,' Mohammed croaked from below them. 'You make a Chinese the village headman of this island ...' He looked around at some of the people who were staring at him. 'ASEAN solidarity!' he added loudly.

Judith and the other two ignored him.

'What are you doing here at the airport?' she asked the Australians.

The ABC man dropped his voice even lower. 'We can't put anything on the wire or over the air or even over the phone, for that matter. But Moh is leaving on the MAS

56

flight to Sydney tonight. He'll take the stuff down, and our Canberra offices can start stirring from that end.'

'Great,' she said. She was thinking of the advantage she would have in being on the spot, in Kuala Lumpur. Then she frowned, 'Actually, I know Minou Hobday,' she added. 'I hope nothing has happened to her.'

The two men became alert. 'What's she like?' they asked at once.

The Reuters man said, 'At the High Commission here they say she's a Saigon bar-girl who's got the old man by the short and curlies.'

Judith shrugged: there was no simple way to describe Minou. 'She's . . . different,' she said, and felt annoyed with herself for the dismissive tone in her voice. It had produced knowing grins from the two men. 'But I really admire her,' she added warmly. It was difficult to know if they had heard her, for just then the flight to Kuala Lumpur was announced.

7

The Selangor Cricket Club, a well-kept Tudor-style building in the centre of a thriving Asian city, was a place of peculiar charm for Ralph Hamilton. To him, the romance of the British Raj – the rubber boom, the sporting sultans, the servile Chinese – was woven into the fabric, starched and ironed and now worn tissue-thin, of the club's white damask tablecloths.

Its back verandah steps led down on to a large, grassed playing field, the *padang*, also neatly maintained. On the other side of the *padang* was a busy thoroughfare, Jalan Sultan Hishamuddin, and the Sultan Abdul Samad building, a Victorian Moorish folly of pink-and-white arches and black onion domes, with a clock tower. Despite the royal names, no sultan had been responsible for the construction of street or building. They were the handiwork of the Empire and the names they bore were an example of British colonial finesse – a polite reference by recent foreign rulers to earlier, native ones. Now that the wheel had turned and Malays were once more rulers – if not of their economy, at least of their Constitution – the name-game had taken a new direction. The government of Malaysia was busily stripping the patronyms of colonial administrators from places and replacing them with the names of local trees and flowers. This would, it was felt, encourage in Malay, Chinese and Indian a love of Malaysia, solidarity and nationhood.

The importance of names in times of flux and reflux was evident too at the Selangor Cricket Club, and added to its mystique. The club was never referred to under that name by Ralph Hamilton or anybody else who took pride in membership or even local knowledge. It was The Dog, a title that had arisen from a pet Dalmatian which a member of earlier years had chained each evening to a front verandah post. He was obliged to do this by a sign of those days which said, people claimed, 'NO DOGS OR CHINESE ALLOWED'.

A Chinese was now captain of the club's cricket team.

On most evenings after work Ralph dropped in at The Dog for a drink, confident of friendly company. He was a man whom other men liked, having maintained, as an adult, the playfulness of boyhood – a love of sports and *badinage*. And he was a boozer: KL was a boozing town. Head down, he crossed the worn black-and-yellow tiled floor through to the back verandah with its bamboo blinds and its soothing view across the *padang* to the traffic jam on Jalan Sultan Hishamuddin. The strain that made slashes on his forehead began to smooth away. He usually arrived at five-thirty, when the dusk air felt like warm milk, vigorously stirred inside the club building by rows of ceiling fans, and was punctuated outside by the shrieks of little bats.

The fans fluttered his fine, fair hair and disturbed the leaves of the pot plants on the verandah, but had no visible effect on the knot of Chinese waiters, who were dressed, like the club's facade, in black and white. Their hair did not move, nor their expressions. Without shifting their eyes they knew when a member wanted another *stengah*, or a bender, or a beer. The oldest sporting club in the city had the best waiters and also the best curry tiffin on Sundays.

When Ralph strolled to the verandah and joined his friends – a Chinese, two Sikhs and a Tamil – a waiter detached himself from his motionless group and went to fetch a *stengah* for him.

'I'm on beer tonight,' Ralph called out. He noticed, as he looked after the waiter, that there were two or three women seated inside near the bar, and his expression became irritable again. The Dog's polished long bar, on which planters had formerly ridden their bicycles on Friday nights, had once been out of bounds to women. Ralph considered it a blight on a good club to allow women in the bar.

'What's this, you bugger, drinking beer? Too mean to buy whisky now?' Johnny Kok said. His round, bespectacled face squeezed up with delight at his own wit. Johnny was in excellent spirits: his accountant had told him that morning that he was a millionaire in Malaysian dollars. Not bad, for a fellow of twenty-five.

Ralph's face creased again with irritability. 'Doctor's orders. I'm not meant to be drinking at all, with this gut of mine.'

'You go to bloody lying Sikh witch-doctors,' Johnny said. 'You should go to a good Chinese doctor. A few little herbs, a bit of acupuncture, and you're fixed! Isn't it, Dr Singh?' He poked the Sikh in the ribs.

Dr Devinda Singh gave a big, slow grin and settled his feet more firmly on the floor tiles. A plump pod of genitals bulged the material of his flannels, his Sikh virility as undisguisable as a bull's. 'Listen to the Chinaman,' he said, turning to his co-religionist, Dr Lukbir Singh.

Dr Lukbir was not as modern as Dr Devinda and still wore the turban and beard. He was shorter and fatter, and giggled. 'You should *not* be drinking, Ralphie,' he said. 'Better for us lions to drink! Alcohol is milk to us.'

Ralph relaxed into the evening game. The creases that ran from his nostrils to his mouth and gave his face a look of handsome bitterness flattened out. 'The bloody warrior race,' he replied amiably. Swearing was *de rigueur* in the group but four-letter words were avoided, for this was neither a club nor a city in which working-class mannerisms

60

were admired. Ralph's voice moved carefully around vowels which rolled with ease from the Oxford-trained tongues of his large, dark companions. 'All you buggers are called . . .' Ralph added.

'Yes! Yes!' Dr Lukbir became excited. He had been drinking with Devinda and Johnny for an hour already and was in the mood for recalling Sikh greatness. He beat at his chest with a brown dimpled fist like that of a giant baby's. 'We are called Lion. Our ladies are called Princess. We are warriors.'

Sometimes, on the hockey field, Dr Lukbir used his stick as if it were a sword and so did Dr Devinda.

Terry Donleavy, a third secretary – immigration – from the Australian High Commission had walked up to them and stood there, limp-armed and grinning. Ralph had invented his nickname, Opium, 'which stands for Slow Working Dope,' as he would explain.

'G'day, Terry,' Ralph said.

'Hullo, boss. Hullo, chaps,' Opium said eagerly. He was restraining within his body some momentous secret. In a second he would let it out, Ralph realized, for Terry's blue eyes, always prominent, were bulging with excitement.

Ralph felt a stab in his guts. Opium was a master of the foot-in-the-mouth statement.

'You've heard? Her Ladyship's disappeared,' Opium said.

The Sikhs smiled at him indulgently, familiar with the undisciplined jabbering of white trash. And of yellow.

'You're shickered, Terry,' Ralph said. 'Come on, I'll buy you another beer.'

He rose and escorted Opium to the bar, where a Malay was saying to another Malay, 'Did you read that the Tamils threw chairs again at a political meeting in Petaling Jaya, last night?'

When Ralph and Opium were a safe distance from the others he said tartly, 'That's for Australian ears only. The cables about it are classified secret.'

'Jees,' Opium said. 'Other people know.'

Like an anxious, blue-eyed puppy, Ralph thought. His own eyes were a cool grey. 'Who told you?' he asked.

'That Malay from Reuters. He asked me to go for a drink at the Brass Rail and then he said, "What's the latest on the search for Lady Hobday?"' Opium's expression was hurt. 'You could have knocked me down with a feather. I didn't even know she was missing.'

'Forget he told you,' Ralph said. Opium was gazing at him with awe; its unconscious stimulation of egotism worked. Ralph added unwillingly and irritably, 'All anybody knows is that she didn't arrive at the Pantai Motel the night before last. Neither she nor her driver has been seen since they left KL on Monday. Special Branch is checking the villages and *kedais*.'

'Jees,' Opium said.

Ralph wished sometimes that he was not Terry's boss, so that he could flatten him. Instead, in the office, he imposed small humiliations on him and suffered moments of revulsion for both of them when Terry, cheerful and innocent, carried out unnecessary tasks. 'They're also checking the East Coast camps,' he said, to cover his animosity.

'Has there been a ransom note?' Opium whispered.

'No.' This idea – that Minou had been kidnapped – had not occurred to Ralph himself. He wanted to add, Your moments of intelligence, Opium, are more frightening than your stupidity.

He was about to abandon Opium at the bar when he thought of something else. 'There is an Australian journalist, a sheilah called Judith Wilkes, coming in on the Qantas flight tonight. Don't tell her anything about the boat people that isn't official information. Nothing about the coppers or the blackmarket, understand?'

Opium winked at him. Ralph thought his head would explode. The indiscreet little shit.

'Can I buy you a beer?' Opium asked.

'No thanks. I'm getting the drinks for our group.' Ralph signed a chit and returned to his peers.

They had entertained themselves in his absence with more play. One of the main rules of their game, of which they never tired, was that Johnny Kok, being the youngest and unmarried, and the richest, should be oppressed by the older men. His role was to provoke them, up to a limit. None of them doubted that when at last the Chinese came to power that Johnny would be among the leaders. Already he had established a mess for useful friends; the girls there, people knew, were Javanese and Thai, and remarkably proficient. Ralph was the only member of The Dog whom Johnny had invited to the Kuala Lumpur Film Distributors' Association Mess, and he had been shocked by the politically radical conversation there. He had spent the night talking, reluctantly leaving the sitting room for a five-minute bang only once, despite Johnny's hostly urgings to try the Thai girl as well. Johnny had not invited him again, but had said, 'You're like me, man. Not really interested in the ladies,' to which Ralph had replied, 'You've got to be joking!'

Judging from the way Johnny's arms were jerking in the air and from his yelps of 'Bloody black-faced buggers!' his teasing by the others was now well advanced. The only one who was not either talking loudly or laughing was the Tamil, Dr Kanan, whose title referred to philosophy and history. Ralph's eyes rested on him. No Caucasian could resist for long the temptation to gaze at Kanan, although he spoke rarely and hid, rather than sat, in chairs. An Englishwoman had once remarked to Ralph, 'He looks as if even his eyelashes were made personally, by God', and Ralph had replied tersely, 'Yes. And he keeps them for his wife.' It had already occurred to Ralph that if he were a homosexual he would fall in love with Kanan. Once, thinking of his friend, he had tried a Tamil girl and had been sickened to see that

63

his skin looked pale green against her purple blackness. The envy he had felt for her body had kept him away from Tamil girls afterwards.

Kanan's eyes seemed to admire whatever they rested upon; for the moment this was Ralph's haggard, handsome face, already marked by death. It embarrassed Ralph, this grave, tender regard of Kanan's. He returned it with a grin and an up-your-arse hand gesture, then turned to the Sikhs. His tone was confidential: 'You know, of course, that Kanan comes from a very strict religious background, where beef is eaten only on Fridays?'

They all chased this new hare, baying with merriment. More drinks arrived. The backcloth of sky turned grey for a few minutes then invisible stagehands whisked it away to replace it with a dark blue and, seconds later, a black one. Change was swift and uncompromising close to the equator. The bats disappeared and the outer darkness became luminous from orange public lighting.

Kanan was laughing. At length, run to a standstill, he said, 'To be very frank with you, Ralph, I am named after the god of Thaipusam. He discovered "OM". One of the names of the Lord Subramaniam is Discoverer of OM'.

'All you cow-worshipping buggers have got dirty names!' Johnny yelped.

The Sikhs chuckled and swayed about on their fat bottoms. They had no problems with names, like the Hindus, who were called improper things such as Great Sex. Dr Lukbir Singh began crooning softly, using the tune of a famous Indonesian song, popular among the Malays.

Bengali one is so long
Melayu one is *potong*
But China one is like *sontong* . . .

There was laughter from another table. Ralph looked over, saw Tunku Jamie and raised his hand in greeting. The prince returned it with a jolly, regal nod.

64

'Say hullo to the opening batsman, Johnny,' Ralph said. As everyone knew, it burned Johnny that for political reasons the captain of the Dog's cricket team, his brother in race, had been forced to make 'that useless Malay bugger' (as he referred to Jamie in private) opening bat, instead of Johnny. Johnny regarded all Malays as useless. He had recently discovered a way to avoid the government's instruction that one-third of all employees must be Malay. It was expensive – he had to pay a double set of salaries and keep another set of books – but it was worth not having the lazy, privileged buggers in his offices. He retained a couple of sleepy minor nobles on his board and sometimes took them to the mess, where they spent the whole night making love with the Javanese girls. It was well known to the Chinese where the Malays' brains were.

'Good evening, Your Highness,' Johnny said. He slunk down in his armchair and stared with eyes grown as small as cracks behind his spectacles at Dr Lukbir's blue turban. Two metres away the prince was giving out rich gurgles of amusement at the song.

The song ended. Johnny Kok stood up and knocked Dr Lukbir's turban off his head.

For a moment it seemed as if even the ceiling fans had stopped spinning overhead. Then Dr Devinda Singh rose to his feet. Johnny's spectacles went flying across the tiled floor. 'You Mao Tse Tung bastard,' Singh bellowed. He glanced at his co-religionist whose skull, streaked with sickly strands of metre-long hair, was shamefully exposed as he scrabbled beneath a chair for his turban. Dr Devinda Singh thumped his heart. He trod heavily on Ralph's foot as he launched himself across the verandah, down the steps and on to the *padang*. Johnny had not bothered with the steps, but had vaulted the verandah rail.

'I say!' said Tunku Jamie. 'Old Dev is giving Johnny stick!' He sauntered to the rail, squinting across the darkened

65

field. 'Do you think he'll catch him?' he asked conversationally. 'Damned shame we can't see.'

Only Kanan made a reply: he shook his head. Ralph was doubled up, stretching towards his injured foot. The sudden pain of it had flashed upwards into his bowels and had exploded there.

'Kanan,' he whispered, 'Kanan.'

'You are very ill,' Kanan said as he walked beside Ralph to the lavatory. He knew it was futile to tell Ralph the truth written in the clenched lines of his body, that he was dying. And so he said nothing. People who brutalized themselves died in this horrible way, by ripping themselves apart and calling it frustration or illness.

'Come off it, mate. All I've got is a dose of the shits. Lousy Indian food.'

Kanan waited for him outside the lavatory.

'You're immune,' Ralph said when he emerged.

Kanan had experienced his friend's pain and felt faint himself. He decided to try to help. 'Ralph, it's your job,' he said and saw that Ralph understood him and accepted his fond concern; they had been friends for fifteen years.

Ralph reached forward and touched his fingertips to Kanan's cheekbone, then withdrew his hand quickly, and snorted. 'You think I should give up work and live off Sancha's dough? Not me, mate.'

Kanan said mildly, 'But you married her for her money. If one's wife has a big dowry . . .'

'It's not as simple as that, is it?' Ralph muttered. They'd discussed it all before. As an immigration officer posted overseas Ralph could offer Sancha the benefits of expense-account living: a vast house paid for and maintained by the Australian government; servants; a duty-free Mercedes; duty-free booze; subsidies for the children's school fees; free holiday travel. And for this self-respect in the role of husband-provider, Ralph had undertaken a job that gouged

66

at his humanity, bit by bit, hour by hour, using to himself and others the excuse 'I don't make government policy. I only execute it.' The alternative was for him, Sancha and the four kids to live on an unenhanced Australian salary, assuming he could find a job in some other area of the public service or in a university, and that was not good enough. When her sister, who'd married a stockbroker, came to stay with them in KL, Ralph had been flooded with uxorious affection and well-being as he heard Sancha sympathizing, 'How devastating for you, Di, not to have a cook. Can't Tony write one off as a typist, or something?' Di, who was a bloody good sort, had replied with exasperation and a coquettish smile at Ralph, 'We're not millionaires, you know.' Such comments weighed in as huge deposits in the account books of one's life; keeping them balanced was the process by which you strove to stay alive.

'It's easy for you,' Ralph added to Kanan.

On the verandah Ralph shouted, 'Goodbye chaps. It's been wonderful knowing you. I've just agreed to let Kanan drive me home.' It raised a few laughs, but not from the Sikhs. Devinda had rejoined his friend and now four other Sikhs, all turbaned, were sitting with them, holding cricket bats between their knees.

'Johnny over-reacted,' Ralph said as they walked back past the famous dog-chaining verandah posts. 'Chinese nerves are at breaking-point with this refugee business.'

Kanan nodded. 'The boat people are their kin. When the villagers stone them the Chinese feel they are being stoned. It's back to '69.'

Outside in the still, warm air Ralph felt well again; his body was at peace after the tearing attack. 'They're frightened of them, too. Johnny said to me the other day, "We Chinamen don't like any limitations on us. We like to make money all ways. Bloody Chinese Vietnamese made so much money, under Diem, under Kee, under Thieu. Now they can't make money, so they come here." Making dough is a soft option in Malaysia. The local Chinese don't want competition from real pros.'

In the car Ralph went on, 'The refugees are phase four of the Vietnam war. Thailand will collapse from the weight of their numbers. The King will be assassinated, or become an exile, like Sihanouk. Malaysia will be up for grabs by combined local and northern communists, or from the south, by the Indonesian generals. It's only a matter of time. Maybe five years.'

'Everything is only a matter of time,' Kanan said. He was manipulating the gear stick with deep concentration, as if it were a dislocated shoulder joint. The car jumped forward and smashed a headlight on the tree trunk in front of it.

'Poor tree,' Kanan said. He got out and examined the broken bark. 'I think it will be all right,' he said to Ralph, doubtfully. He watched with curiosity and delight as Ralph put the car into reverse for him. He has lover's eyes, Ralph thought.

They steered slowly through the commercial centre, over roads that were being constantly dug up, widened or altered in direction. The whole city was in a phase of diastole, responding to the demands of the economic miracle brought on by the ten good years the Vietnam war had given the ASEAN nations, and buoyed up now by the booming commodities market. In the commercial centre bigger, brighter office blocks were climbing monthly on the sites of smaller buildings not yet old enough to be dilapidated. In the suburbs the jungle was being torn down and the old rubber plantation trees slaughtered to give ground for Hiltons and housing complexes. The trishaws had disappeared. Around the Golf Club pool English ladies said, 'Every South Chinese coolie is driving a Mercedes these days,' and 'The boarding schools at home are full of Malay children.' Their husbands warned club newcomers, 'You can get a game for a thousand dollars a hole, any day of the week.'

As they passed the Ampang Park shopping complex where red-and-gold Chinese New Year banners, three metres wide, hid some of the smaller advertisements on the facade, Ralph said, 'This was once the prettiest city in South-East Asia.'

'You are a conservative these days, isn't it?' Kanan replied. He laughed softly. 'I still remember the day you stood on a box at Sydney University and shouted that you wanted to be drafted so that you could burn your draft card, too.'

'I was bloody lucky I was already too old for the draft,' Ralph said. 'Sancha's father was convinced I was a communist. If I'd been arrested as well . . .'

'You would have enjoyed that, isn't it?' Kanan said. 'You are still a romantic.' Ralph was used to such assertions from Kanan who, western-educated though he was, was Indian down to the pale yellow tips of his black fingers, and who had an Indian's vanity of omniscience concerning the human heart.

'Get fucked,' Ralph replied mildly.

They had crossed Jalan Pekeliling and were now near Ralph's house. The streets here were poorly lit so that coming in to the area for the first time, at night, one could imagine it was almost uninhabited. In fact the houses here were mansions set in huge gardens, commonly half a hectare or more; they were hidden from the road by high vine-covered fences and giant trees. The suburb was unnaturally cool and quiet because of the vegetation. Whenever one of the trees was cut its stump would be invaded by parasite vines and within a few days the stump would be smothered. All life was constantly alert here, not with circumspection as in temperate climates, striving merely for survival, but boldly, striving for conquest.

The residences of ambassadors and high commissioners were here, a place which only a hundred years earlier had

69

been virgin jungle. The Ampang tin mines had been located a bit further on and sixteen kilometres back had been the river junction, with a collection of ramshackle shophouses. This was now the centre of town. The jungle itself, botanists reckoned, was one hundred million years old. At night when a car's headlights picked out a fence post over which vines had grown almost two metres in the space of a few days, Ralph would sense the violation; the jungle, so staggeringly grand, was paradoxically as tender as a spring bud and, once disturbed in its natural flow of energy, was ruined for ever. In an afternoon a man with a chain saw could undo the work of millennia. All along the roadway to the East Coast the injured trees were choked with curtains of parasites.

He turned to Kanan, who was crouched over the steering wheel, driving at thirty kilometres per hour. 'Lady Hobday has disappeared. Perhaps kidnapped,' he said.

Kanan clicked his tongue.

'Keep it quiet, mate. I really shouldn't have told you.'

Kanan had found the entrance to Ralph's house. He carefully negotiated the gravel drive and stopped under the lighted porch. An amah came out to open the door for Ralph but retreated when she saw he was with Kanan, whose hair and eyes, in the semi-light, shone like licorice.

An inchoate plan returned to Ralph's mind. He continued, however, to talk of Minou's disappearance. 'There will be rejoicing in the coffee party set,' he said.

'The other ladies hate her, isn't it?' Kanan replied. 'It makes them angry that they must treat her with respect. And they are envious of her because she is young and pretty. And she has a mission in life.'

'Yes, well, her mission, as you call it, may have come to an end. She and the syce have not been seen for twenty-four hours.'

Kanan shook his head. 'Impossible. Not if she is with Bala.' Bala, the syce, was some distant relation of Kanan's

70

and had been taken on as Minou's chauffeur on Kanan's recommendation.

Ralph smiled at his friend's confidence. It was, he recognized, part of the extreme form of narcissism which Kanan's background had fostered, that Kanan should find it inconceivable that any protégé of his would be foolish enough to be kidnapped. One night Ralph had watched, fascinated, as Kanan lay against his mother's lap, being fed with her fingers. His great, lustrous eyes had been drunk with well-being, like a baby's at the breast. Kanan was thirty-six years old at the time.

Ralph changed the subject. 'Listen, mate,' he began 'there's somebody I would like you to meet. She's an Australian journalist, a friend of Sancha's, who is going to cause me a helluva lot of trouble about the camps. She's one of those bloody women's libbers.' He paused and leant back in the car to look at Kanan. 'I've got a theory about that sort of sheilah,' he added.

Kanan nodded, politely attentive.

Ralph almost sniggered as he said 'I think all they need is a bloody good screw. Why don't you take her mind off work?'

Kanan laughed. Ralph shocked him often with his destructiveness and although Kanan knew its source he was still caught unawares.

'You know my wild days are over, Ralph,' he said, then softened the rebuke with, 'You are the playboy these days.'

It was not the reaction Ralph had hoped for. He tried again, 'Sancha showed me a school photograph of her. She's not bad looking. Tall, blonde, big norks . . .' His voice trailed away, for Kanan had averted his face. 'Well, see you, mate. How about we go to Brickfields for dinner next week?' The image of the Brickfields stall they both loved – with its little chipped dishes of vegetarian curries served by fat waiters who hitched at their dhotis, and shouted and cleared their

71

nasal passages loudly – made Ralph's gut churn once more. He clenched his fist, then punched Kanan lightly on the shoulder. 'Goodnight, you chaste Indian householder. Bastard,' he said, and jumped out of the car.

8

When Judith arrived in Kuala Lumpur her luggage did not.
Or perhaps it did and was mislaid somewhere in the terminal
building. The Malay girl from Qantas was winning in her
smiles, but uncertain.

'You are the unlucky one tonight,' she said as Judith stood
by the baggage roundel. When she climbed on to the
machinery and peered down the chute she could see a group
of Malay boys lying at the bottom, playing cards. They
smiled and waved at her.

'They are on go-slow,' the Qantas girl explained. 'The government is threatening to put the ringleaders in gaol.'

A northern Indian Malaysian, a passenger from another
flight who had already questioned Judith closely with that
extraordinary presumption which was as much a part of
Asian good manners as was the soothing lie, said, 'Go-slows!
Now we are developing the diseases of Western affluence,'
and he went on loudly to attack the Qantas policy of cheap
fares to Europe, which did not extend to ASEAN member
states. He had discovered Judith was a journalist half an
hour earlier and now lectured her on her responsibility for
arguing the ASEAN case in the Australian news media. He
ended quietly, pleasantly, by offering a lift in his Mercedes.

When he moved off an Australian businessman pressed
his card on her and invited her to dinner at his hotel for
the following night. 'You need friends in a place like this,'

he said and patted her shoulder. She heard him calling the Malay girl 'Little Blossom' and she and the girl later exchanged looks of shared resentment.

'The company must give you seventy-five dollars a day if your luggage is lost,' the girl murmured to Judith when, after an hour and a half, it became clear that the suitcase with her typewriter, her background notes, her very *raison d'être* had vanished. Judith walked out of the terminal to find a taxi thinking, It looks different but underneath it's the same bloody chaos and confusion.

There was a system for hiring taxis from the airport now. One paid the fare to town in advance at a kiosk and handed the receipt slip to the cab driver. By midnight only a few old black-and-yellow Peugeot taxis were waiting outside. Judith approached the car at the top of the rank. A Chinese, whose body was shaped like a squashed loaf of bread, levered himself from the front seat and stood looking at Judith with his square head lowered, as if preparing to charge at her.

'Hotel Malaya, please,' she said and handed him the receipt slip. The driver took it. Judith got into the cab. The driver got into the cab. Nothing more happened.

'Hotel Malaya,' Judith said.

The man nodded and sat there.

'I want to go to the Hotel Malaya,' Judith said.

'We wait,' the driver said.

'No. You give me back my receipt,' Judith said.

The driver shook his head. 'We wait.'

Groups of people were getting into other taxis and driving off. Judith opened the door; the driver turned around.

'You get out? You no get out!' he shouted. 'I sick man. I very sick. I work.'

She managed to snatch the receipt from him and scrambled from the back seat. The driver ran after her down the roadway, towards the one remaining taxi.

'I take four person only! I need money. I very sick,' he yelled.

The driver of the other cab looked at her and made the honking sound which puzzled Malaysian Chinese make.

'Please take me to the Hotel Malaya,' Judith said, thrusting the receipt at him.

The driver shook his head. 'You, him,' he said, pointing to his huge colleague.

The first man had caught up with Judith. 'O.K., O.K., O.K., O.K.,' he panted. They returned to his taxi and set off at irate speed.

There was nothing to see except an occasional ghostly row of rubber trees. The old plantation stretched for kilometres, then there was complete blackness again, and after a while a luminous glow, then factories with the names of British companies on them. Independence or not, the colonial master held still, as Judith knew, the lion's share of the economy. She glared at Crosse and Blackwell in neon lights. Houses and a hotel – the Sahid – appeared. The driver swerved into its drive and stopped.

'This is not the Malaya,' Judith said.

The driver opened the door. 'You get out. You get other taxi.'

They had a scene about the receipt slip but Judith, through the sheer energy of desperation that is the traveller's aid, won. Somebody who was asleep on the front steps of the Sahid, when tempted with a *ringgit* note to do so, got up and whistled her another cab. Half an hour later she arrived, shaken, in the centre of Kuala Lumpur at the Hotel Malaya. The left-hand back door of the second taxi had, on a curve, flung open and Judith had saved herself from falling out on to the roadway by clinging to the seat. The driver, a Malay haji, had chuckled, addressed Allah, and reached back with one arm to slam it shut again. Judith was too flooded with adrenalin after that to pay attention

75

to the streets they were passing. The stupid, unfocused feeling that compounds from physical and nervous exhaustion and which reduces concentration to small nips at the environment had overtaken her. She noticed the red-and-gold *Kong Hee Fat Choy* signs plastered in the foyer, the plastic New Year peach and mandarin trees, and a sign by the lifts saying 'Special Raw Fish Dinner', but not much else.

There was no room booked at the Hotel Malaya for Wilkes or Wilkinson or Wills. The desk staff seemed thrilled about her lost luggage. 'Qantas. Lot of trouble, la!' they said, grinning.

A young Malay escorted Judith to her room and he stood grinning at her when he had – more for his own amusement than for her education, she thought – operated all the electrical gadgets there. She was too stupefied to understand his instructions about the airconditioner.

'You travel alone? You stay alone?' he asked.

Judith nodded.

'You like a drink?' He was a very pretty boy and his expectations of success were evident.

'No. I just want to go to sleep.'

He looked from her empty hands to the bed and grinned some more. Half an hour later when Judith was just dozing off he knocked on the door. 'I bring you nice drink. Still early, la. You have nice drink', he called.

Judith tiptoed to the door and put the safety chain in place. She could hear him muttering nastily outside and was shivering with nerves when she got back into bed, naked. She was unable to go to sleep for another hour and in that time her brain jitterbugged with ideas so dejected and bitter that at one stage she began sniffing in misery. She thought, When women everywhere were downtrodden at least they were in the main treated gently, like pets, because they were so vulnerable. Now we have claimed equality but we've not won respect, merely hostility. She recalled suddenly what it was that she had disliked about the Singaporeans. They had been no more brusque than Australian airport staff; they had, however, not been submissive. One expected Asian flunkeys to be submissive, like women. I'm a class traitor, she thought, and, I should have been more supportive of Minou to those drunken bums in Singapore.

She awoke with a jolt from the sound of something being slid beneath the bedroom door. The room was in darkness. She lay still, waiting for the next noise, taut with the sense of vulnerability that nakedness causes.

Nothing happened.

After a few minutes her fright abated. She switched on the bedside lamp and saw that a newspaper, printed in Chinese characters, had been pushed into the room. It must be morning. A photograph of Deng Xiaoping shaking his fist accompanied the lead story. Judith found her watch on the bedside table. It was six o'clock local time, which meant she had had about three hours sleep after being awake for almost twenty-four. She felt ratty, as if her brains had been fried, and when she recalled the events of the previous evening she snivelled with rage.

She went to the window and drew the blackout curtains. The sky was tenderly coloured, on the flood from dawn to daylight, which happened in a snap as she looked at it. The sky turned pale blue and the grey shapes below and in the distance changed into buildings. Here and there, on hilltops, there were patches of black-green jungle: monkeys had frolicked in them before, she remembered. On that first day, with Ben, she had asked him to stop the car and had coaxed a tiny monkey to scamper from the troupe and accept a peanut from her palm. It had eaten it squatting not far away from them, constantly flicking glances at her, its little jaws working overtime.

The jungle ink blots looked smaller, now. Seven storeys down men in pyjamas shuffled out of front doors and silently

77

spat on the roadway. A man on a bicycle delivered a butchered pig to a woman who appeared to be shouting at a knot of young men wearing white singlets and baggy khaki shorts. A few cars passed noiselessly, though they could well be honking their horns at nothing in particular, Judith thought. Sound and heat were occluded from the room by the sterile blast of the airconditioner. The view was of utterly normal Chinatown activities, and yet, back then .. She shivered, cold from the airconditioning and dirty, stripped of the comfort of even a toothbrush. She had picked this hotel from a travel agent's list because it *was* in the centre of town, where everything had been boarded up and great curls of fire had flowed upwards into the night sky. There had been a sickening stench of burning rubber. Ben had said that usually this area smelled of sandalwood incense, curries, drains and 'the Indian favourite, attar of roses'.

It was still too early to ring anyone to enquire about Minou's disappearance. Judith made the best toilette she could and set out for breakfast in the street.

The air outside the hotel felt as sticky as warm beer and was laden with the sounds and scents of intense, competitive small-scale capitalism. In flower stalls children were wrapping coloured tissue paper around individual chrysanthemum flowers, attempting to outdo the children at adjoining stalls. A dozen metres further on was a collection of food stalls. There were few customers but the young men in baggy shorts and singlets flashed their cleavers over chickens and shallots and ginger with an urgency which suggested Armageddon was at hand and that they, personally, were in charge of feeding their army before the battle. Every boy over the age of eight seemed to be smoking.

Judith took a seat at a footpath restaurant and within seconds a waiter appeared in slapping sandals beside her and said, 'Aaagh?' Seconds later he slapped a bowl of chicken rice on the table, splashed tea into a cup by holding the pot about sixty centimetres above it, cleared his sinuses, spat, and slapped off again.

It is because they are here on sufferance, Judith thought. They know that any day the Malays might again take out their parangs. Every minute counts.

A newspaper boy walked up to her and held the *Straits Times* in front of her face. The lead story, she realized from the photographs, was the same as the one in the Chinese newspaper delivered to her hotel room. It said 'CHINESE TROOPS MASS ON VIET BORDER'.

At a nearby table a light-skinned Indian bought a newspaper also and sat stroking a fantasy beard as he read it. He looked up at Judith. 'There is only Thailand between us and Vietnam, isn't it?' he said. He added, 'And you Americans left the Vietnamese such a good arsenal. Many Hercules, Chinook helicopters and Iroquois gunships, isn't it? Even the poor boat people when they arrive here have beautiful M16s.' He swayed his head from side to side and Judith thought, We're all going mad. He uses gestures as old as his race and refers to military equipment like a snotty wire-service reporter.

The waiter honked 'Aaagh?' and smiled at Judith with astonishment when she paid. The astonishment was, she recalled, another local peculiarity. Ben said the Chinese had known for almost a century that Western women did not have long, hairy tails - as they had previously believed - but they still seemed to find it odd that they obeyed the laws of gravity. Or the conventions of commerce, Judith thought now. She tried honking back at the boy, which affected him with a crescendo of quacking and giggling.

She turned the corner and walked slowly down Petaling Street, groping back into memory. There was a shop here, she recalled, which Ben had shown her on the afternoon before, as she referred to it mentally, 'we rescued the Indian'. The shop had been particularly horrifying. It was still there, though no longer locked with an iron grille with the caged animals dying inside from lack of food and water, as they had been then when the proprietors had been too busy saving their own lives to care for their stock. A sign said 'Pets Shop', in English, which was, Ben had told her, a poor translation.

A Chinese woman invited Judith inside now. The first stacks of cages held little dogs, stub-tailed orange cats, baby monkeys and birds of all sorts. Judith followed a narrow alleyway between the cages into gloom and the sharp smell of reptilian ordure. There, as Ben had warned her, were the other pets: pythons, cobras, kraits, civet cats with mad yellow eyes, wells filled with snapping turtles and cage after cage of giant monitor lizards. On the floor a hessian bag heaved and bulged from the life inside it.

Judith knelt in front of a lizard wrapped upon itself in a cage that was far too small. Its blunt snout rested upon its front paws and it looked into Judith's face with an expression of desolation. It looked ill, for tears dribbled from the corners of its eyes.

'Hullo, old friend,' she said, and the creature raised its head slightly and flicked its tongue. You could talk to any animal, she'd discovered in childhood. You had only to wish them well, and they responded, even creatures whose intelligence was ancient and dim recognized something, some common vibration of the heart.

The shopwoman startled her. 'You buy? Him very good.' She had a thirty-centimetre-long chopper in her hand. She reached to open the cage.

Judith jumped up. 'No. No. I don't want it.'

The woman looked at her with incomprehension. 'You buy frog,' she said.

Judith shook her off and went to look at the pythons coiled up into beehive shapes in their tiny prisons. Some were ordinary brown-and-black ones, but there were others coloured

80

lemon yellow, and one immense snake whose coils surged and contracted as she approached, trying to move but constricted by wire and iron. Its scales were rose pink, silver and white.

'We are a horrid species,' she said to the python.

Looking back towards the shop entrance she had the sensation of being deep inside a cave and wanted suddenly to escape into daylight. As she hurried forward she came upon the shop woman again standing at a wooden table. A set of old-fashioned scales with brass weights was beside her. She had opened the hessian bag and was plucking huge frogs from it. With one movement she decapitated them, with a second stripped the skin from their halved bodies and with a third tossed them on to the scales, where they continued to flex their flayed hind limbs.

'You buy frog?' she called. Her hands kept on killing and skinning. Like a machine, Judith noticed.

The little dogs fawned and tried to flirt with her as she dashed out into the street. She thought, They are harmless. Why can't we be?

Standing there, she remembered that smooth, silver-haired Foreign Affairs man. He'd said, 'They are wicked people, to our way of thinking. They live with a power structure different from ours and have internalized, as conscience, a different type of authority. Conscience, I feel, defines a culture ... For them, family law rather than impersonal, state law is the internalized authority. To us, they appear flawlessly immoral, and I rather gather they hold the same view of us. It's really a conflict between differing consciences.' He had gazed at her speculatively, to Judith's irritation, because clearly he was thinking that she would be an innocent abroad. 'The temptation for us to condemn them is remarkably strong,' he said, then added, 'Oh dear, I do sound like the Moderator of the Presbyterian Church!'

Judith stood outside the pets shop calming her urge to

retch. The street was filling with gaudy new motorcars and the pavements were becoming crowded with small, neat, fast-moving people. Chinese girls in pairs clickety-clacked past, as slick and pretty as dolls. Ben, she remembered, had called all Chinese girls 'Mini Poos', all young Chinese men 'Hung Fat' and he and everyone else had referred to the Malays as 'the bloody bumis' – an abbreviation of *bumiputera*, noble sons of the soil. These mildly unsavoury satires on race were invented by people, unconsciously, to let off steam. Recalling the silly names Judith herself was calmed by them. She set off to find the exact place where they had rescued the Indian, but soon became lost in a maze. There were Chinese department stores, Indian cloth merchants, street markets, curry houses, noodle restaurants, and shophouses in the depths of which Chinese families could be seen engaged in trivial, mysterious activities. The streets smelled sweetly of incense and spices. She walked for an hour. The Indians and the window displays of poisonous-looking delicacies aside, it could have been a hot summer morning in Sydney's Dixon Street. The mob and the flying boy were lost, like a dream.

She retraced her steps back to the Malaya, thinking it would be time to make some phone calls, to start work.

Three members of the foyer staff rushed at her as she entered. 'Mrs Wilkes! We have found your luggage!' They looked almost as triumphant at its discovery as they had on learning of its loss.

The most important male – one wearing a suit not a uniform – led her to the desk where he unfolded a telephone message slip. 'We rang Qantas for you. Your baggage is located. It is going to London!' He was overjoyed by his cleverness but skilfully adjusted his face when Judith replied, 'Shit.'

'Aaagh?' he said.

'How long before I can have it back here?'

He held one hand in the air and rotated it swiftly. 'Four–five days, la.' He saw this caused displeasure. 'One–two days, la!'

On the way back to the Malaya a cloth merchant had beckoned her into his shop with a bolt of pretty fabric.

'Will this feel hot?' Judith had asked him.

'Very hot, la.'

'I want something cool,' she'd said.

'Very cool, la. Cool, cool,' he had assured her.

She thanked the desk clerk now and returned to her room. It took some determination to discover from the telephone company the phone number of the local Reuters representative. Judith began to tremble as she reached to dial the number, imagining that Ben might answer. Then she realized how ridiculous she was being. Ten years ago he had already packed up his flat and was on the point of leaving Malaysia for a new posting in Karachi. A couple of years after that, in the non-member's bar, a journalist had said, 'Met an old mate of yours in Bangladesh. Ben ... Ben?' 'How was he?' she'd demanded. The man had grimaced. 'Wanted to get home to London, to his wife and kid. That's all any of us wanted when we went into a village after the Pakistani army had been through it.' A sense of betrayal had filled her skin for days; at home she'd been surly with Richard.

A Malay answered the phone and Judith thought, Of course, the Malaysianization programme. She found it a relief to hear a voice which did not chop up sentences as though they were lengths of vegetable to be stir-fried – even when excited, as this one was. There had not yet been a ransom note for Lady Hobday, nor any sightings of her, the syce or the car.

'But I tell you the government cannot hold the embargo for another day,' he said. 'Every journalist from Singapore to Bangkok knows.' He dropped his voice, as if Special

Branch bugs might be hard of hearing, and added, 'You see, the theory is that this is an act of the *dakwah*.'

'The what?'

There was a note of rectitude at the other end of the line. 'I am a Muslim myself. But these *dakwah*, they go a little too far. And with the example of Iran . . .'

Judith did not have even a notebook. On the back of a breakfast menu she roughed out a few paragraphs about the kidnapping of Lady Hobday by Islamic fanatics who objected to her work for the Vietnamese refugees.

9

There was a rain tree in the front of Ralph and Sancha Hamilton's house. Its trunk was perhaps four metres in circumference but nobody was able to measure it because it was clad with creepers, great-stemmed vines with leaves like breast feathers from huge black-green birds. Its lowest branches, which spread in a straight line twenty metres long, carried whole greenhouses of staghorns and ferns and were mottled with lichens, so that from the ground the tree looked endangered by its own mighty capacity to sustain parasites. It seemed doomed.

From the upper storey of the house, however, one could see its canopy of pale green leaves and its profusion of small pink flowers. From this vantage point the rain tree had an unexpected appearance of gaiety and vitality. Ralph, who knew nothing about trees and flowers, found the rain tree inexplicably attractive and would look at it each morning through the upstairs bedroom window as he was getting dressed.

When the servants reported that snakes were nesting at its base and Sancha had suggested that the creepers, if not the tree itself, should be cut down, he had become enraged and had afterwards felt foolish. He was unaccustomed to shopping, which he regarded as a female occupation, but the next day had gone to a market and bought a mongoose which he had released beside the tree. His tone had held the spite of triumphantly recouped dignity as he said, 'You *see*, Sancha?' when the animal, after only a few minutes, had reappeared from the undergrowth with a snake in its jaws.

This morning Ralph was standing at the bathroom window, which also faced the front garden, dawdling over his shave as he looked at the tree. Sancha was still in bed, where she would stay for breakfast, since the amahs were expert in dressing and feeding the children, despite their resistance. This process was now in train and shouts of 'I'll kick you, Ah Moi' were coming from their bedroom. Like other white children whose mothers regarded the locals with grim patience – it was, after all, convenient to have servants – the Hamilton tribe had become uncontrollable after a fortnight with Chinese nannies. Ralph laid into the eldest boy with his belt every so often, and had accustomed himself to the child's dislike, which was mutual.

The telephone rang and Ralph said, 'For Christ's sake, answer it.'

'It's for you, darling,' Sancha called. 'Mr Hussein.'

'It must be about Minou,' Ralph said. He ran back to the bedroom, holding the towel he was wearing around his waist with one hand and grabbing the receiver with the other from his wife. '*Selamat pagi*, Hus. *Apa kabar?*'

Mr Hussein from Special Branch did not respond with the friendliness that a few words of Malay would usually elicit from a Malay. Ralph frowned deeply as he listened in silence, saying 'I see' and 'You think a press conference will be necessary?'

He replaced the receiver and stared at Sancha but she might as well have been a blank wall. Then he began to swear.

'Ralph, please!' Sancha said.

'Shut up. I'm thinking,' he replied.

He returned to the bathroom, finished his shave and took a shower. Always when showering now, his mind, intoxi-

86

cated by water, roamed freely for a few moments then created an image of Lan. For five minutes her silky little body pressed against him as he stroked a lather of soap and warm water over his chest and belly. When he stepped out on to the bathmat his thinking was focused. Hussein's news had been good, and bad. Minou had been found, safe, on a beach close to the village of Dungan on the East Coast. She had spent two nights sleeping there, having neglected to cancel her booking at the Pantai Motel in Trengganu, thus alarming its manager, who had contacted the local police. She had, she'd claimed, been waiting for giant turtles. Hussein's voice had been cool as he said 'We have informed Lady Hobday for her future reference that no leatherbacks will be coming ashore to nest there for another four months.' Ralph's face wrenched itself into a smile. Next to the statistic that Malaysia had the world's greatest supply of rubber and tin, the turtle-nesting season was the most often repeated fact you could hear in KL. Tourists came from Okinawa and Arkansas to see them. Hussein had not needed to rub it in further but had paused, then said, 'There was an extraordinary coincidence. On Lady Hobday's second morning – just a few hours ago – a boat carrying two hundred Chinese from Ho Chi Minh City arrived. There has not been a refugee boat for several weeks. The local villagers were . . . surprised by this coincidence.' 'I see,' Ralph had replied, holding his breath for the next bit – that the villagers had stoned the boat people. But Hussein had continued, 'Luckily the Trengganu police arrived quickly and there was no trouble.' His voice had become friendly for the first time. 'There have been some irresponsible rumours about kidnapping. Fanatical groups and so forth. The Department of Information will hold a Press conference this morning and explain it was nothing more than a wild turtle chase. Sir Adrian, of course, will not want to be distracted from his duties for a minor matter like this.' Hussein had that special suaveness of the

Malays; he had too the toughness of the Brits who had schooled him during the Emergency in the most efficient way of eliminating Chinese terrorists. He was still rather high on the Communist Party assassination list, people said. Smiling into the telephone he continued, 'It occurred to me, Ralphie, that you might come along to answer any questions. This is only an informal suggestion, from a friend. You would have to clear it with Sir Adrian, but you could assure him you would be welcome. As well as, naturally, your Press officer. Still Fred Sykes, is it?' Hussein paused. 'Such a well-meaning fellow, Sykes.'

Ralph returned to the bedroom where Sancha, propped on pillows, looked at him in the nervous way he found infuriating. He said, 'Minou is O.K. She went walkabout for a couple of nights, that's all. The Malaysian government is angry but they want to keep a very low profile on it. For the time being. They've picked me out for a hiding, as Hobday's proxy, at a Press conference this morning. I've been chosen so that they can make their irritation with our miserly immigration policy on the refugees known, without stating it.' The Press would get the point, Ralph knew, but would probably not report it until there was a more substantial show of irritation by the Malaysian government. They would store it away in memory, however, as a straw in the wind. He could not be bothered explaining all this to Sancha, whose involvement with politics was restricted to ticking the ballot papers every few years.

'Darling!' she said.

For a moment her sympathy stirred him and he moved closer to her upstretched arms, then he saw the pelt of long fine hair on them. He sat on the edge of the bed, concentrating on pulling on his socks.

'I'll have to have it out with Hobday. Minou is heading for big trouble. This can jeopardize Hobday, me . . .' He held his head, thinking, The Malaysian government might choose to make me the scapegoat and demand my recall. His guts began to churn.

Sancha was saying 'You know, darling, Minou practically ordered me to go with her to the Bellfield camp last week. I told her I wasn't going to risk my health by traipsing in there to show so-called educational films, which they can't understand, anyway. She was quite unpleasant about it. She didn't say anything, but her look! I told her that the Hamilton family does quite enough for the refugees. I mean, look at you. Your tummy trouble. There's no doubt you caught that up at Pulau Bidong, living on nothing but noodles for days, sleeping on a table.'

Ralph made a gesture of annoyance.

'The refugees live on noodles. They don't get sick.'

Sancha replied in a tone which indicated that she was determined to be reasonable. 'Ralph, they're used to nothing better', and he turned to stare at her. He had told her often enough that many of them had been millionaires – bankers, factory owners, film stars – with wealth beyond her understanding. They had lost everything but their courage and their integrity. 'The bravest people I've ever met,' he'd said. He looked at her now, lying in bed, letting the servants do her job as a mother, too lazy for anything more than tennis and shopping and beauty treatments. The last somewhat ironically named, he thought, glancing at her early-morning face.

'Darling,' Sancha said softly. Once she had been so pink and white. 'You're like a piece of china,' he'd said to her, his wonderment at her skin and shiny hair swelling terrifyingly, as he spoke, to another feeling – hostility. He'd had to keep it secret, as he'd fingered the texture of her Italian clothes, him, without even a suit to his name. 'Ralph's fiancée is a real socialite,' his mother had confided to her cronies. But after the headiness of victory in marrying her the maddening excitement – it was like rape, he'd say 'I'm

89

going to rape you', and she'd be flattered, eager – had just vanished.

It was weeks now since he had been able to bring himself to approach her obediently outstretched body.

'Darling,' Sancha murmured. A flush like an echo of her early pink and whiteness had returned to her cheeks. She was glancing at his crotch which, beneath the blue bathtowel was swollen. He knew her legs would be smooth, because once a month she had the hairs ripped out of them by hot wax, applied by a Chinese masseuse who came to the house. Ralph moved towards her but suddenly his genitals hung dead.

Her pale eyes looked like cold mirrors and he was used to the chocolate colour of Lan's. 'Why do you think the French, then the Yanks, fought so hard to keep Indo-China?' he would joke up at Bidong. Sancha's appeal abruptly seemed an invitation to something repulsive, like mating with a fish.

He clasped his forearm over his waist and belly. 'My guts,' he said, and hurried back to the bathroom.

The slight twinge he thought he had felt disappeared as he locked the door. He spent five minutes standing at the window, looking at the rain tree, and thinking of Lan. When he had first interviewed her as a refugee he had known only that she was a widow and that her child had been murdered by pirates. He had given her a recommendation for priority entry to Australia. When later he had learnt the full story he had advised her never to speak of it again, especially to Minou, explaining, 'I know she seems sympathetic, but deep down she has one idea only: her own family. The rest of the world comes second.' 'Of course,' Lan had replied, puzzled at his implication that there could be any other way. Minou had once told Ralph that all her family was dead; refugees rarely told the truth, until they felt safe.

He heard the telephone ringing again and Sancha talking

animatedly. He went on gazing at the tree's mysterious vitality while he fingered his belly. There were no terrifying lumps in it, though here and there it jumped and fluttered eerily, like a pregnant woman's. The Sikh doctor, a man of bovine calm, had looked at him reflectively after the examination and had said, 'You have an illness of the soul, Mr Hamilton. You aggravate it by alcohol, cigarettes and spicy food. No drug can cure it.' He tapped his head and his heart. 'It will become a cancer – what we call a cancer – quite quickly if you cannot resolve this . . . this problem of conflicting desires.' He had given an indolent shrug.

Ralph stared at the lovely pink flowers on the rain tree and thought, I will live! I will myself to live! He turned away from the rain tree, flushed the lavatory for effect, and went to see what Sancha was gabbling about on the telephone.

'Here he is now,' she said and covered the mouthpiece with her hand. 'It's Judith Wilkes. She's heard the most extraordinary stories about Minou, but I've told her it's all nonsense. She can't get to the Press conference because she's got to buy some clothes. They've been lost by Qantas, wouldn't you know? She says she's beginning to smell.' Sancha raised her eyebrows at Ralph to indicate that such an admission, from Judith, should be taken seriously.

Ralph smiled involuntarily as Judith went through her patter of introduction. He had imagined she would have the same upper-class nasal twang that Sancha had, but her voice was soft and breathless, as if each word were snuggled in fur, and despite his decision to dislike her he grinned at her projected presence. He told her everything about Minou's adventure that Hussein had told him, realizing only at the end of it that he had responded to a professional interviewer's telephone blarney, and that she had conned him. 'You smart bitch,' he thought. Judith was bemoaning her ill-luck in being held up because of the loss of her clothes and typewriter.

91

'I wouldn't worry about it,' Ralph said. 'There are three days of religious festivities coming up – the Prophet's birthday tomorrow, Thaipusam on Saturday, and the Chinese St Valentine's on Sunday. Most officials are taking a long weekend and their minds won't be on the job after this morning. You may as well relax.' His carefully rounded voice became avuncular. 'Look, Judith, there is a wonderful travel story for you in Thaipusam, the Hindu festival.' He almost ruined his spiel by laughing as he added, 'It's very colourful. Everybody should see it at least once.'

Sancha was looking at him fretfully, but he flapped his hand at her to keep quiet. He ended 'O.K. If you promise to get up at 2.30 am, I'll fix it with a mate of mine to take you,' and rang off.

He poked an index finger at Sancha. 'Not a bloody word out of you. It should come as a surprise.' As he began to dial Kanan's telephone number he added, 'You've never been to Thaipusam, anyway. You only yap-yap hearsay about it.'

Ralph sat on the edge of the bed with the handpiece to his ear, grinning. Kanan, whom he loved like a brother, was a sucker for a soft voice. Like a lot of Indians he attended to a woman's voice and her walk as marks of beauty. Ralph hoped that Judith had a nice, undulating walk. The vibrant days in Sydney in that Ultimo flat he and Kanan had shared – 'Those times have seized upon my imagination for ever,' he'd once admitted to Kanan. He smiled broadly, inwardly, as his most cherished picture of Kanan came back into mind – black arse in the air and what looked like a dozen white arms and legs flashing around on the bed. There had only been three of them – a couple of freshers and a psychology tutor – but in 1963 getting just one into the cot had been a major operation. Kanan had turned round and said, 'Ralphie, Ralphie, come and meet my milkmaids.' They'd had to move on to the floor for lack of space.

A year ago, when they had met again in KL, embracing at the airport, Sancha and the kids forgotten, and then Christ knows what ... an afternoon, a night and another day talking and on the piss together ... Ralph had said, 'Now for a couple of milkmaids, eh Kanan?' Kanan had replied, bewildered, 'But I am married, Ralph' and for a moment they had looked into each other. Kanan added, 'I must go home to Mariam, isn't it?' That look of his had been like a hot needle. Ralph had stared into his beer and said, 'You don't want to play up?' His question dropped between them, a rock dropped into a chasm.

'This will be two birds with one spear,' he muttered to Sancha. Then he began swearing when he realized that Kanan's telephone had gone unanswered for twenty rings.

10

The auntie with a nose-jewel had gone around grumbling after she had finished her prayers at five am and these grumbles had developed into a thunder storm of Tamil at six-thirty when Kanan displayed little appetite for his breakfast of *chapatis*.

'Alcoholic,' she said. And 'Cow-eater,' and having made the egregious accusation, she worked herself into a frenzy. She was a small, wiry woman past child-bearing age and she chewed betel, so that her lips were scarlet and her teeth dark brown. This gave her a frightening appearance like a mandrill's, Kanan thought, when she was angry.

He sat at the table watching the *chapati* become soggy while auntie raged about his sins. They were numerous and had begun five years before his birth, when Kanan had refused to be conceived.

'Five years! Five years your parents asked you to come, but oh, no! Mr Stubborn. You made your father carry the *kavadi* five years before you were ready. Mr Too Proud To Be Born! You didn't care about how your mama suffered. You wanted to come out of a lotus. Then, one day you turned up, Mr Little God, for your mama.'

Kanan pulled off bits of the *chapati* and fed them to the cat, which was a vegetarian. The auntie had progressed to his era of Mr Everything Western (which included a truly delinquent stretch of Mr Listening To Elvis Presley) and

94

had got on to Mr Lover Of Cow Murderers. Kanan fed the cat lime pickle, which made it sneeze and made auntie pause for a moment. Mr Kill Cat would be included in future, he supposed. The auntie finished in a hurry, since it was almost seven o'clock and time for Kanan to leave for the polyclinic.

'Now your wife is in pain, pain, and you are Mr Run About Town, Mr Drinking All Night.'

'Would you like to come with me to the polyclinic?' Kanan asked.

'Nephew,' the auntie said, 'you are a good boy at heart.' She started to grumble again, quietly, while she collected the mushy packages of herbs she had already prepared to take to the polyclinic, in case Kanan should invite her. As a widow whose sons were plantation workers, she considered herself a servant in Kanan's house. It had not occurred to her that she could ask him to take her to the polyclinic.

'What have you done, nephew, to get only daughters?' she muttered. 'Why are you being punished?'

'I like daughters,' Kanan said.

The auntie gave him a sharp look and went off to change into her nose-jewel for visiting.

A bank occupied the first two storeys of the building which housed the polyclinic; the surgical theatre was on the third floor, and the labour, maternity and nursery wards were on the fourth, at the top of the building. From the footpath below passers-by could observe women leaning out of the top-floor windows, shouting at men in the street.

As Kanan was gingerly steering his car into a parking space he was distracted by the screams of a Chinese woman above, which were being returned by a Chinese man cooking at a mobile stall. The smell of frying garlic, which Kanan enjoyed, was hard to detect even at this early hour when the air was soft and easily imprinted with aromas. For, across the road from the polyclinic building sprawled the Kuala

95

Lumpur Pasar Borong, the city's wholesale market, and from it came the smell of rotten shrimps. Kanan's auntie poured some rose-essence scent on her handkerchief and clapped it over her nose.

A Malay strolled past and she muttered, 'Eater of rottenness'. The street cook made a rude gesture at the Chinese woman, who threw a pink plastic bag out the window at him. It landed at the Malay's feet, bursting and splattering his high-heeled shoes with wet noodles. The Malay spun round and looked at Kanan and his auntie. The Chinese cook was giving minute attention to his frying vegetables and the Chinese woman had disappeared back inside the window.

The Malay advanced, glaring from his fouled shoes to Kanan. He was making the tiger noise of the angry Malay, Kanan noticed. 'Please, sir, to tell you frankly, I have not thrown noodles,' he said, but the Malay, who had now noticed a sliver of shallot on his trouser leg, was not paying attention.

He took Kanan by the throat and slapped his face. Kanan's eyes watered and the Malay slapped his face again. The auntie screeched in Tamil – fortunately she could speak no other language – 'Hit him, nephew! Hit the eater of rotten shrimps!'

Kanan stood still. The Malay spat and walked off.

The Chinese woman leaned out the window again and the street cook gave her a wave, shouting, 'O.K., O.K. Pork. No prawn,' and began tying up a new pink plastic bag of noodles for her.

There was no kitchen in the polyclinic and the ravenously hungry post-partum mothers relied on the street vendors for their meals.

All the way up in the lift Kanan's auntie said 'Mr Harmless. Mr Wouldn't Protect Himself. Mr Scared Of Malays.' It was known in family circles that Kanan had never beaten his wife. 'Mr Harmless' the auntie repeated.

'The *Gita* says we must do our duty, not the duty of others. I am a lecturer in history. It is not my duty to hit Malays in the street and thereby start race riots,' Kanan said and after this speech was silent.

His wife's room was filled with the scent of bunches of tuberoses and the even stronger smell of his mother-in-law. She was a big, powerful woman and she liked big, powerful colours: this morning's sari was watermelon pink, edged with gold. Two folds of mauve-brown blubber filled the space between the bottom of her lime-green choli and the top of her sari skirt.

'Get out! Get out, boy!' she shouted at Kanan when he put his head through the door and smiled. She and three other women were clustered around his wife's bed, performing rites of extreme, feminine delicacy. These mysteries were being observed by his two young daughters, seated together on a chair. The women whipped back the sheet over Mrs Kanan's naked, puffed belly and flexed legs. Kanan withdrew, charmed to have stolen a look at her, for it would be months before he would be allowed to see her naked again. Even his mother, who referred in private to his mother-in-law as Maharanee-Ride-On-An-Elephant, would combine forces with her on this point of marital protocol. Already she had snatched his daughters from him, carrying them off for a month with the authority of supernatural wisdom which descends upon Indian females when they reach grandmotherhood.

The auntie slipped through into the room, carrying her bags of mushy herbs. Maharanee-Ride-On-An-Elephant said 'Oooooh' up and down the scale and Kanan heard his wife whimper from what they were doing to her.

He stood in the corridor, unsure of what he should do.

An Indian nurse with a long black plait came by. 'Not

allowed in?' She was amused, as women always were by the irrelevance of men in these female strongholds. Then she became severe. 'They are putting herbs on your wife? Doctor will be angry, la! He says it is a filthy practice which does not promote healing.'

'The herbs are clean,' Kanan said.

The nurse rolled her head at him. 'I know. But doctor is modern.' They understood each other perfectly. 'Come, I will show you your daughter,' she said.

A Hakka nurse, as neat as a doll, was guarding the nursery entrance, inside which twenty iron-framed cradles, half of them painted blue, half pink, were on show behind a plate-glass window. Inside each was a bundle of brown- or yellow-skinned, new-born baby wrapped in white flannel. With their squeezed-shut eyes and shiny black birth hair they looked more like kittens than human infants, Kanan thought.

'Your name?' the Hakka said.

Kanan told her and stared at his shoes, for the Hakka's glance had been a frank invitation to see her later. She ran an orange-painted fingernail as long and sharp as a claw down her list.

'You have daughter. Pity, la.' Her smile now indicated that she, if given the opportunity, would do the right thing and would provide him with a son.

'I have three daughters,' Kanan said.

The Hakka decided he was unlucky, and shrugged. From the row of pink cradles at the back of the room she picked out a bundle and walked to the glass window, where she held the bundle up for a few moments for Kanan to admire. He swayed and his eyes half-closed, for he felt faint with joy. The baby was as pale as a lotus and a tiny hand, like a bud, was curled up against its mouth.

'Nice,' mouthed the nurse through the glass and took the bundle away again.

Kanan continued to stand at the window, transfixed by the glow from the new-born souls which he could see now shining around each one of the babies. Every tiny black head had a golden envelope of light. As his gaze wandered from one to the next he lost awareness of the limited world and floated upwards and hovered, looking down at the shimmering lights.

In Hakka the nurse quacked to another who had come by, 'They have such big penises but they only get girls out of them', and they giggled.

Kanan understood some Hakka from schooldays. He sighed. He had been celibate for two months already and it would be another three or more before his wife would receive him again. She was a simple girl, ten years his junior, and although he had the right to demand of her whatever he chose he would not frighten her by challenging her beliefs.

He returned to her room where Maharanee-Ride-On-An-Elephant said, 'So! You have seen your daughter! One disaster after another, with you. The child is white!'

'She is fair-skinned,' Kanan agreed.

Seven pairs of black female eyes looked at him disapprovingly. The eighth pair, his wife's, were lowered in shame, for although her husband was a partner in this misfortune, the blame was really hers.

'You are pleased! You have no pity for these poor children!' The Maharanee rushed to the two young girls on the chair and flung a protective arm around them, giving off as she did so a blast of body odour which made Kanan dizzy. 'How will they find husbands, these poor babies, when they are dark-dark and little sister is pale-pale like buttermilk?' she demanded. 'You better start praying now. Millions in dowry you'll have to pay. And how?'

'I will not pay dowry,' Kanan said. 'I will educate them. Then they will not have to get married at all, if they don't want to.'

The room filled with flapping coloured wings as the women raised their arms and their sari scarfs fluttered upwards.

'Mr Modern Man!' they shrieked at him. The abuse lasted for several minutes, then the mother-in-law took control of the floor again and jabbed her finger at Kanan.

'You go to the cave tomorrow, boy. You pray to the Lord and get your hair cut and show you are a decent man who will bring up his family properly. Hair *shaved*!'

They let Kanan look at his wife and press the present he had brought her between her palms, but he was not allowed in nose-rubbing range. When they jostled him and auntie out of the room again Maharanee-Ride-On-An-Elephant was muttering about carrying the *kavadi*, a theme which auntie took up on the drive home.

Kanan said to her in English, 'The *Gita* expressly warns us against excessive practices. Those who bear the *kavadi* are indulging in a vain and disgusting ritual which has been banned in Mother India since Independence, isn't it? To tell you frankly, the Malaysian government allows and even encourages us Hindus to admire the *kavadi*-bearers because it understands our weakness for God and for self-abnegation and it knows that if we are free to express this in the most difficult ways we will have no energy left to do anything but tap rubber. Soon Thaipusam will be promoted abroad as a tourist attraction, so that the sophisticated will be appalled and the naive impressed while the government makes money and laughs.'

In Tamil, he said, 'Yes, auntie.'

11

At dawn the sky and the South China Sea formed an unbroken pearl-coloured expanse, without horizon. The water, which could be deadly along the East Coast beaches for it had hidden undercurrents, especially strong at ebb tide, lay as smooth and lifeless as a sheet of tin and it was only by looking directly overhead that one could know that the silver-grey liquid had changed at some point to air. This was a miraculous place, no one understood why – though Mama would have an explanation, Minou knew – but something attracted the giant sea turtles to swim from far-off oceans to this one beach. In KL Minou had once asked a man at a cocktail party, who'd said he was studying turtles, what it was about this stretch of sand. 'Maybe it is a species memory they have. Distant ancestors hatched there, perhaps fifty thousand years ago, and somehow the geography of the place is patterned into their brains.' He'd pulled a silly face, adding 'Lamarck, you know,' (she didn't) 'is being rehabilitated. We understand very little, really.'

Bala, who was a good boy, had fixed up one of the beach shelters for Minou before she had sent him off in the car to sleep in Dungun, with instructions to return with her breakfast at 6.30 am. He'd arrived on the dot the morning before and would again this morning, in another hour. She lay propped on her elbows, looking at the straight wall of sea-and-sky, wishing she had told Bala to come earlier, for she was already hungry and there was nothing out there, nothing to wait for.

Then, it happened.

Minou started upright at what seemed at first an illusion, for with distances distorted the boat looked to be floating high up, in the sky. Then a pink thread defined the horizon, many kilometres back behind the dark blob, and she realized that the boat was real, and close in. She went rushing to the water's edge. The sun, rising above the sea, shot forward a red-gold spear. Suddenly the whole expanse turned to molten metal, blinding her. She stood clenched against herself, feet glued into wet sand beneath the incoming tide, willing it to be their boat, for Mama and the boys to be on board.

When she opened her eyes again she knew they were not. The air did not feel right, even now when the boat was close enough to hear the beat of its engine. Failure, again. Minou studied her feet, turned unfamiliarly pale beneath the cool lick of sea water. She had said to them, 'He'll only take me on the plane. But I'll get you out, when I've escaped. Don't let them take the house or we'll lose contact.' But they had taken it, of course, the bloodthirsty bumpkins. She still wrote every week to the old address in Cholon and in four years had received no letter in reply – so the house must have been requisitioned.

'*I* was requisitioned, the first time,' she'd told Adrian. 'That is – oh, you don't understand much, at twelve. Mama came to me and said "The military governor has asked for you". We were living in Song Be then, before we moved to Cholon.' Mama brewed herbs for my complexion – they were sickeningly bitter and I choked trying to drink them. She said, 'Learn now to swallow bitterness. Everything changes. Your beauty is today a curse for you; it will become a blessing.' The governor was kindly. When I had Quoc Quang he said, 'A doll with a doll'. Then one dawn, with

102

this same grey refracted light, when I was feeding Quoc Quang I looked out into the courtyard and saw the governor lying in his dressing gown under a durian tree with a note attached to the handle of a knife that stuck out of his back, like a flag.

'I wrapped up Quoc Quang,' she'd told Adrian, 'put him on my hip and walked home to Mama. Fifteen kilometres. I wondered all the time if anyone had seen me leave and if I'd be arrested and questioned. Quoc Quang was hungry – something had happened to my milk – and I had to steal a banana for him and chew it up and poke it in his mouth.'

And now . . . the boat was close enough to shore to anchor . . . now he was only a few years off military age, and he was a big boy (from the French blood of his grandfather, probably) and they might not believe that he was only thirteen. They were drafting the Chinese, especially, as front-line troops for the Kampuchean war. Chinese boys were expendable. And in the north . . . Adrian said there was going to be a Red Army invasion within another few weeks; it was in the top secret cables.

At least I've got Papa Adrian. He says 'You are *not* a failure. You have done everything you can to try to help them. This sense of shame that's instilled into you neo-Confucian children. It's worse than guilt. Guilt is for trespass. People can decide not to trespass, but they cannot, by an act of will, succeed against impossible odds. Can't you see that, Minou?' And then he gets exasperated and talks about history and stuff and the Japanese shame about losing the war and their emperor being made into an ex-god by General MacArthur. If I want to stop him, I have to say 'Papa,' and look at his cock.

Minou shook her head and jumped backwards – the water had crept up over her ankles, to her trouser-legs.

She looked up and saw the boat was anchored now, and some of them were climbing down a rope ladder into a

103

dinghy. That was smart. They'd brought a dinghy for the ones who could not swim. Some of the men were jumping overboard. The tide was coming in fast, and they were, too. She began jumping up and down, suddenly wildly exhilarated for them, for herself.

'Oh, you're like a spaniel!' She said that to the first man to reach the shallows and come rushing with a bow-wave in front of his shins to embrace her. A stranger.

And then it was all joyous confusion. Even when the fishermen came running along from the village, shouting, and the police arrived and fired shots in the air, and Bala came rushing saying, 'Quickly, Madam, there is trouble with Special Branch. Let me drive you away. We will say the car has been broken down and you have been staying in Mersing for two nights.' But she could not drag herself away from them – they had photographs from home and bottles of fish sauce. And finally when the police realized she had not arrived on the boat too, they said, 'Lady Hobday! We have been searching for you.'

They forced her to leave, took her off by police car to the airport, while Bala drove the Citroen back to KL. Her exhilaration had lasted throughout the flight, but as the taxi from the airport crossed the boundary road, Jalan Pekeliling, and rattled and clattered into streets which were like paths in a garden, so lush and green was everything around, she began to be frightened of what she had done.

Then she was home.

The Australian Residence was designed to impress, as were all of the houses in this area. Like most of them it was double-storeyed, with a semi-circular drive. Minou darted out of the taxi, leaving the servants to collect her luggage, and ran into the cool of the main reception room. It had white stone floors, was large enough to hold two hundred people and was, thanks to its fans and french windows, as light and airy as the seaside. But she felt suffocated by the room. Her mind had been suddenly forced to constrict on entering the house. The laughter she had shared with her compatriots, the expanded sense of life, was squeezed out.

A group of High Commission wives, jubilant with scandal, was seated at the far end of the room, taking morning coffee. On seeing her they fell silent abruptly then gathered their wits and rose, one of them crying, 'We've been so worried, Lady Hobday.'

Minou sauntered over to them. They took in her spike-heeled sandals and pencil-thin trousers and white shirt tied in a knot over her navel.

'I'm glad that worry has not ruined your appetites, la!' Minou picked up the last of the curry puffs and ate it noisily. 'Yum, yum,' she added, looked at the empty silver dish and then at each of the women, with their floral dresses exposing fat arms mottled by sun.

'Do sit down.' She raised her arm, sniffed her own armpit and said, 'Ouf!'

The wife of the military attaché stood up again, for Minou had remained standing. 'We called in to see if there was any way we could help.' She was unable to contain her moral outrage and added, 'Poor Sir Adrian has been frightfully anxious about you.'

Once, feeling a chord of sympathy in this woman, Minou had said, 'From the age of twelve I've had no compass for my life, except . . . well, anyway, it's been very confused and I've had to invent stories about it.' Within a week strangers at cocktail parties were approaching her, their feigned seriousness barely concealing their anticipated thrill as they said, 'Do tell me about your life. It must have been interesting.' Minou had not trusted any of them since, and grinned to see that they were bursting to know what she had done, and why.

In her Senior's Wife's voice she said, 'I'm going to have

a bath. Would any of you like to scrub my back?' She smiled to imply that this was not to be taken as entirely offensive, but that it was nevertheless their notice to clear out.

Minou's favourite servant, an old Black and White amah whom she called 'Aunt' in Cantonese and whom Hobday called The Wrath of God – she did have a face like a toad and her life of celibacy may have been enforced had she not voluntarily embraced it in childhood – panted up the stairs behind Minou. As she did, she muttered, loudly enough for the departing ladies to hear, about the consumption of curry puffs and 'fat'. A former high commissioner had warned Hobday, 'The Black and White considers it beneath herself to speak anything but bad English to her employers.'

Aunt or Wrath of God would stand at the breakfast table with its white napkins folded into fans, by her, and command Hobday, who was taller than she even when seated, 'You eat, Master. You got young wife. You need strong,' and would reel backwards, cackling. Once when she was massaging Minou – the woman had hands and wrists as powerful as a woodchopper's – she had said, 'You clever girl. Why you marry, Missus?' and when Minou replied, 'Love, Aunt,' had squeezed up her gargoyle face in derision.

'Master's new plants come,' she said to Minou as she ran the bath. She looked as though she were going to spit into the bathwater. 'No good. No flowers.'

Minou shrugged. Her husband was an enigma to her. He protected her, that was enough. That was all a woman wanted from marriage – a man who would not abandon you when you were pregnant (as had happened to Mama) or get murdered, like the governor, or turn out to be married to somebody else, like a certain American. From intuition, refined by years of study of male behaviour, she knew how to amuse Hobday and to what limits she could go before he would be alarmed by her. Beyond that she understood

106

little about him, and was incurious. As a matter of common sense she kept potential rivals at bay and encouraged all his passions, which included football and growing plants in a greenhouse, as well as the usual ones in men his age. When in company his conversation bored her or made her uneasy, but alone together they lived a life of rich play. Initiating the games was her side of the contract and the guarantee of Hobday's continued devotion, for he was addicted to them, as she had discovered on the night she had first been to bed with him, in Canberra. She had had an intuition that he was ripe with stored-up fantasies and had reached some point of despair which games would release. Hobday, with an air both of fear and exhilaration, had taken over from then on.

On the third night he had pleaded urgently, 'Will you marry me? I will divorce my wife if you will.' Although she had sworn off men for life, after that 'husband' from Atlanta, she had the healthy avarice of poverty, which was the reason for being in bed with Hobday at that moment. She had departed from the warm burrow of the Glebe sisterhood with few regrets.

Minou telephoned Hobday from the bathtub. '*Papa? C'est moi,*' she murmured. 'Why don't you come home? Baby wants to give you a kiss.' She made some soft purring noises into the receiver.

Hobday evidently had somebody with him in the room, for he said stiffly, 'My dear, I'm delighted you're home.'

Minou crooned, 'I want to fuck you, Papa.'

'I'm sure that would be in order, my dear,' he replied. 'Mr Hamilton has been giving me a most interesting briefing, which he has almost finished. I think, then, I could come home for an early lunch, as you suggest.'

'Ooooh, la! That again,' Minou said, giggled and hung up. She rang through to the kitchen and told the cook to prepare the luncheon trays. Then she painted her face, dressed herself in the pink gingham nightdress with matching frilled panties which Hobday had purchased for this game, and half-dried her hair. He – she thought of Hobday as 'he' – would want to dry it properly himself.

There had been no rain for more than a week, unusual for Kuala Lumpur, where it normally rained every couple of days, all year round. Despite the ceiling fans the bedroom would be too hot for him, in his suit, Minou realized. She shut the windows and turned on the airconditioner, then crouched under the bedclothes, rehearsing the most dramatic events of the story she would tell him. He had known in advance that the turtle story was a blind, that she was hoping to see a boat come in. But then she had made the silly mistake of forgetting to cancel her hotel booking, and this had led to all the fuss with Special Branch.

'He's angry with me,' Minou said aloud, for thinking back to her telephone conversation with him, she had realized his voice had been more stern than she might have expected.

He strode into the room without knocking and his expression was, as Minou saw with a fright, grave. She began to cower under the bedclothes then noticed that old Aunt was immediately behind him, carrying the luncheon trays. Minou sat still and contrite in the centre of the large bed, waiting for the servant to leave. Hobday paced up and down, also waiting. When the woman departed, he spoke.

'You have seriously embarrassed me, Minou. I've had to make a personal apology to the Foreign Minister and to explain the nature of your, ah, interest in turtles to the head of Special Branch. I did that as soon as I was told you were missing. For their own reasons the police chose publicly to pretend to go on looking for you. There's been hell's own delight with the Press.'

Minou began whimpering. Hobday merely noted her condition.

'I am in the middle of delicate negotiations on the boat

people. Embarrassment like this leaves me vulnerable to pressure from the Malaysian government to take more of them than Australia is willing to accept. I can't afford things like this. How you dress, how you treat the other wives, I don't care about. They are the tiresome trivialities of diplomatic life and I'm senior enough to be able to ensure that you can be as free as you wish, socially. But *this is different*. I cannot afford to become vulnerable, to be in the debt of a foreign government. And you, my girl, can't afford this obsession with your family.'

Minou was crying frantically now, for the terrifying thought had come back to her that she had gone so far beyond the limit of his tolerance that she would lose his protection.

Hobday's manner softened. 'It's over. Forget about it. I'll play golf with the King after lunch, and that ought to close the matter. Now stop crying.'

She dared to look up and saw that his face muscles were relaxing. He had a wet sponge in his hand.

'You know it has been worth every social inconvenience for me to ... uh ... have you,' he said. He sat on the bed to pat her face with the sponge. 'You mustn't be naughty like that again.'

Minou sniffed and gave him a look of brazen appeal. 'Baby is hungry,' she murmured. To her immense relief, he smiled. 'Open up,' he said.

After he had fed her, he dried her hair with a towel while she squealed and wriggled and he told her to keep still. He led her to the bathroom where he finished the grooming with an electric dryer; he was an expert now in rolling the circular brush through her hair. Minou watched him in the looking glass with wonder. She did not understand his pleasure in this mother-baby game. She knew only that it was necessary to him, for during it his large body became peaceful and his stony face took on contentment.

109

'You look seventeen years old,' she said and Hobday, absorbed, chuckled to himself.

He rang down to the kitchen for coffee. The play was over but he still had a luxurious afterglow, and lolled on the bedroom chair, cheerfully calling, 'Come in, come in' when there was a tap on the door. He even patted Wrath of God on the back of her yellow strangler's wrist as she set down the coffee cups.

'I had an interesting lecture from young Hamilton this morning,' Hobday said. He had crossed his legs at the knee and was holding his coffee cup daintily; these delicate gestures too, Minou had noticed before, were part of the afterglow of the game.

'Yes?' she listened brightly.

'Yairs. He seemed to be wound up in a way which I found . . . hmm . . . irrational in a man whose political sense is normally acute. He said he's afraid our refugee immigration programme will be cut out or cut down. The refugees are, of course, unpopular with the Australian electorate. Hamilton says that the ALP may make a promise to scrap the programme – give money, but allow no immigration – which would oblige the Australian government to make a similar pledge before the next election. I told him it would be a diplomatic impossibility for any government of ours to carry out such a policy. ASEAN retaliation against us for such an unfriendly act would be . . .' Hobday waved a hand languidly. 'No landing rights for Qantas? Oil blackmail via Islamic brothers in OPEC, which they could then extend to demands for lowering of our tariffs? Anyway he got very excited and tried to argue with me. Union pressure, fear of wage dilution and so forth.' Hobday paused. The marvel of being able to cosset Minou, yet also at times to talk to her as an intelligent equal, pierced him with pleasure. 'I got the idea that he has some personal interest in the refugee programme. Do you know anything about that?'

110

Minou was alert. 'He goes to Pulau Bidong more often than he needs to.'

'And does he have a special . . . friend there?'

'There was an interpreter a couple of months ago.'

'Ha! The spoils of power. Immigration officials are kings in those camps. And what else?' Hobday looked at her mildly. She was, he knew only too well, an habitual liar and even a thief, if she got the chance. Yet she was his other half, the part that lay dormant.

Minou shivered, nerving herself for betrayal. 'There's a woman called Lan who's his mistress now. He's given her a priority assignment but it will be three months at least before the backlog is cleared and she can go to Australia. And he shouldn't have selected her. She's got no job qualifications.' Minou was looking sulky. Hobday enjoyed her histrionics; years of self-discipline had robbed him of the power to express emotion. When she cried and sulked and giggled he was attracted to her by a force which seemed instinctual, it was so strong. 'You are my fatal solipsism,' he said to her once. She had smiled prettily.

'Go on,' he coaxed. Sometimes it took him weeks to get the truth out of her; sometimes he never did.

Minou burst out with it. 'She's a killer, la! Their boat was attacked by pirates and some people got killed. She worked out a trick to play on the pirates. Her people managed to get the pirates' pistols and knives, then they killed all of them. Lan herself shot five men. Everyone was talking about it on Bidong.'

'Hmmm. Justifiable self-defence, I'd say.'

'No, Adrian. She also killed her husband. She didn't like him.'

Hobday raised his eyebrows. 'Did she indeed? You're a fierce lot, aren't you?' he said amiably. He glanced at his watch and rose.

'By the way, I spent half an hour with your journalist

friend, Judith Wilkes, in the office this morning. Quite an attractive girl – that Marilyn Monroe voice – and sharp. Definitely sharp. Now, now, don't look at me like that. You are not Lan.'

Minou, in her pink baby's dress, propped up in the middle of the bed like a child's night-time doll, waved her long arms at him. 'Papa! Your plants came,' she shouted as he went off for golf with the King.

She sulked for a while over his remark about Judith, regretting her impulsive gesture of insisting that she stay at the Residence. She liked her, and she didn't like her. And the feeling was mutual.

'Book, Book, what will I do?' Minou said aloud, then hopped out of bed and went to the chest of drawers where, wrapped always in the piece of yellow silk that a great-grandmother had spun, woven and dyed, she kept the Book and the pouch of coins. 'The *I Ching* is all that's left of my life,' she had told Hobday when, shyly, she had first shown him the parcel. 'Be guided,' Mama had said. 'The Book tells us that which is hidden inside us, the wisdom of our hearts.'

Minou sat on the blue Tientsin rug on the floor to throw the coins, asking, 'What will happen when Judith comes to stay in my house?' and concentrated. Her hands, pressed together like butterfly's wings as she shook the three pieces of money, then flapped open to let the coins roll out on to the rug. She threw Revolution, changing to Obstruction.

Minou sometimes cheated with The Changes; she threw again and got a change to Possession in Great Measure. 'Goody,' she said aloud, in English, and rang downstairs for Aunt to come to the bedroom to give her a massage. It was no good puzzling what Possession in Great Measure might mean. That would become clear, in time.

Aunt entered the room and planted her hands on her hips, making a noise in her throat as if bringing up phlegm. Her

112

disapproval was caused by the fact that Minou was not yet prepared for her massage; she was still wearing her baby costume.

'Sorry, sorry,' Minou said, pulling the silly thing off and tossing it on the floor.

Aunt, kneeling beside the bed, squeezed her naked buttocks in silence. At length she said, 'You clever, Missus. Master very angry. Later, smiling.'

She continued her massaging, muttering to herself, slowly increasing the volume of her voice as the limbs softened from kneading, a rhythmic pressure that Minou experienced as sunshine rising through her body.

After a while Aunt was speaking aloud in the dialect they both understood. She said, 'You poor child. It is such a strain for you to be continually amusing an old man. I can feel the tenseness in your muscles when I rub them. Why don't you go home to China? Life is good there. It's so clean and beautiful and there are plenty of handsome men if you want to get married again. I go back every year now to the sisterhood's shrine and each time I feel more joyous. On my next trip I will die. China is safe. It is the only safe place in the world now for us Chinese. Everywhere else they want to kill us. We are the scapegoats for all their stupidities.'

Minou replied quietly, 'I know. In Ho Chi Minh City they treat us Chinese as if we were alleycats. But my mother and my three sons are trapped there. They can only escape to the south. I must stay here and wait for them. While they are trapped, I am also.'

'You chain yourself up,' the old woman sighed. 'I have nobody. I'm lonely sometimes. But I'm free.' In English she said, 'You lie on back now, Missus.'

12

Sancha Hamilton was fond of saying, 'The Club is a life-saver when the servants are away.' People knew immediately that she was referring to the Royal Selangor Golf Club. Her clothes and accent debarred her from interest in the Lake Club, nice enough as it was, even smart, these days.

The Golf Club was off Jalan Pekeliling, conveniently close to the Hamilton house, its gateway set in a part of the thoroughfare lined with huge trees which, if growing in a less luxuriant country, would have been considered miracles of nature. Their trunks rose twenty-four metres, massive and fluted like columns of grey smoke which, at a sudden moment while moving upward, had solidified. Awestruck newcomers to the city would often say, 'It's like The Garden of Eden' when they first saw the giant waringins and the rain trees, their outstretched arms dripping with ferns, giving shade to the club's lawns. Sancha would reply, 'More like the better parts of Brisbane, really.'

Sancha had invited Judith to lunch at the club, rather than at home because, as she had explained, 'The wretched cook expects a holiday for the Prophet's Birthday, and frankly I'm too desperately out of practice to manage more than fried eggs.' She had added brightly 'There are super people at the club. I'll introduce you to Tunku Jamie – he's one of the modern royals. Sure to be playing golf instead of going to the mosque.'

114

By the morning of their luncheon appointment, when Judith had been in KL thirty-six hours, she had received two cables from her editor. The first had said 'APPRECI-ATE YOUR URGENTEST ON KIDNAPPED WIFE' to which she had replied 'KIDNAP STORY A FURPHY APPRECIATE YOU DONT HASSLE'. But she had sent a seven-hundred-word backgrounder, marked 'HOLD'. The second cable, delivered an hour before she was to meet the Hamiltons, read 'REQUIRE YOUR PROFILE ON NON KIDNAPPED WIFE STOP IMPLICATIONS OF HER ETHNIC BACKGROUND COMMA INFLUENCE ON HUSBAND COMMA CONSEQUENCES FOR OZ REFUGEE DIPLOMACY STOP DEADLINE WEDNES-DAY STOP APPRECIATE FINGER OUT'.

She stood at her window looking down seven floors to where the Chinese mother from the pork shop was scolding her teenage sons who were leaning, as limp as boiled noodles, over their bicycle handlebars. A pink facsimile of a pig's head – a real pig's head, Judith realized – lay on the ground. Neither boy seemed inclined to pick it up. Just as insolent as my brats, Judith thought.

'You are sabotaging me, Bill,' she said aloud, as if Bill in his editor's glass box, thousands of kilometres away, could hear her – or would care. This sort of thing always happened. The minute you were out of his – any editor's – sight he got ideas for half a dozen stories, all of which would conflict with the main assignment. 'Require' in a cable was an order. She would have to produce the piece and jeopardize her chances of getting into the camps by offending Minou – or try to talk him out of it.

She rang through to Sydney. A photographer answered the telephone. 'Jees, dear, it's Friday lunchtime here,' he said. 'Bill's taken everyone to lunch in Dixon Street. I'll give you the number.' The photographer must have been looking over notes on Bill's desk, for he added, 'It says here, "Page 5 held

115

for Wilkes' story on Lady Hobday, 'The One Who Got Away', spill to page 6 with government, opposition views on boat people". Mean anything to you?'

She groaned. 'Listen, don't tell him I rang, O.K.?' She knew, from that note, that the machinery would already have been thrown into gear: two or more journalists would already be working on the domestic political angle. The mere fact of their interest would have alerted the politicians, who were always keen to get some publicity at this time of the year, when Parliament was not sitting and they were suffering from Attention Withdrawal. The government and shadow ministers would issue Press statements the moment they realized there was some benefit to be gained in the news media. This would attract the TV boys, which in turn . . .

Judith glared at her hired typewriter, then sat down to write. She typed 'YOUR REQUEST FOR PROFILE JEOPARDIZES CO-OPERATION OF LADY COMMA HUSBAND STOP PLEASE DELAY'. She thought of trying to explain in cablese that any half-good profile of Minou would need to be carefully etched in acid; that Minou would be unlikely to speak to her again after such a story had been published; that as Hobday's houseguest she would get the whole story, anecdotes, internecine diplomatic manoeuvres . . . Bill would always listen with curiosity to explanations of why an assignment was impossible. At the end of them he would say, 'Now you've told me why you can't do it, you can do it.' He was nicknamed The Zen Master. By general consent he was known as A Great Editor.

She took the cable form downstairs where a uniformed employee was wiping dust from each leaf of the plastic peach and mandarin trees in the foyer. In the morning light the female desk clerks looked even more like advertisements for cosmetics. One pincered the cable from Judith's fingers with her long nails. On impulse Judith snatched it back from her. She crossed out what she had typed and printed instead

116

'GONE TO EAST COAST STOP INCOMMUNICADO FOR ONE WEEK'. In the surprised silence this produced from the desk clerk Judith felt she could hear the shouts of rage in Sydney.

'If they ring?' the girl asked.

'I'm not available,' Judith replied. He would know it was all lies, she realized. Bill fought with the management when it perceived a left-wing bias in her Canberra profiles and he fought with the politicians when they complained of right-wing bias. He roared at libel lawyers. He had only once sacked a senior journalist – for lying to him.

'I'll take local calls but no international calls,' Judith added.

Sancha and Ralph Hamilton arrived a few minutes later. Ralph was seated in the front passenger seat of the powder-blue Mercedes, and leapt out for the introductions. He was affable, even effusive, as he helped Judith into the back seat. He had a small overnight bag at his feet and chatted about his trip to Pulau Bidong. He was to leave immediately after lunch. There he would interview the new load of boat people whom Minou had encountered during her beach adventure.

When Sancha swerved past a Sikh boy on a bicycle, saying, 'Watch out, Sambo', he jerked round to face her.

'Are you blind?' he shouted. He turned back to Judith. 'I don't drive a car in this city,' he said.

Judith thought, Just as well, with a temper like yours.

She looked at his pale grey eyes and his well-cast features, deformed almost to ugliness by the anger in his face, and wondered, What does a job like yours, having power of happiness or misery over thousands of people, do to a man born enraged against the world as you obviously were? The thought gnawed at her for the rest of the car trip, Sancha gingerly navigating between bicycles and motorbikes, until the distractions of the Royal Selangor Golf Club took over.

117

The golf course came to within a few metres of the swimming pool which had a wire fence and some long grass to keep stray golf balls off those bathers who chose to sit on the lawn under the umbrellas. Those who did this were nearly all Caucasians; other races preferred the shade of the poolside dining pavilions. A first impression of the place was one of apartheid. All the sunbathers, whether well-tanned, biscuit-coloured or pink, looked strangely etiolated, Judith noticed. The sunlight was too intense here for skins designed for more subtle illumination. Under the glare of noon, when black shadows shackled the feet, people's bodies looked gross and unhealthy – open-pored, hairy, fissured, spotted with pimples which the heat drew out on their shoulders and backs. Most of them seemed too stunned to swim or even talk but lay in sodden trance states, jerking their wrists occasionally for the attention of waitresses.

When Judith and Sancha returned from the changing sheds Ralph's eyes lingered on Judith's bosom but he soon lost interest when a Chinese waitress came to take their orders and stood gazing at him with admiration and promise. His chin went up and he flicked off his sunglasses to look back at the girl, a half-smile cracking one of his cheeks.

Judith had seen this expression often before, in Canberra, on the faces of men conscious of their power – big-time fixers, ministers and business lobbyists. But Ralph was no tribal warrior. He was a bully of small-fry – his wife, his children probably. She thought, His job must corrupt him; it gives him power beyond his capacity.

'What effect does interviewing refugees have on the morale of immigration officers?' she asked.

Ralph shrugged. Sancha was fussing with her hair. 'I wish I could find that new Mason Pearson brush,' she said.

He glanced at her irritably. 'Go to the hairdressers again,' he said. To Judith he added, 'Lee Kuan Yew answered that. He said "You must have callouses on your heart or you bleed

118

to death." After you've heard the first one thousand sob-stories you don't listen any more.'

'But the refugees are desperate. If they don't get accepted for a country they know they're facing years in the camps. They've risked their lives to escape. Surely they're going to try to bribe . . .?'

'Oh, it's awful,' Sancha said. She was referring to her hair.

'Shut up about your bloody hair, Sancha,' Ralph returned his attention to Judith. 'What are you trying to suggest?' he asked coolly. Judith thought, I've hit a nerve.

'I'm really trying to work out the morality of the whole business,' she replied.

The drinks and food arrived. Sancha pulled a face as she sucked her straw and said to the waitress, 'I ordered gin in my lime.' To Judith she added, 'God, they're hopeless. Back in the fifties, people say, there was one servant to every three members in this club. You'd only have to lean back slightly in your chair and a little man would appear at your shoulder. Now you have to shout your lungs out, and they can't even get the orders right.'

'Very sorry. I get gin-lime,' the waitress said.

Ralph had relaxed. 'There is no morality. One million Chinese, the Hoa Vietnamese, are going to be forcibly exiled from Vietnam in the next year, and when they arrive off the coast of Thailand and Malaysia and Indonesia their boats will be pillaged and capsized. So many of them will drown, and those who manage to swim will be shot or stoned to death.' His mouth was set in a hard smile. 'And that process will go on until China can't stomach it any longer. Then she will attack. And the whole of Indo-China and South-East Asia will blow up.' He leaned back, sipping his lime drink, satisfied. 'In ten years Australians will say "If only the West had taken more refugees this war wouldn't have broken out".'

'Darling, don't be morbid,' Sancha said. He didn't bother to glance at her.

'Hitler wasn't stopped. People always realize too late. You know that the Chinese are known as the Jews of Asia?' He laughed. 'There is already a staggering breakdown of international morality. The shipping code, Christ! It's hundreds of years old, but it has shattered in a few months. Ships of every bloody country simply sail past refugee boats in distress. In defiance of the rules – they're not just rules, they're the laws of humanity – they *ignore* distress signals. I've interviewed people who were dying of hunger and thirst, who were seen by ten, twelve ships, and *ignored*. We always think it doesn't matter if it's somebody else copping it in the neck. But it does. It will be our turn next.' His face muscles were tightened, pleating the flesh between his nose and mouth.

'What do you think it does to us here who care, spending all our time with people – the bravest people in the world – who are being hacked up by Thai corsairs, while we can't do a thing?' He suddenly doubled over.

Judith turned to Sancha, who was sitting up rigidly on her sun-couch. Her eyes warned Judith not to speak.

Ralph straightened up. 'Bit of gut trouble,' he said to Judith. He managed to smile, although his face was still grey. 'Were you asking what I personally do during the selection process in the camps?'

She nodded, dumbfounded. She found him appalling. What he said and what he did – his cruelty to Sancha – were so at odds.

'I take the strong ones,' Ralph said. 'The ones who've proved they can survive this mess. They're women mostly. I don't know why, but they're tougher.'

'We've had years of practice at surviving,' Judith said.

Sancha gave a little scream, 'Jude, you must not get Ralph on to that. He can't bear women's lib.'

I bet he can't, Judith thought. It probably scares him to death. He's only a mangy tomcat in lion's clothing. She and Ralph grinned at each other, bonded by mutual dislike.

Not far away an Indian, teaching his son to swim, was saying in a Cambridge voice, 'I shall now turn you on your back, isn't it?' and over on the golf course a group of Chinese in jaunty peaked caps were slapping each other and laughing. A light breeze rustled the palm fronds and the pink leaves of the crotons planted at the edge of the lawns. Although the sunshine was still strong outside the shade of the umbrellas, cool air came in light puffs off the pool's surface, momentarily drying the sweat which had broken out all over their skins. More fresh lime drinks arrived.

'This is bliss,' Judith said. 'I was so tired.'

'Yes! And I've found my hairbrush,' Sancha said. She had been fossicking in Ralph's overnight bag and now waved the brush aloft, triumphantly. Judith glanced at her and saw that she was blushing.

'The servants must have packed it,' Ralph said.

Sancha sat bolt upright. 'Darling, how could they? They weren't in the house this morning.'

Ralph grunted. He made a small, uneasy gesture. 'I don't know how it got there. Perhaps you packed it.'

'Ralph!' Sancha had become pale. Her arms were weirdly tensed, Judith saw. Jack-knifed upright on the sun-couch, she looked like a corpse that had suddenly sat up in a coffin. 'Ralph!'

Ralph said quietly and distinctly, 'Shove it up your cunt, Sancha.'

They were all silent. People at other tables were looking at them, aware from the aura of tension that something was happening. The three of them sat, as if paralysed, staring at the plump Malay in a peaked cap who was strolling along the lawn towards them. He was light-skinned and seemed rounded with self-satisfaction as much as with fat. A golf club rested casually on his left shoulder.

He was almost upon them.

The spell broke.

'Sancha, old thing,' he said. 'And Ralphie!' It's the rich prince, Judith thought.

Ralph leapt to his feet. They all began talking at once.

'Bugger of a game I've been playing this morning. Lost three balls.' Jamie chuckled at Sancha. 'You didn't know I had three, did you, Sancha?'

Tunku Jamie looked at Judith with the interest of a collector at an offered *objet*, then looked away. He sat down on the end of Sancha's couch, forcing her to draw her legs up sharply to make room for him. He grabbed one of her feet and squeezed it for a moment, an easy gesture of possession. It announced, All women are mine, if I want them.

While Jamie held Sancha's foot he gazed at the long grass beside the wire fence. 'One went in there,' he said. 'The caddy said there was a snake there and got frightened. I offered him two *ringgits* to find the ball.' He waved a jewelled hand, dismissing the whole affair. 'For God's sake sit down, Ralph. You make me nervous standing up.'

Ralph sat, and Tunku Jamie smiled around himself at his small court. 'We're having a little dinner up at the house tonight – just family and a few friends. Why don't you come along?' He nodded towards Judith to indicate that she was included in his largesse.

Sancha's face lit up. Jamie was no ordinary Sambo, and Sancha was not, Judith realized, often invited to dinner by him. She glanced nervously at Judith, obviously thinking that she, with her cheap, locally bought clothes, would be an embarrassing companion at a grand social event.

'I'm afraid I've got no suitable clothes – my luggage has been lost,' Judith said.

Jamie regarded her tolerantly, as if she were confessing to an irrational belief – that the world was flat, for example. How did people lose their luggage? And have no suitable clothes? It didn't make sense.

122

'And anyway, I've got to be up at three in the morning to go to Thaipusam with Dr Kanan.'

'Kanan! Old Fourpenny Dark! Splendid. He'll come, too,' Jamie said. He made a helicopter movement with his hand and a waiter appeared. 'Go and call my chap,' Jamie said.

The waiter see-sawed off on bandy legs and after a few minutes, during which the prince fretted about his lost golf ball and talked about World Series Cricket to Ralph, he reappeared with another Malay. This man was younger and military in his bearing; he bowed slightly as he stood before Tunku Jamie.

'You all know Rashid?' Jamie asked affably by way of introducing him. 'Look here, old boy, I want you to ring Dr Kanan and invite him to the house tonight. Tell him Miss Um here – his Thaipusam friend – will be with us. And Sanchie Hamilton. Kanan can sleep at your place, Sanchie.' Jamie flapped his diamond rings at Ralph, who had stood to depart. 'Give Ralph a hand with his bag, will you?' he added to his secretary. For a moment they went through the polite confusion of farewells. Then Jamie said, 'You and your refugee buggers. Eating their heads off up there on the East Coast. You know, the price of fish in Kuala Trengganu has skyrocketed since these boat people have been coming. The UN High Commission for Refugees has been buying fish from the local markets to feed them. It's caused inflation. Well, bye-bye, Ralphie.'

Ralph ducked his head deferentially and began to move off but the Malay bag-carrier hesitated. 'Sir, you know several Dr Kanans. Which one do you wish me to contact?'

Jamie's face expanded sideways like a ball of potter's clay flattened between the palms. For him to distinguish between one man and the next was, clearly, as bemusing as distinguishing one sheep from a flock was for a city-dweller.

'Fourpenny Dark, you know!'

123

'They are all dark, Sir.'

'God, so they are!' Jamie looked around him in delight. 'Well, the cricketing one. The vegetarian one. That's it, the one who is always such a bore when we have Beef Wellington. Has to have large servings of the Wellington. You know!'

The secretary by now did know. He bowed again and withdrew, following Ralph towards the club-house.

Jamie moved to a chair and relaxed after the mental strain. His body spread to the contours of his seat like a slowly deflating balloon. His eyelids slid down, and he sighed. 'Bloody hot,' he said.

The shavings of brown iris left exposed beneath his plump lids were focused, Judith noticed, on the body of a teenage English girl lying with her mother under the neighbouring umbrella. The girl was so young and slender that her hipbones formed two little peaks under the skin and her bikini pants were strung above them, raised just above her belly. Slowly the eyelids rose; slowly Jamie sat upright again and gave the merest inclination of his head towards the mother. She responded with a dazzled smile and Jamie looked away.

He said to Sancha, 'If ever I were in real trouble' and paused to smile at the fanciful improbability of this, 'say, a plane crash, like those people in South America, or kidnapped, or lost at sea – I do a bit of sailing, you know – if ever that happened, the person I would most like to have with me is good old Kanan. Amazing fellow.' He nodded at Sancha and Judith, agreeing with himself. 'Some of those Hindus, you know, they've got that what do you call it, Sanchie?' He turned to Judith. 'My English is getting worse and worse. I'm taking Malay lessons and now I can't speak anything. What *do* you call that Hindu thing, Sanchie?'

'Integrity?' Judith said. The word had come out of the air to her.

'Integrity!'

For a moment there was interest in those eyes as shiny as beer-bottle glass, but it dulled. Judith thought, What do men like him see when they look at me? How do they know I'm unable to respond? The uneasy feeling arose that she was in an environment where people played with words while operating on a deeper, unfamiliar level of perception. Even this brown frog of a nobleman, with his lazy mind and wrist-watch with a ruby in the centre of its dial.

Jamie said, 'Old Kanan has magnificent integrity. Of course, it means he doesn't care . . .'

The English mother had given a whoop of alarm. Sancha leapt off her couch, her arms jerking around her. 'Quick!' she said. 'Quick!' She grabbed up Jamie's golfing iron. 'It's there. I saw it, too.'

People were standing up, some running away, some moving forward, enclosing the two adjacent tables and their occupants.

'Move back, la!' a Chinese man said.

They were all staring towards the long grass beside the wire fence.

'You give me,' the Chinese man ordered Sancha, trying to take the golfing iron from her. She shoved him away with such force and such ease that they froze. She was possessed.

'Come out,' she muttered. Her eyes did not move from one spot in the grass and as if they had some energy force, it shuddered under her gaze. Then the cobra swept forward and up the bank, and reared. Sancha got it with the iron before it even had time to steady itself to strike. It jumped from the earth as she broke its back, twitched and danced as she continued to batter it.

'It's dead already,' a woman murmured.

'Filthy, filthy beast,' Sancha breathed as she chopped at it. People were moving away.

Her shoulders slumped and she looked up, bright-eyed. 'Here,' she said, grasping the corpse, which broke in two as

125

she pulled it from the ground. 'Here, you can eat it now.' She handed the snake to the Chinese man. Jamie's face was aglow with merriment.

Judith took Sancha by the arm and steered her towards the changing sheds. People fell back for them to pass.

Sancha began to tremble as they entered the shed, then sat down suddenly on the cream-painted benches inside. She was spattered with blood and yellow-green guts and shit. The mixed colours dribbled down her thighs and chest, like child's waterpaint flung about in a tantrum.

'Look at what I've done!' Judith felt ill at the sight, and from the knowledge they both shared that it was no snake that Sancha had battered to death.

The changing block was empty, except for the Malay girl attendant who had followed them in from the door, curiously, then shrank back again on flopping sandals. The tiles and paintwork were clean, but the wet concrete gave the place a graveyard smell.

After some minutes Sancha was quiet, and Judith was able to coax her to her feet and lead her to a shower. She emerged smiling apologetically, restored.

'Jude, I've been desperately worried about Ralph. He's got ulcerative colitis, you realize. The doctor has told him that if it gets any worse he'll have to have surgery. One of those ghastly bag things.' She sniffed, then began to cry again. 'Ralph says he'll kill himself if that happens.'

Judith hugged her.

'It's beastly. And he's so beastly,' Sancha said. Her eyes were bulging with indignation. 'It's these refugees. Ralph's so bloody romantic! He hero-worships some of the men. I think he's gone crazy.' She tensed and relaxed her long fingers. 'He'll do anything for them. He's taking things from the house – *from our house* – for them. You know that hairbrush? I'd hidden it. I've lost so much recently – clothes, a radio, my Piz Buin sunblock that I had to order from

126

Singapore. And I know Ralph is taking them. I hid that hairbrush. He's been through my drawers to find it.' She was ploughing her hair with her fingers. 'You don't know how dangerous what he's doing is. It's absolutely forbidden to give or take anything from the refugees. Even letters. The camps are virtually prison camps. The police regard the boat people as criminals. If any of the women are caught smuggling they get their heads shaved. The men get beaten up. And bloody Ralph! He could have us all thrown out of the country at forty-eight hours notice.'

Judith hugged her again. They were both dumb with bewilderment; but Judith, at another level of her mind, was committing all Ralph's indiscretions to memory. If Minou failed her on the camps, then Ralph . . .

After a while Sancha said, 'I'm not much of a hostess. You've only had one swim so far.'

Beneath their umbrella Tunku Jamie was explaining something interesting to the English schoolgirl. Her pink baby lips were parted and her eyes wide; Jamie's diamonds throbbed with rainbows as he talked.

13

When Kanan said that after the visit to the polyclinic he would be dining out and probably would not be returning to his house to sleep, Auntie pressed her palms to her temples then flung herself down to a corner of the kitchen floor where she crouched, as if warding off blows.

'Mr Adultery!' she wailed. 'The night of the spears begins and he pollutes himself. He drinks poison, he eats cow flesh, he fornicates with casteless women on the very night the Goddess gave the spear to Lord Subramaniam. Already the Lord is riding out on his peacock, preparing to vanquish the demon king with his invincible Vel. But does Mr Atheist pray for victory? Does he want human beings to be saved from the forces of evil? Oh, no! He goes out to indulge his body in filth!'

She had quite a lot to say on this theme; Kanan went on correcting his third year students' essays on twentieth-century cultural interchange.

Five years ago he would have failed the lot, but the rules were different now and it was his duty as senior lecturer in modern South-East Asian history to find reasons for passing them. One boy had written 'The re-birth of Islam as the World Religion, led by Colonel Gaddafi of Libya' (he had written Gaddafi's name in Arabic script) 'and pushed forward by the Great Revolution, which will take place when the self-styled Shah is exiled from Iran,' (he had written

'Iran' in Arabic script) 'will provide the solution to the non-Malay problem in Malaysia.' The boy's father was a Minister.

Kanan sighed and drained his glass of tea.

Auntie leapt up and put the kettle on for a fresh pot. 'You work too hard, nephew,' she said. 'A man must work, work, work to feed his family.'

'Your sons work harder than I and they are not paid thousands,' Kanan said.

Auntie shook her head in disbelief as she held the match to the gas-jet between fingers like charred sticks.

'You are talking about wages now, nephew? How it is possible that you worry about the wages of rubber tappers and you don't care about the demon Bhasmasura? Ill will come of it.'

She repeated this last phrase often during the afternoon until Kanan, who knew that cosmic justice was not an idea but a fact and did not like Auntie's reminders of this, said, 'Be quiet or I will send you away from my house.'

At times during the same afternoon – particularly after the Hamilton children were delivered to the club – Judith thought, I must go back to the hotel and get some sleep. But Sancha's continuous chattering and the stream of introductions she forced upon Judith detained her. The heat did, too. The sky was a white fog by two o'clock and shadows had turned pale. People levered themselves from sun-couches, their faces fuchsia-coloured from dilated capillaries, and stumbled into the chemical-tainted water to emerge not much wetter than before their plunge. Each swim provided a revival of energy for Judith, a sense of well-being that dissipated quickly, leaving her body processes working on a lower plane. She thought, I should not have sent that cable, and, If I don't rest I'll get panicky again. But the heat was a phantom boulder pinning her to her chair.

At four o'clock there were, abruptly, no more shadows. The sky had become livid. A crackle of crystal-pink lightning ran through the storm clouds, for a moment giving a neon glare to the pool and the drooping banana palms.

'The *bumiputeras* will be turning up now the sun's gone. We'll pick up your dress from the pub, first. Come on,' Sancha said.

'Australia calling you two times,' the man at the hotel desk said. 'Urgent, urgent problem.'

'It's your children. Something must have happened,' Sancha said, 'Perhaps a car . . .'

Judith telephoned Richard from her room. When there was no answer she telephoned a Canberra neighbour, who reported that she had seen the family an hour ago, looking normal.

'Perhaps I should ring his office,' Judith said, but Sancha was looking anxiously at the sky and the Hamilton children had begun to vandalize the hotel's furniture. 'Oh, tomorrow,' Judith added.

There were forty-eight green-paned windows in the Hamilton house and they had to call the servants, who were officially on holiday, to help them rush around shutting each one before Judith could accept Sancha's invitation to take a nap in the guest bedroom. Its airconditioning muted the children's noise, but nothing could protect her senses against the energy of the storm. The house shuddered from each burst of thunder and the dark bedroom jerked like a disco under strobe lights. At every lightning flash the bedside telephone rang.

'Don't answer it,' Sancha had warned Judith. 'You could be electrocuted.'

Judith lay staring at the light pulses on the green panes, thinking that most humans had lost the emotional stamina for this sort of climate. These storms pull us back to the era

130

of caves, but we haven't got the wherewithal now to enjoy or defy them.

The rain stopped and she opened the windows. It was still dark outside, the sky draining from the purple of the storm to the pale grey of twilight. She lay down again and must have slept for she found herself back in the pets shop, with its disgusting caged-animal smell. She moved her hand across her breast and unexpectedly felt membrane and spiky bones. Touching the knitted mess she released from it a sour smell so piercing that her whole body made a huge jump back into consciousness.

The room was quite dark now but she could see clearly the thing that had attached itself to her breast and she shrank backwards from her own body-walls. As she clawed at it, it clung tightly and she heard it scream. She shouted to Sancha who ran in and said, 'Oh God! It's a bat!'

They unhooked it at last and Sancha, holding it by a wing-tip, flushed it down the lavatory.

'It must have been sick,' Sancha said. 'Bats only come into the house when they're sick. You'd better have a brandy,' she added, looking at Judith's face.

They had several, downstairs in the drawing room, before they set out for dinner. The room's stone floor was covered with rugs as rich and vibrant as stained-glass windows, and there were Chinese antiques – marvellous rosewood tables and carved cupboards decorated with gold leaf.

'You'd go crackers here if it weren't for the shopping,' Sancha said. She gave a long-suffering look at a red lacquer cabinet, 'But the prices!' One had to thank Heaven that the *nouveaux riches* Chinese had not yet twigged to the value of carpets and antiques, Judith was given to understand. But when they did . . .

The storm had cleared out the sky, which was needle-pricked all over with stars in its western quarter, and blazing

131

with a full moon in the east. In the moon's white glare the shadows of the giant trees were as black as the shadows of midday.

Sancha was saying, 'It would take more than the bloody *bumis* to put me off driving.' At the wheel of her Mercedes she had become the chin-up, square-shouldered white woman battling the tropics. Only the timid and the extravagant bothered to have chauffeurs. She went on, in a tone of less conviction, 'You don't *have* to go to Thaipusam, if you're too tired. People say it's pretty ghastly. The devotees go into a trance and stick things into themselves.'

The brandy had flowed in a soothing tide through Judith's system; the Mercedes' airconditioning helped. 'I feel great now,' she said. She clicked her fingers and turned up the volume on the cassette deck and she and Sancha sang along with Rod Stewart – Judith boisterously, because Richard would not allow 'your regrettable taste in music' at home.

'This is just their KL *pied-à-terre*,' Sancha explained, rolling her eyes as the car crunched over raked gravel and the proportions of Jamie's house came into view. 'Jamie's in timber. His father, the sultan, has absolute control over the lands in his State. He's let Jamie chop down the jungle and ship it off to Japan. There's nothing the government can do to stop him.'

The house was large for a house but modest for a palace; there were plenty of servants. Two Malays, wearing silver-woven tunics over their black trousers, bowed to Sancha and Judith at the front door and showed them into a reception room with chandeliers, fake Chippendale and a dead cockroach, Judith noticed, almost concealed by the fringe of a silk carpet. Sancha muttered to a third Malay, who announced them.

Jamie came forward with outstretched arms.

There were about thirty people in the room, all Malay

132

except for an English couple, and all as similar as beer bottles on a shelf, within the limits of their sex. 'They intermarry a good bit,' Sancha had said.

Jamie steered Judith around, introducing her to his wife, Faridah, and then Billy and Alisja and Anwar and Mudzaffah and Charles, saying things like 'Alisja is just over from Oxford for a few weeks', and 'Billy's in base metals', and that somebody else normally lived in France. The men gave their knowing frog-prince smiles and the women, arch and roguish-looking, inclined their heads. Judith knew she looked like Orphan Annie, in her makeshift clothes, and smiled back defiantly.

Jamie then abandoned her to someone he referred to as 'Tunku Berenice, my naughtiest cousin', who at once said, 'What a cute dress. Did you buy it locally? How brave!' She glanced down at her own little bit of Nina Ricci. Hobday had said to Judith yesterday, 'The revolution in Malaysia will be against the royal families. That's off the record, too.'

Another silver-uniformed servant, with bare feet, offered sherry. A man near Judith turned to her saying, 'She'll know. She's Australian. How much do you think they'd want for Leilani?'

'I don't follow horse-racing,' she said. He looked puzzled, then turned away.

The naughtiest cousin's eye was wandering. Sancha, a few metres off, was giving an animated demonstration of how she had killed the cobra. We've been summoned here to amuse them, like dwarfs, Judith thought. The idea tickled her.

'Why are you the naughtiest cousin?' she asked.

The Tunku, who said 'Call me Bibi', laughed and tossed her head. Her hair was cut into the soft little curls which were the rage in Europe. She might have been any age between twenty-eight and forty-three, a woman past the luminosity of youth and in her physical prime.

'I've had rather a lot of husbands,' she said gaily and

133

paused. Her vivacity, which had the magnetism of a child's, moderated. 'I work, these days. I'm a counsellor-therapist at the Human Relationships Centre. It's very important, very fascinating work. We get all sorts of people – business managers, students, housewives. You know, middle-class people.' She said 'middle-class' eagerly. It proved her sincerity, Judith gathered, her devotion to the wretched.

Bibi added, 'I've had a lot of therapy, myself. I had primal in the States, with Janov. And I've done TM, of course, about ten years ago, and I've been into Subud . . .' Her little hands fluttered, displaying rubies in a bunch. She gazed into Judith's eyes. 'I was a searcher for many years. But not any more!' She was almost singing. *'I've found my level!'* She threw back her head and laughed. Her amusement amplified Judith's own sense of vitality. The last time she'd heard a laugh of such pagan robustness was from an old nun at school who used to take them fishing down on the rocks at Rushcutters Bay.

Bibi recovered her seriousness. 'You know, I used to have all sorts of hang-ups about being, well . . .' She gestured vaguely at the black silk dress and at shoes which, Judith noticed with sudden, fervid interest, had the tail feathers of some wonderful bird shooting up the back of the calf. They were of a type she had seen once only in an Italian glossy. Bibi was saying, 'But right here in KL I did a special course in mind control, and I know now that nobody needs feel guilty. About anything.' Her hands moved in downward sweeps, as if she were a conductor muting an orchestra.

'There is no such thing as one person taking advantage of another against their will. People *ask* to be taken advantage of. They *believe* they are badly done by.' She took Judith's hand and pressed it between kitten palms. 'Do you know, you can be happy living on a handful of rice a day? I do it myself at home. I sleep on a mat on the floor of a tiny room.'

134

Judith wished she had a tape recorder. She kept her face straight as she replied, 'Yes, only the very rich these days can live really simple, human lives. In Australia when people have made their pile in the cities they buy a little place in the country where they get back to nature, breathe lovely clean air, eat wholesome biogenetic vegetables.

'*Touché, touché,*' Bibi squealed. They reassessed each other.

'What you're suggesting,' Judith said, 'is that victims of the social system should be blamed for being at the bottom of the heap. They're there because they're lazy or stupid, or both. You're inventing scapegoats to soothe your own conscience about having so much wealth.' It sounded tough.

Bibi's response was unexpected: she trilled with laughter. 'You Westerners! Such materialists! Happiness is having a paid job, for you. Even your own prophet, Jesus, said . . . look, here's Kanan. He'll explain.'

Judith had pictured Kanan as an Indian version of her own history lecturer, who had been a plump little man with spectacles, fussy manners and a passion for harpsichord music. When she turned to look at her guide for Thaipusam she did a double-take. He was standing in profile, chatting to Jamie. His eyes were like those of a figure on an Egyptian frieze, she thought, and knew before he came towards her that he would be wearing scent. And he was. An almost palpable cloud of the smell of violets moved with him. This is a 1920s Hollywood version of the East, she thought. Mystical princesses, and men who tart themselves up like whores.

He said, 'How do you do?' nicely enough and inclined slightly for Bibi to kiss his cheek.

'You're as gorgeous as ever, Kanan,' Bibi said and he shrugged, a man acknowledging a fact.

Then dinner was announced.

'Faridah has forgotten to do the *placement*, chaps. It's liberty hall,' Jamie called out.

Judith had a mind to seat herself beside Kanan, but Bibi

135

carried him off to one of the smaller tables at the end of the terrace, and Judith found herself seated with the Tunku Faridah, whom everyone seemed to call 'Fred', and eight others, including the royal in base metals. There was a toast to the King (of Malaysia) followed by a toast to the Queen (of Great Britain and Australia). Then Jamie proposed 'the Sultan' and all his children and nieces and nephews smiled as one.

'The food will be appalling,' Fred said without apology. 'I had to give most of the kitchen staff the day off.' But there were three bare-foot waiters serving at table.

'What's this?' Fred asked, looking at her soup bowl as if she had never seen one before.

'Soup, Tunku Yang Mulia.'

'What did I tell you?' Fred nodded round to her guests in a way which indicated that soup confirmed her worst fears. Later she said, 'I think this is meant to be chicken. Billy, does Kanan eat chicken? One never knows with him.' She addressed the table at large. 'He's so polite. I saw him eat a big beef-steak at the German Ambassador's Residence one night. I ticked him off afterwards, I can tell you. Do you know what he said? "In my heart, it was vegetable."'

The conversation swung to anecdotes about tense moments during house-parties in England when bacon had been served for breakfast. The Arabs had made lots of improvements in Britain, but really, the place was finished except for shopping, they told one another.

Somewhere in all of this there was a story, Judith realized, on the complacency of people whose countries were rich in resources. She could work in Billy's remark, just now, 'Korea? Can't stand doing business in Korea. All their food is on sticks. I make 'em come down here to do business.' She asked two of the princes if she could interview them about their companies on Monday morning. They replied languidly, 'Why not?'

The wines had been good, though warm, and champagne

was served with the fruit salad. Judith was so engaged by Billy's story of how he had swapped a (small) rubber estate (plus workers), for an uncle's polo pony with which he had fallen in love, that she did not realize that the women were leaving the terrace.

As she hurried after them she heard Jamie begin what promised to be a ribald song. She was smirking as she caught up with Sancha, who said with alarm, 'I was afraid you were going to stay in there.'

Fred's bedroom suite, up a flight of stairs, had a pink marble bathroom and lamps with pink frilled shades. On one wall was a huge gilt-framed mirror, carved with lounging cupids. Above the flounced, satin-covered bed there was a painting of a Middle Eastern scene, with camels.

They repaired their makeup and one of the Tunkus ripped off then restuck her eyelashes. Judith noticed that she and Sancha looked as plain as grass-stalks in this bunch of sensual blooms. They sat about for a bit, waiting for their turn in the Cecil B. de Mille bathroom. Two ladies massaged each other's shoulders and one said to Judith, 'You're going to Thaipusam?' and shuddered delicately.

'The holy Koran forbids that we attend infidel festivals,' she added.

Then Fred announced, 'Come on, then. We've all done wee-wee,' and they marched off. Coffee and the men were waiting for them in a downstairs drawing-room. Jamie sang a song which he said was 'Sawf Airfricane' and one of his cousins sang 'Twinkle, Twinkle Little Star' in a Punjabi accent, snapping his fingers and rolling his head.

Sancha whispered to Judith, 'Can you do "Waltzing Matilda"? They'll ask us to, in a moment.'

Judith moved off to a settee where Bibi was talking animatedly to Kanan, who nodded now and then. The cloud of violets had lost some of its pungency, Judith noticed, as she allowed Bibi to pull her down beside them.

137

'I was trying to explain inner consciousness to Judith, but she's a real politician. She switched the conversation to scapegoats,' Bibi said. 'Now, scapegoats. How do people become scapegoats?' She looked brightly at Judith and Kanan. 'I'll tell you. They have desires, and for those desires they make a bargain. And sometimes the bargain does not pay off. Look at your own prophet, Jesus. I don't mean to be anti-Christian. I respect all religions, but look at the prophet Jesus. *He* made a bargain to be called Son of God. And what happened to him? He was eaten by lions!'

Judith felt her eyeballs bulge. 'Actually, he was crucified,' she said.

Kanan nodded at this correction.

Bibi conceded the point. 'O.K. But if he had had no desire to be a leader nothing bad would have happened to him. It's always our *own* fault.' She looked triumphantly from one to the other, smiling brilliantly.

Judith said, 'Is it the fault of the Chinese minority in Vietnam that the Hanoi government has embarked on genocide against them? There are tens of thousands of corpses in the South China Sea. What does that justify? Being kind to fish? And here in Malaysia . . .'

Bibi had covered her ears and murmured, 'Cancel, cancel, cancel. No negative thoughts or negative suggestions will have any influence on me', and having said this patted Judith's hand. Her expression was pitying. 'Kanan, *you* explain.'

'I don't need an explanation,' Judith said. 'This Indo-Chinese refugee problem is an international crisis. When modern people like you, Bibi, resort to wit's end reasoning, to fatalism, we all must know that the situation is hopeless. The next step, usually, is war.'

She turned unwillingly to Kanan, who had made no attempt to gain her attention. For the first time he looked Judith full in the face. She had the sensation of a sudden

138

decrease in her metabolic rate, as if an internal barrier had abruptly been lowered.

'The Tunku does not suggest that suffering should be ignored,' he said. 'Her point, I think, is that ethics must arise from a pure inner source, dissociated from ambition, desire from esteem, fear, and so forth. If not, our actions are vulnerable to the passing fashions of society and only sometimes, when fashion and ethics coincide, will they be good. But to achieve an inner purity it is necessary to look into the unconscious mind, and deeper. That is difficult. It happens only in dreams, in fantasies, or, as in Tunku's case, in modern Yogic meditation.'

'Bravo, Kanan,' Bibi cried.

He gazed at Judith, who wanted to say, 'What superlative garbage! India is recognized as the most irresponsible society in the world, and now I know why.' Pure inner source! Cosmic consciousness would be next. It was a great excuse for staring at your navel, while people starved. She supposed he believed in rebirth, too, so that death in the here-and-now did not matter. Judith noticed that at the outer corners of his eyes there were hair-thin lines and she realized he was not in his early twenties, as she had first imagined, but nearer middle age. His physical beauty was distracting, making it difficult to concentrate on his elaborate philosophy. I'm still exhausted, she thought.

He was saying. 'If people have absorbed violence they resist looking into their unconscious minds, for they know intuitively that the violence is stored there and that they will have to re-experience it. So she', he turned, to Bibi, 'tries to prevent its storage by saying "Cancel, cancel". She does not mean to ignore the boat people. She means their plight pollutes us all.' He smiled with charmingly exaggerated warmth. 'Hindus worry a lot about pollution.' It was impossible to tell if he were embarrassed about this, or proud.

Judith was able to pretend to listen as Bibi chattered feverishly about her new techniques, aware that Kanan was watching her. As he had gone on speaking she had allowed cynicism to unhook from her mind, had even ceased grasping for the meaning of his words, and had felt herself carried along by a river of communication flowing from him at a different level. He had seemed to ask 'Who are you?' and his unspoken question had plucked out of her a memory, just a few weeks old, but forgotten until now — Gail shouting 'You were a wasted fuck!' and the man's backward glance, appalled, as if he'd glimpsed the damned.

She's been at an abortion rally in Canberra, outside the House. The Festival of Light had bussed-in their supporters. Judith and a Sister from Queanbeyan were holding a banner reading, 'Catholic Women for Abortion', and were talking and laughing with their group. A man carrying a clumsy sign saying 'The Festival of Light Supports Life' walked up to them and said, 'Good afternoon, Ladies'. He was badly dressed and had decayed teeth. 'Piss off,' they'd said. The man had replied, 'I'm glad your mothers didn't abort you, so that you can be here today.' Judith had muttered at him 'It's a pity yours didn't get rid of you' and her companion had yelled 'Yes! You were a wasted fuck.' They'd laughed wildly. Judith had joined in but had felt so shaky that she had left before the speeches were over. By the next morning she had completly forgotten about it. Until now. Judith glanced at Kanan, furtively.

Bibi was saying, 'I'm never bothered by mosquitoes these days. I simply go down to my Alpha brain-wave level, visualize the mosquito, ask the mosquito to leave, and it flies away.'

Kanan was nodding.

'You can communicate with trees, too,' Bibi added. 'My mangoes! Since I've been communicating with my mango tree . . . You two must come round and eat some.'

It was off-putting, the way Bibi had confidently linked them together: you-two. Judith said quickly, 'Doesn't the

140

tree raise objections?' and realized that she was being pur-
posefully crass, that most of her behaviour that evening had
been a kind of version of the loud, slow, pidgin English which
Australians abroad used. They were all more unnerving than
she had cared to admit.

'We should leave,' Kanan said. 'You look tired and you
will have only a few hours of sleep before we go to the caves.'
He lifted his hands from his knees in a gesture of helplessness.
'Unfortunately my car is being repaired. Perhaps Sancha?'

Sancha was singing 'Waltzing Matilda', with Jamie join-
ing in the choruses. She was rosy from exertion, and other
things. 'Billabong! Jumbuck!' Jamie was saying. 'Extraw-
dinrary!'

He called out 'Don't get caught up in the *kavadis*' as he
waved the three of them off.

The air outside was warmer, and tender on their skins.
Judith began to vibrate with laughter when the front door
closed as if, released from etiquette, her spirit had been
liberated, and was soaring.

'What a madhouse! Bibi thought Jesus was eaten by lions!
Oh, Sancha!'

'I'm sloshed,' Sancha said, victoriously.

The moon was flying high overhead. They danced a bit
as they approached the car. Even Kanan was giggling, a
high rippling noise. 'You've stepped off a star,' Judith said.
For a moment the three of them clung together in the tinselly
light; Judith, leaning against Kanan, felt a brotherly
warmth from his shoulder. She realized that she was nearing
the limits of exhaustion and that recklessness was overtaking
her.

As the car went lurching off through the moonlit garden
film clips were speeding through her head, but too fast for
her to see them.

14

To Kanan's look of inquiry Judith said, 'I feel jittery. I had dozens of jumbled dreams.'

He nodded. 'You are a sensitive person with many problems. The knights of self-knowledge are battling with the dragons of fear in your mind. Isn't it?'

Judith grinned. 'Do you read palms, as well as minds?' She had managed to keep the irritation out of her voice, and too well, apparently.

Kanan replied, 'I can.' He was confessing to another of his virtues.

She wanted to laugh. He was so astoundingly beautiful and gentle. So unlike a man, she thought. There was no room in her imagination for someone who looked and behaved as he did, and it occurred to her suddenly that for ten years, more than ten years, Richard had defined for her what a man was and did, that she judged all of them by how closely they resembled or departed from him, the norm. Perhaps everyone turned a mate into a prototype?

He had not slept at all, Kanan was saying, but had spent an hour or so talking to Sancha, and then had meditated for two hours. That was as refreshing as sleep.

'Sometimes I see the future when I meditate.' His great black eyes moved at leisure over Judith's head and shoulders, making her say pertly, 'You'd be a red-hot journalist.'

They were standing in the living-room of the Hamilton

house, waiting for someone whom Kanan described as 'my relation' to arrive with a car. The windows were all shut – against oily men, whom, Sancha had explained, were the local cat-burglars who worked naked and covered with oil which made them impossible to capture. The house was airless and to Judith seemed hot, even at this pre-dawn hour. Their footsteps made loud, metallic sounds on the polished stone floors and when Kanan moved out of the pool of yellow light from a table lamp he merged with the dark, so that she had the sensation of communing with a poltergeist.

The car, a rackety vehicle of venerable years, arrived. They stepped out into a night no longer suffused with thin white light but black and heavy. The moon was as small as a tennis ball now and its valleys and craters were blue. Kanan and his relation sat in the front and burbled in Tamil to each other sounding, Judith thought, as if their mouths were filled with marbles.

Every now and again the relation, the middle-aged man with spectacles whom Judith had expected Kanan to be, turned right round to face her. He had long yellow teeth which escaped the covering of his top lip, like a slipped petticoat. In English he made remarks like, 'I'm telling you, Madam, it is a wonderful sight to see the amazing things these people can be doing with the spears', and 'All this wisdom is coming from India and even Western people are following it now'.

Somehow they had no head-on collisions with the other vehicles careering towards them.

Judith took notes to calm her nerves. The Lord Subramaniam had six heads and twelve arms ('Some gods have ten thousand arms – he's modest with only twelve', Kanan said); he was forever youthful; his elder brother was the elephant god; white oxen drew his silver chariot with his image in it from the temple in High Street out to the

143

caves once a year for this festival, the Lord's day of victory; more than a thousand devotees – nearly all Tamils, but some Chinese and Sikhs as well – would carry the *kavadi*; Subramaniam had thirty-seven names; his mother was Parvati, his father was Siva; in the luni-solar calendar it was now the tenth month, Thai; and the lunar station was Pusam, governed by the planet Brishaspati.

They argued in Tamil about the planet's name in English, and agreed on Jupiter.

'In southern India now the moon is at its most beautiful,' the relation told Judith, just missing a truck. Traffic was getting heavier.

'And this festival – originally celebrating the winter equinox – is banned in India,' Kanan added quietly.

It was the first indication Judith had had that something was amiss, but Kanan only shrugged when she asked why it was banned, as if things Indian were so unknown and unimaginable to her that they were beyond her questioning.

They had been travelling over dead-flat land and had come to a village of some sort. From the car's headlights and from spots of other illumination, made by kerosene lamps, it was possible to make out coconut trees and shophouses and people walking or sitting around on the roadside, grinning at nothing in particular. The relation parked the car in front of a Malay garage, and they set out on foot, following the flow. There was a continuous soft murmuring from the people around them, a collective, beehive hum.

'Soon you will see the caves,' Kanan said.

They turned sharp right and Judith stopped. The land, as flat as a table, leapt up ahead in a single mountain. Suspended above it was the small blue moon, a stage-light aimed down on the mountain's jungle and white limestone cliffs. Two parallel threads of fairy lights ran part-way up the mountain side.

144

'They mark the stairway to the cave,' Kanan said.

Unconsciously, they had all quickened their pace. Everyone had. Women with flowers plaited into their hair and gold bangles from wrist to elbow moved past them. When Judith bumped into one she turned, startled but smiling, a glass ruby flashing from her nostril. They were moving like parched animals heading for water. But there was more to it than that – there was joy in the air. Or maybe love.

Judith turned her face up to Kanan's and saw him smile.

'Do you hear the drums?' he asked.

She could, just. The double heart-beat thump off in the distance, perhaps a kilometre away. And there was something else, a sweet smell. Incense. Even on this still, warm air its smoke was perceptible and was drawing them on, to its source. It was narcotic, Kanan said. It helped the trance.

Judith knew the way without any help from him now, she was ahead of him already, almost running towards the lights off to the right of the roadway where hundreds of people moved in the dark, and where the music was loud, and there were shouts and fires burning on the ground, with clouds of incense billowing up from the flames.

Kanan caught hold of her arm. 'Later,' he said. 'First we must go to the cave. You can see what happens at the river later.'

He pulled her back to the centre of the roadway in to the crush of soft bodies. They were crossing a bridge over the river. Ahead and above them the fairy-lights on the stairway stretched up the limestone cliff. From the distance it had looked like a toy ladder. Now its true dimensions were revealed – a funnel hundreds of metres long leading in to the belly of the mountain.

'Up there?' Judith said.

'Oh yes, up there.'

There was more noise now. Indian music was swirling out of microphones rigged up above the food and drink stalls which choked either side of the roadway. In the extra light that came from the stalls Judith saw that Kanan was one-armed; his other embraced a brass pot. The relation too had a pot. He must have brought them in the car. People in the crowd smiled at them when they saw the pots. But there was hardly time to notice anything, they were all moving so swiftly, carried forward towards a new area of darkness before the base of the stairs. And pushed, too. Judith knew something was pushing her, something different from the soft, hot bodies. It was an urgent noise, musical instruments – cymbals and drums – and a shout 'Vel! Vel!'

People in front of her parted. She could feel the force pushing her against her back and moved sideways against Kanan to give it passage. There was a rush of energy, five or six men in a circle, running forward, shouting, thumping their drums, and in their midst, something strange, a dancing tower of tinsel and peacock feathers. It twirled past her, gyrating, this fairground thing, a pink kewpie doll at its peak a metre and a half above her head. Then the bodies closed in again and the shouts of 'Vel!' faded. They were crowded in darkness now, close to the stairs, when the shouts came again, very wild and mad. She moved aside for them, but there was no dancing tower in the circle of yelling men: it was a long, cold flash of silver, a spear held. Held how? She could not see, but her hair was rising on her scalp.

Then they were at the base of the stairs and Kanan was saying, 'Stay close to me, stay close.' There were hundreds of people, flesh rubbed on flesh, they were all pressing together, jerking upwards in unison as their feet felt for each new step. 'Don't fall,' Kanan said and Judith thought, Oh God, I'll be trampled to death. They can't stop. None of us can stop. She felt a moment of panic, then laced her fingers in to the hand she knew was waiting and was drawn against his side, so that they moved together, her hip heating on his thigh. The fairy-lights turned their faces yellow, red

146

and green. Ahead a woman shrieked, her back arched in a rictus. People grabbed something from her, some bundle. A sleeping baby. The woman had gone dashing up the stairs. The crowd felt her coming and moved aside. It went on, this hot, rising movement. How long? Twenty minutes, an hour? The sky was still black. At times they all rested and Judith closed her eyes. Every sense seemed overwhelmed, even on her lips and tongue she felt the ebb and flow of breath as she panted in the scented air.

The crowd in front of them had thinned abruptly; they were in the vanguard now, high up above all the hundreds below. There were only twenty or so steps to go, with nothing in their path.

'Let's run,' Judith said. She had recognized something, some memory from decades ago, an earlier life or childhood, of two people rushing together, the excitement of one spurring the other, a back-and-forth exchange.

She tugged Kanan's hand and they ran, then paused, then ran. Then Judith stopped, frozen.

They had reached the mouth of the cave. Deep inside it there was smoke and fire, but here at its entrance there was a cold, sour breath. And a smell, a piercing foetid odour. She knew it too well. 'Bats!'

'Bats love caves,' Kanan said.

They dropped their hands apart.

'What will you do with your milk?' Judith asked, glancing at Kanan's brass pot.

'I present it to the god.'

She dawdled behind him as they walked forward into the cathedral of rock, with its great sails and curtains of coloured crystal. The confusion and noise was at a crescendo some hundreds of metres further inside the cave. There was chanting and mumbo-jumbo from priests in white dhotis, things were being flung into open fires, and grey clouds of camphor incense floated into the air.

147

'I'll wait for you here,' Judith said.

'Don't you want to see the idol?'

She shrugged. 'Is it worth seeing?'

'Frankly, no. Just a small plaster god with garlands of marigolds round his neck.'

She found a ledge of stone and sat on it. A man, exiting from the shrine, walked up to her and suddenly collapsed on the ground. He was naked except for a pair of yellow shorts, a red headband and ankle bells. His back and chest were smeared with ash. He just lay on the cavern floor. Dead? Asleep? Drugged? Nobody paid any attention to him. Judith felt too tired to be interested. She was angry with Kanan for going off with his pot of milk. He had seemed apart from the crowd when they had been together on the stairs and yet he had abruptly rejected her to return to a superstition which, when discussing it in the car, he had held in contempt.

She stared down to the lights by the river and wondered vaguely why he had been so insistent that she should not see what happened there, as if he were protecting her from something. She would see it soon, nevertheless.

He returned after a few minutes, alone, swinging empty hands. The relation had been lost ages ago, on the stairs.

'We'll have breakfast, then go to the river,' he said.

The descent – there were 272 steps – was speedy. They went in to the first stall they came to and ate free fried bananas and curry puffs. The stall holder was giving away his food on this holy day.

'As a penance for being so greedy the rest of the year?' Judith asked. Her ill-temper was abating, and settled completely after a glass of tea mixed with condensed milk. 'I was starving,' she said.

Kanan nodded, in that infuriating way he had, as if he understood everything one was about to say before it was actually said.

148

Outside the stall it was as noisy and as aimlessly active as Saturday at the Royal Easter Show. Music was blaring overhead. An old party wearing nothing much asked Judith to buy a calendar showing a fat blue baby seated on a lotus leaf and holding a cobra in each pudgy fist. More of the weird tinsel towers were wheeling past, their bearers hidden in the throng. The night was fainting away.

Judith got out her notebook. 'Now, what about the *kavadis?*'

'Are you strong?'

'Look, I covered the riots here in '69.'

Kanan smiled. 'There will be no blood. That is, very little blood. And they are not in pain. It's important that you know that first. They feel no pain. They are in ecstasy.'

Judith wanted to say 'Don't *look* at me like that. Don't ask me those questions with your . . . oh God, your beautiful eyes.' Instead, she said, 'You make ecstasy sound more frightening than pain.'

They rose and began walking back towards the river, over wet grass. The sky was now a thin wash of grey; the phantom shapes of coconut and banana palms were glowing faintly green. Faces could be seen more clearly now. Judith leapt aside from a man with a naked chest as hard as a gymnast's and grey snakes of hair to his waist. He glared at them and jumped up and down on the grass, rattling his ankle bells. A mindless, concentrated malevolence seemed to emanate from him.

'A man of Siva,' Kanan said. 'Siva destroys the universe by dancing it down to atoms.' He looked admiringly at the devil.

She moved away from him, pushed through the crowd, and was suddenly witness to the things that happened on the river bank. It was dawn and she could see it all very clearly, this orgy. This abomination.

149

Later she tried to explain it to a hippy girl who also had fled and had joined her in a search for transport back to the city.

'It was when I saw them doing it to the children,' Judith said. 'I thought either I'd vomit or I'd rush and stop them. There was a little girl of about five. She looked starving, her arms were like sticks, and her eyes were too big for her face. They screamed "Vel! Vel!" in her ears, held the incense under her nose, and she closed her eyes and began rolling her head. They just grabbed her, her mother held her still, and they speared her tongue. Everyone looked as calm as if they were threading meat on to a skewer for shish-kebab.'

The girl said, 'I couldn't stand the young guys. They're so bloody beautiful. Their bodies are so smooth and lean after all the fasting. Did you see? When their eyes roll up, showing only whites, and they start dancing they don't have any expression at all. No joy, no excitement, no fear. Just nothing. When the priests put those big spears through their cheeks they don't register anything. They aren't there, they're out with the cosmos somewhere.' The girl picked distractedly at a patch of bleached skin on her arm – she said she'd caught a skin fungus in Bali. 'I wonder if they fuck like that?'

Judith snorted.

'No, I'm serious,' the girl said. 'Those guys really let go. They let go of the whole world, they look like they're coming. I kept on thinking, Jesus I'd like to fuck with a guy who looked like that. And then I'd think, but Jesus, it's scary. You'd be alone.'

'We'd better start thinking of catching a bus,' Judith said.

The traffic from town was bumper-to-bumper on the road that ran past the village, but it was flowing freely enough in the other direction. Some family groups were already going home. They strolled along, chatting contentedly, smiling with accomplishment. They had discharged their duty by helping a relation into the trance, helping the spearing or skewering or fish-hooking – dozens of silver fish-hooks were run through the flesh of backs and chests to act as anchors for the towers of tinsel, peacock feathers, plastic dolls and other glittery rubbish that made up the big *kavadis*.

'I thought I saw you earlier with a Tamil guy, a tall guy wearing one of those shirts with a high collar,' the girl said. 'You were talking to him on the river bank. What happened to him?'

'He did something I didn't like,' Judith replied. 'I left him.'

'Yeah?'

'Maybe I imagined it,' Judith muttered.

'Yeah? Well, he's no good for a lift. We'll get groped on the bus. Let's hitch.'

A Sikh succumbed to the girl's demand for a lift back to town. His son, a man in his twenties, was slumped comatose on the front seat alongside him.

'When his sister was sick he vowed to carry the *kavadi* for three years if she became well,' the father said. 'Now he loves the *kavadi* so much he has vowed to carry it for the rest of his life. My son is a wonderful boy.'

'Did you see the Chinese who went into a monkey trance before he was speared?' the girl asked him. 'He turned into a monkey before my eyes. He ate bananas with the skins on, and ripped a coconut husk off with his teeth, and they beat him with whips.'

'There were European devotees also, this year,' the mother said. 'They are discovering some of the secrets of India. You see, there are natural body substances called endorphines which we are knowing about for millennia but only in the last couple of years is Western medicine discovering them, how they act like morphine. We Indians do not need painkilling injections because we know the secret of self-production of these substances. I, Madam, am a medical worker. I read the journals.'

151

She jabbered away as the car moved off. The landscape, revealed now, was shattered – wastelands of grey sand, the abandoned land of former tin mines, that once had been jungle. It was already suffocatingly hot in the car, although it was only about nine in the morning. One of her fellow passengers – perhaps the hippy girl – stank, but even that was preferable, Judith thought, to the nauseatingly sweet incense down by the river – and the fruit abandoned to be trampled under foot, and the music and screams which had shuddered through her. Everything in excess for these people. There had been young men who cut their tongues with metre-long knives. Their eyes had bugged out as they danced around displaying their bloodied tongues. One had tranced while sucking a cheroot, until it burned his lips; a white rope of congealed saliva had hung from his mouth to his navel. He'd rolled in convulsions on the ground, making people leap backwards from his flailing limbs. 'And Kanan . . . oh, Kanan.

'Would you open the window?' she said urgently. She leaned her head back on the seat and closed her eyes. A few minutes later the car drew up outside the Hotel Malaya. The hippy girl was accepting an invitation to stay at the Sikh's house, and Judith was stumbling out, saying thank you, then tottering up the front steps into the glorious, air-conditioned, efficient world of the Chinese business class.

'Your suitcase delivered. In your room already, la! Another cable. Also a telephone message from Australia.'

Judith took the slips of paper and her key. Five minutes later she was asleep.

When Judith had refused to go with him into the cave and later, when she had run away from him, down by the river, Kanan had not taken offence. He knew that she had not meant to give offence, but was frightened.

At the river, he had explained to her, 'All of us want only

152

two things: power and protection. That is the human condition – the desire for dominance, the craving for succour. These devotees, who are mostly from the socially oppressed classes, satisfy both in their trance. The god takes away their pain; they have his protection. But they also unite with him, they have his strength. So they are as strong as a god, isn't it?'

She had not understood a word he had said, for she had asked about Bibi and inner consciousness, so he had explained that Bibi's ideas were Hinduism for non-Hindus, the husk only. But because of them Bibi no longer wanted to commit suicide. And when Judith had still not understood he had said, 'There is no god in the cave. There is only yourself. Power over yourself is the only power. All this', he had pointed out a young boy having fish-hooks put in his back, 'is the workings of a mind in darkness, an excess called piety, nothing but an illusion of piety.'

She had cut in, 'I'll say it is. It's not religion either. It's mutilation of children!'

It was like reasoning with an imbecile. He had merely replied, 'His parents don't mean to harm him. They believe they are doing something wonderful for him. The philosophy of Hinduism is harmlessness to all living things. Frankly, you are wrong about religion, also. Religion is – I am quoting Marx, isn't it? – a system of ethics, a source of consolation and an explanation of the unknown. So, you see . . .'

She had not run away then, but later, when he had begun to dance. Kanan liked dancing, liked the feeling of his limbs flowing loose and his hair giving soft blows to his cheeks as he shook his head. It was lovely dancing on the wet grass with all the other dancing people, the sky pink and blue with dawn, incense rising from the altar fires. He had watched her running away, her hands covering her ears against the drums.

153

Later his father-in-law had turned up, and danced also. Then they ate some noodles and drank kopi-O and drove back to town.

'The Australian lady is in love with you,' Father-In-Law said. 'That is my opinion.'

'Oh, yes. What will I do, Father?'

They both laughed at the dilemma. 'Let's go to a *kedai* and have a beer,' Father-In-Law said. 'Ranee won't know the difference if I have one beer. She's so pleased that I delivered the milk that she won't complain about one beer.'

So they drank for the rest of the morning. Mother-In-Law shouted at Father-In-Law when he got home and auntie with the nose-jewel shouted at Kanan, who did not listen to her and fell face down on his bed and went to sleep.

15

There was only one sensation: heat. As if his thigh were a warm iron being pressed against her side and the heat from it were spreading across her pelvis. And there was one image: a semi-naked youth as slender as a palm tree dancing in the trance and behind him, Kanan dancing, too. Kanan's eyes had been half-closed, he was slipping away, going back to the drums and the silver spears. There had been orgy in his half-sleeping eyes.

'Anyone can go into a trance,' he had said to her.

Sunset blossomed in the picture window of Judith's room. She was between sleep and wakefulness, physically inert. She looked at the sunset that filled her room without seeing it; the gaudy veil of that other world was still binding her eyes.

He had asked, 'What do you feel?'

'I'm frightened.' As if she had to tell him.

'Frightened of poor people enjoying themselves? If they were not so crushed by life they would be more moderate in their enjoyments. We Hindus . . . ' he had looked secretly proud and embarrassed again, 'we Hindus take a pessimistic view of life. It must be lived, that is all. These things, these hours of release, make it seem more bearable.'

She had shaken her head. 'I can't think like that. I believe that if life is unbearable, change the system, do something to *make* it bearable.'

'*Make* it?' He had laughed. 'Come and dance.' His body was already swaying, like that half-naked boy's whose pectorals had the smooth, rounded shape one saw on ancient Hindu statues. The nipples were small, hard currants. Those statues invented nothing, she saw. They captured these strange, suave bodies and these thousands of years of dancing away anxiety. Dancing the universe to atoms, he'd said.

Judith blinked. She could see the sunset now. She turned to the bedside table, taking up the cablegram first. It would be from Bill, she knew, and she grimaced while opening it. It read: 'EXCELLENT BACKGROUNDER STOP IN LINE WITH MY POLICY OF LAISSEZ FAIRE YOU CAN GO INCOMMUNICADO FOR AS LONG AS NECESSARY.' She panted out the breath she had been holding: he realized I was in a knot. Then she had another good thought – I won't have to write up that gruesome festival. I can forget about it.

The telephone slip said that Mr Richard Wilkes had called and requested his call be returned. His voice saying 'Wilkes speaking' had that heavy, purposeful tone which Judith used to think was manly. 'David has the mumps, my love,' he announced.

From some musty locker-room of distrust she found herself shouting at him across four thousand kilometres: 'I don't believe you! He hasn't got mumps!'

There was a lapse in communication, caused either by a hitch in the line or his instant anger. She did not care which. He was millions of kilometres away, this disembodied bully. She'd escaped from him.

'He *has* got mumps, Judith. Sebastian will get them too.'

She knew what would be next. 'I'm not coming home,' she said. 'You'll have to take time off and look after them yourself.'

'I thought that would be your attitude. I'll tell David you're too busy with the Vietnamese.'

Judith replied calmly, 'Tell him what you like. You've devoted yourself to belittling me in their eyes.' Then abruptly, 'We both know why. There's no point in going on.' She slammed the receiver down and fell back on the bed, laughing. She'd done it! The words rehearsed over and over ... 'By the way, Richard, there's something I feel I should tell you ...' And after the initial explosion they would sit down together, rational adults, and discuss what would be 'for the best'. They would have to keep it entirely *entre nous*, of course; explain that they were separating just like everyone else; that marriage was impossible these days when roles were so confused, in this interregnum in social history; that they were victims of societal instability ...

She was trembling, holding a scream inside herself, but with sudden relief tears rushed out of her eyesockets and sluiced down her face. She sat down, heavy, tired, like a sick person and wept. She felt neither happy nor sad now, only stunned by what she had done. Her head felt drum-full and pulpy as a tomato.

In the bathroom mirror her face gave her a fright: her eyelids were puffed and her mouth had been pulled out of shape into an oblong opening. When she blew her nose grey particles of incense came away in the kleenex. What had someone said? For a fortnight after Thaipusam the incense you've absorbed through your body membranes continues to work its way out. The incense penetrates the tissues. The way the drum music did, and the other things, the spears, the heat.

The telephone rang while she was drying her hair after showering. For a moment she thought 'Kanan', but it was the receptionist saying, 'Canberra, Australia, calling. Connecting you now.'

Richard said, 'I will find you a flat next week, Judith. Our separation can begin as from Wednesday, the day you left. We can be divorced by February next year. You will, of course, be wanting to move to Sydney or Melbourne, having complained for years that you've only stayed in Canberra because of my job. I will get custody of the children, naturally. You can see them in school holidays – if you wish.' And he hung up.

'Well,' she said aloud. 'Well, will you now?' She felt peculiar, as if her mind had climbed out of her body and was perched over on top of her suitcase, on the luggage stand, watching her. She moved around self-consciously as it continued to observe her going about the business of grooming and dressing as if everything were normal.

Outside it was growing dark; the moonless sky was filmed over with the reflection from city lights caught in the humid air. Judith checked her face once more in the bathroom glass: she no longer looked as red and swollen as a screaming baby. Clean hair, clean clothes, fresh make-up. She was outwardly all right. She had dropped Visine into her eyes four times and the whites were now clear and glassy. She wished she could stop the sensation of being in two places at once – inside her skin and elsewhere, flitting around the hotel room, in bed on Sunday morning trying to read the newspapers, with the kids climbing all over her and complaining, 'You never take us to the swimming pool'. But the feeling would not go away, so as two identities she caught the lift to the foyer and asked directions to Campbell Street.

'You catch taxi, la!' the commissionaire ordered, and finger-snapped one out of the air.

The cab driver had 'Wo Hai Bei-jing' – 'I love Peking' as he explained – playing on his radio. He sang along with it, driving with one hand, with the other lighting a cigarette, adjusting the nylon-furred animals that bobbed from his rear-vision mirror.

'You eat Penang fried oyster,' he said. He swerved the car to a stop adjacent to one of the first of the pavement stalls in Campbell Street. 'All foreign peoples eat Penang fried oyster.'

158

Judith did not argue. She was not hungry, not even sure why she had come down here where traffic fumes billowed over the steamed chickens, red ducks, squid, shallots, noodles, lemon grass, satay roasting on charcoal fires, and all the other Chinese-Malay-Thai ingredients hanging in the glass cases of lamp-lit stalls. It was a largely Chinese food area, a place of frenetic noise and activity. Whole families of Chinese children rushed out from glaring neon-lit rooms behind the stalls, ordering customers to sit down, eat *laksa*, drink lime juice, try chilli crabs. Judith let them push her around, shouting to their parents the names of dishes they had decided she should eat. They banged things down on the table – little bowls of chilli and soy sauce, jabbed their fingers at cylindrical containers of chopsticks, indicating she should use them, quacked, yelped, and were off again after new quarry. It was comforting to submit responsibility to this clamorous authoritarianism. She was watching the people going by, and knew she was watching for Kanan, and that he was not there.

Her food was growing cold. The tepid, greasy soup seemed a final injustice. A few tears of self-pity dropped from her cheeks on to its orange, coconut-milk surface and lay there, trapped in the oil. She pushed the bowl away and a Chinese girl said, 'You no eat chilli. You cry,' and thrust a warm face-cloth into her hands.

She managed to eat some of the glutinous oyster omelet and drink an iced lime juice. Then she wandered off down the row of stalls, staring past the glass cases of squid and ducks at the customers seated behind them. People said, she now recalled, that if you sat long enough at the Campbell Street stalls everyone you knew in Kuala Lumpur would eventually come there to eat. But he was not eating there tonight.

I'm alone, she thought. No husband, no children. The sensation was that she had been physically ripped, and that

159

her habits of dependence on Richard and the boys had become close and ghostly, like the phantom limbs of amputees. It was not the way she had pictured it. She had imagined, once she had had it out with Richard, that she would feel light and free. The irritations of motherhood – the sticky fingers, the noise, the Saturday afternoons spent in movies called *Battlestar Galactica*, instead of in art galleries – were nostalgic memories now. She wondered how they would talk about her to their friends when she was an arthritic old lady and they had just rung her to say that they were too caught up at work to visit her this Christmas. 'She never had time for us when we were young. She was always impatient. A real bitch.'

She realized that a man in a white singlet with a cleaver in his hand was addressing her: did she want to try his squid? Judith shook her head vehemently, and felt abruptly as if she had shaken a single, unsuspected coin from the pocket of a dress. 'Bugger Richard,' she muttered. '*I'll* get custody.'

The stall holder pulled a face and glanced at the boy standing next to him, a warning that here was another deranged tourist.

At nine o'clock she caught a taxi back to the Malaya and rang the Australian Residence. Minou said '*Don't*! Don't tell me,' about Thaipusam, then asked, 'When are you moving in here? Tomorrow? That would be great. We'll have *dim sum* breakfast in town.'

'Actually, I'd like to go to Mass,' Judith said.

'Mass! Ooh, la, I haven't been for years. We'll both go.' The idea became an exciting excursion for Minou, and for Judith, also. She too had not been for years.

After Minou put down the telephone, still rolling her eyes at Judith's peculiar outburst about the Hindu festival and wanting to get it out of her system by going to Mass, Hobday had said, 'We all believe in sympathetic magic. And it's no bad thing, either, as long as you recognize it for what it is.'

160

Minou pouted because she did not understand what he meant. 'Convent girls never leave the church, they just become feminists. I learned that in Australia,' she replied challengingly. 'I'm a Buddhist, *at heart*,' she added.

Hobday nodded, tolerant. Minou was what she said she was at any given moment. He was pleased that she was going to Mass, for although Buddhist *at heart*, a visit to church might rekindle in her an enthusiasm for Western ways – she'd spent six years in a convent school herself. Since they'd arrived in Malaysia, six months ago, Minou had become increasingly 'oriental', sometimes speaking to him not in English or French, but in Cantonese, without realizing it. And she was redeveloping old superstitions. He'd caught her out secretly counting things for lucky signs, and eschewing clothes of a certain colour. She would never admit to any of this, which, if questioned, she passed off as unconscious caprice.

But it was there all right, as exotic and unnerving as the thing she was doing again now, slowly and carefully, to him. Which Mrs Wilkes had interrupted.

16

'I'd imagined it would be the same as it was at school. I thought I'd slip back into a routine,' Judith said as she and Minou shuffled out along with the Goanese ladies in saris and the Chinese businessmen with blue mohair suits and digital wrist watches, their spiky hair glued with brylcreem.

Neither Judith nor Minou had taken confession. 'It seemed so flat,' Judith added. 'I'd even forgotten it isn't in Latin these days.' She had thought, This is like sex without lust, like Richard and me, and had been utterly bored from the first words of English. The sermon, mercifully brief, had been on the topic of racial harmony, with references to our unfortunate brothers and sisters who were cut off from Christ by the delusions of other 'religions'; the necessity of enlightening them without breaking the law (Render unto Caesar) by proselytizing among Muslims. And so forth.

Minou maintained the look of secret amusement she had worn throughout the service. She thought she should tell Judith the Buddhist saying, 'You cannot step in to the same river twice', but could not be bothered. Instead she said, 'I thought you'd bore a hole in the priest, la, you stared so hard at him.'

'He came as a bit of a shock.'

They exchanged grins and Minou jabbed Judith's ribs with her elbow. 'Shut up, whitey,' she hissed. She could roll her eyelids down as if they were canvas blinds.

Judith thought, She's going to curtsey to him.

'A beautiful service, thank you, Father,' Minou said.

The priest swayed his head. 'Delighted you are coming, Madam. And you, also,' to Judith, 'are being most welcome in our congregation.' His sermon had been couched in the same Goanese English, making it even more remote and meaningless.

'Just like a black-and-white minstrel,' Minou said before they were quite out of his earshot. Then, 'And here is my Bala. You know, he's only nineteen and already he has a son, la.'

The Indian syce ducked his head, overcome with modesty. Minou transformed herself into Lady Hobday as she reached the black limousine. 'Bala loves driving Adrian's car,' she confided to Judith, in the tone adults use to praise children in their hearing.

'Where is His Excellency?' she asked the syce when she had finished her routine of arranging her legs and skirt as if television cameras were ranged waiting for her signal to roll.

'He is marking time for you at the Merlin Hotel already, Madam.'

'Best *dim sum* breakfast,' Minou assured Judith.

'I stayed there, once,' Judith said. 'It was the only high-rise hotel in KL then. It had the biggest, gaudiest restaurant I'd ever seen – like a warehouse decorated with red and gold, and there was an ornamental pond.' Ben and I ate there, the next morning, she thought. It had been empty except for some American tourists. A man had pleaded reasonably with the waitress, 'Look, can't we just have eggs-and-corfee? You know, eggs?' The woman with him had started to cry. He'd said, 'We'll get out of this country. Damn the curfew. We'll go to the airport. Today.' She and Ben had exchanged glances; they did not want to get out.

She did not listen as Minou talked about the merits and

163

demerits of the city's other eating houses: the Malacca Grill at the Hilton, the Ranch at the Regent where all the waitresses were dressed as cowboys, the snake restaurant, the Mongolian bear's paws restaurant, the noodle palaces. People said Kuala Lumpur, a Chinese city, was one huge cafeteria.

'I'm getting divorced,' Judith said abruptly. 'That is, my husband wants to divorce me.'

Alert, hostile eyes regarded her. 'Oh, really?' After a silence Minou added, 'You'll be on the loose, then. I'll have to find you a new man.'

Judith studied her hands. So this was it: hostility, humiliation. This was the first taste of what she could expect when she returned home.

The road outside the Merlin was being dug up and the car lurched like a ship at sea. Their shoulders bumped together for a moment.

'He wants custody of the children,' Judith said. 'But he's not going to get it. I'm going to fight.'

Minou looked her up and down. 'Custody. That's easy, la. The mother always gets custody. A few tears for the judge is all you need.'

Judith glanced at Minou's composed, unlined face. 'It's not *that* easy.'

Minou replied, 'Just steal them. And fly to the States. If he tries to steal them back . . .' She shrugged.

'Shoot him, I suppose?'

'Why not? I would. Husbands are a dime a dozen, but children . . . We have a saying . . .'

Judith ceased to listen to the wisdom of the East. 'Do you have children?' she cut in.

Minou's eyes shuttered, that same, quick barricading of herself she had executed before, back in the Lakeside, in Canberra. 'I think so,' she replied coolly and Judith, looking at her, suddenly felt something about Minou which made

164

her, without realizing what she was doing, draw back, as one does from a corpse.

'I'm not as lucky as you,' Minou added. 'I can't just ring up and talk to them. I don't know where they are.' She looked bored, sitting there in her elegantly arranged raw silk dress – Lady Hobday waiting for her chauffeur to open the door of the limousine – while Judith said, 'Oh, I'm sorry . . . I didn't realize.'

Hobday was flirtatious during breakfast. It was a skill he used to imagine he had lost much earlier than hope, which had finally abandoned him during those terrible years in Saigon. One day he had said to Hilary, 'This bombing of Cambodia. We are accomplices to murder. As an ambassador, I am no better than a mercenary thug.' She had said something scornful and rallying in reply.

His conscience had roared day and night until it exhausted him and he had found himself no longer wicked, merely absurd and empty. And everyone about him was equally shrivelled and foolish, so that life became a continuum of intense boredom. He alleviated it, late at night, in his bedroom, by getting drunk on liqueurs. He would sing to himself sometimes, songs he remembered from university footballing days, ribald Elizabethan ditties – 'May her bouncing buttocks be marble' – that sort of thing.

She was an ordinary girl, a typist, perhaps one of his typists. He didn't pay much attention, so long as the work was properly done. She was walking down a corridor in front of him one morning when a movement of the flesh under the fabric of her skirt had drawn his attention. He had touched her. Not on the buttocks – he was not that sort of man – but on the soft upper arm. She had glanced up at him with the look of alert opportunism he remembered in girls' faces from twenty-five years ago. He had made some trifling remark, to cover his embarrassment more than any-

165

thing else, and she had leaned her head to one side in that coaxing, submissive way, making her earlobe brush the collar of her jumper – that's right, he was back in Canberra and it was winter. He'd thought then, Flirting is like riding a bicycle. You don't ever lose the knack, you just lose the inclination.

Some months later when he had encountered a scruffy little girl with bare feet arguing with a policeman on the steps of Parliament House, where he had just come from briefing his Minister, he had recognized her accent and on impulse had teased her with the greeting they use in Saigon. She had unleashed a stream of street-Vietnamese on him which he could not understand. The policeman was looking puzzled and dangerous. Hobday had replied, in French this time, 'If you can find some shoes I'll take you to lunch and you can explain your problem to me then.'

In the event he had had to buy Minou a pair of sandals. How exciting that had been! She had pranced around the shop, making it clear from her chatter that he had picked her up off the street, that he was lecherous. 'What about these yummy green ones?' she had asked, as if she were already his mistress. A sales girl had sniggered at them, and he had known suddenly that he had the courage of despair. As they stepped out into a cascade of spring sunshine he had felt as if the world had been made new, and delightful, in half an hour.

The speed of the rest of it had created distrust in Minou. She would say, 'If you were so quick in throwing over Hilary for me . . .' No amount of logical explanation could extinguish her jealousy.

While he flirted with Judith, Hobday noted the flick of Minou's eyes and wondered if the bosomy Mrs Wilkes were aware of it also. She had condemned the Thaipusam festival with nervous, passionate denouncements, had been talking too much and to him, exclusively. Minou had remarked

'Ouf, Tamils', wrinkled her nose and had given her attention to the bamboo containers of steaming food being wheeled past the tables in a peak-hour jam of trolleys. The vast late-Empire restaurant – gold dragons raced snorting up red columns in their eternal pursuit of flaming pearls – was filled with the barnyard racket of several hundred Chinese feasting on *dim sum*.

'The Indian impulse is to fast, the Chinese to gourmandize,' Hobday said. 'Famine was the historical stimulus for both races, but the Chinese response is straightforward and optimistic, while the Indians' is subtle and pessimistic. Jesuitical, one could say.' He raised his eyebrows at Judith to indicate that the subject was closed and turning to Minou, offered her from his chopsticks a prawn wrapped in translucent pastry. She averted her head with drooping sulky lips.

Nonplussed for a moment he turned back to Judith to warn her with a look that she must start paying court to Minou. But the Australian woman was glancing around the restaurant, looking for a familiar face.

In the two days since he had first briefed Judith she had, he noted, lost the bold, careerist air which, combined with her untidy appearance, had given her the appeal of incongruity – of being both single-minded and undisciplined. Hobday now found her disoriented and vulnerable. It unsettled him, particularly since Minou was observing her with calculating spite, and he sighed.

It was glorious, this dangerous course he had chosen, but it demanded unflagging attention. He quailed sometimes before the poison in Minou's system and was appalled that he had allowed her to intoxicate him as well. For she did; a man and wife could not remain immune to each others' illnesses of spirit. On some unperceived level, they languished together. And here she was, intensely jealous now of the Wilkes girl, planning some savage joke on her into

167

which he, inevitably, would be drawn. Worse, it was his fault, for flirting with the girl.

Hobday watched malice sharpening Minou's eyes.

As the limousine turned in the gate they all saw the pale-blue High Commission Holden blocking the Residence porchway.

'Trouble,' Hobday said ruefully, 'And on Sunday.'

He had managed a temporary conciliation between Minou and Judith after breakfast. He had suggested window shopping and in Batu Road had bought Minou a jade bracelet. She had queened it for the next hour and was still chatting gaily as they turned in the drive. The Australian had taken this well, herself contented by extravagant gifts she had bought for her children.

The duty officer, Terry Donleavy, ambled towards the limousine and slapped a hand flat on the car's roof, grinning with friendly stupidity. 'Some urgent cables, Boss. And something for Lady Hobday,' he said.

They had wound down the windows, letting midday steam, like a breath from a furnace, rush into the car. Hobday shivered, his body reacting contrarily to the climate. In Donleavy's hand there was an airletter defaced by multiple addresses.

'Came in the bag last night. A letter from Ho Chi Minh City,' he said. 'Posted in Hanoi.'

So, it had happened at last. For a second Hobday felt relief, then his head began to ache, low down near his hair line behind his left ear. It was the old weak spot, damaged in a football tackle thirty-five years ago, when he had felt his head was being torn from his shoulders. Minou would massage it later. He pressed the spot but her hand did not cup warmly over his own.

She was sitting bolt upright in the seat behind him. She took the letter from him wordlessly.

168

'I think,' Hobday said to Judith as they entered the cool, airy house, 'that we should let Minou go off and read her letter.' The pain behind his ear was acute, reaching its peak. It would be gone in a moment, leaving a low, stubborn ache. 'And I'll show you the garden.' He added this quickly; the pain had lifted.

'What about your cables?' Judith said.

'Oh, yes. I'll look at them now.'

Minou was beside them but not with them: she had become a sleepwalker. Hobday had to push her gently to wake her up. 'Go upstairs and lie down,' he said. 'Send Aunt for me when you want me to come up.'

He nodded at the Black and White amah who had opened the door for them and who now took Minou's arm and led her towards the staircase.

Judith followed Hobday through to a cluster of armchairs and a settee beneath one of the ceiling fans in the main reception room. He sighed heavily again, as he had in the restaurant.

'Minou is, ah, highly strung,' he said. 'You must forgive her excesses. She is the victim of . . .' A regretting smile overtook him; Judith thought he was going to leave the sentence unfinished.

'A useless tampering with history.' He took reading spectacles from the inside pocket of his cream bushjacket – his casual clothes announced the taste of a woman in her twenties, not a knight in his fifties. 'A senseless misunderstanding of the loyalties and blood-feuds that rule Indo-China and which . . .' He was reading the cables in his lap now: Judith could see red TOP SECRET stamps on the paper. He looked up, his eyes mournfully enlarged behind the fishtanks of lenses. She did not have to read the cables to know that they announced disaster.

'Is there going to be a war? Between China and Vietnam?' she asked.

Hobday adopted his ambassador's tone. 'I think we'll have some tea,' he said.

'What does that mean for the refugee situation?' she persisted. 'What about Kampuchea? And Thailand? What will the Russians do if the Chinese overrun Vietnam? What will the Americans do if the Russians . . .?'

He lay back on the settee, amused by her importunity. 'I don't know, I doubt that anybody knows. The only evident fact is that we are entering a period of intense danger.' He tossed a cable across to her. It read 'TEHERAN: THE AYATOLLAH KHOMEINY HAS ORDERED . . .'.

'I used to think – when I was a young man – that these catastrophes could be diverted by people of goodwill, behaving intelligently. Now I know that it is impossible. The enemy is rooted in our inner beings.' He watched her attending him minutely, leaning forward, suddenly becoming aware of the intimacy of their knees and moving back with one of those quick, unconscious movements that signal a whole life-pattern. Hilary had that same rejecting tic.

'Anger,' Hobday added. 'The great gods of anger and war – Zeus, Mars, Siva, the Old Testament God, the Prophet Muhammad. Anger is an imperial human emotion, which we acknowledged once, and which summons our energies in a way that nothing else can. Anger that crops are ruined, anger at death, at unjust systems, anger at a universe indifferent to man: it has dragged us forward from the caves. And the paradox is that anger, a source of creative change, is also the source of destruction. We Westerners have done ourselves a disservice by banishing the principle of anger, the irate Jehovah, and replacing it with an ideal of love, making the prophet Jesus serve as god. When we are angry now we have no explanation for our behaviour, no deity inciting us to destruction and, inevitably, we feel ashamed when the anger has passed. You know, the word "enthusiasm" means "possessed by god". Don't you ever believe that

170

men hate war. They *love* it. It arouses our highest excitements. Siva, you know, is both the god of destruction and the god of sexuality; Venus and Mars were lovers. I went several times on bombing missions, when I was posted to Saigon . . .' He lent back, embarrassed by himself.

'I'd agree with the unjust systems,' Judith said cautiously. What he had just said had in fact made little impression on her. She was thinking that his outer shell of formal sang-froid was as fragile as a cicada chrysalis, that he was a shy man who had chosen, from God-knows-what need for self-mastery, a career which every day exposed his shyness to jabbing. It made, at last, some sense of his liaison with Minou, extrovert, flamboyant and vulgar as she was. His complement.

What of me and Richard? she thought. Nothing more than egotism *à deux*: I'll help you get on, you help me. But it had not always been like that. We'd been in love. Then love had vanished.

Hobday saw that her attention was no longer on him. 'Come on, I'll show you my lilies,' he said.

As they rose the old servant, whose legs were so short that her gait was a rocking hobble, came into the room. 'Master, you go up now.'

He went immediately.

Judith was left standing, stared up at by the servant, who had the face of a gargoyle. The woman's eyes, which were almost as small as the black beans used for sauces, travelled from Judith to the cables which Hobday had abandoned on the settee, and back again.

'Piss off,' Judith murmured. She was sure there was something in the cables about Vietnam and the refugees. The amah was trying to hypnotize her out of reading them.

'We wanted tea,' Judith said, moved to the settee and picked up the cables. A hand crushed her fingers together and there was a horrible noise, a cackle made low in the throat.

171

'Bad girl,' the amah said. She extracted the cables from Judith's hold, refolded them and stuffed them back into the manilla envelope in which they had been delivered.

'Any journalist would have done the same,' Judith said. She didn't expect the woman would understand her, but it helped decrease the fire she felt in her face. The amah said nothing but waddled off, with the cables, towards what Judith supposed was the kitchen. 'Duck-arse,' she muttered after her.

Any journalist *would* have done the same, she assured herself sullenly. Hobday had, after all, given her one top secret cable to read. She tried to work herself into a righteous rage with the amah but no full-bloodied emotion would come, just a whip-lick of irritation.

God, what's come over me? she thought. I've been in the Treasurer's office when he was called away, leaving a pile of secret papers on his desk and I didn't touch them. And when I told Richard later he said, 'Commendable, but naive, my love.'

The Black and White returned with tea, but there was no sign of Hobday.

Eventually, Judith retired to the ground-floor guest suite and spent the rest of the afternoon alternately typing up interview questions and brooding about Richard and the divorce. Each time the telephone rang and was answered by the servants she rested her hands on the keys, waiting to be summoned. She had given her new telephone number to the desk staff at the Malaya, and a twenty-dollar tip.

None of the calls was for her.

17

When he entered the bedroom Hobday saw how beautiful
Minou had been, years ago, as a child, before she was sold
as a concubine to the provincial governor. Laughter poured
out of that thin, supple body as carelessly as music flowed
from a magpie. Her whole being was carolling, sitting there
cross-legged on the bed with her sandals and handbag and
sunglasses strewn all over the place and the air-letter
smoothed over the peak of a knee.

'They're coming! They've got the money and found a
boat! A good boat – an iron boat.'

Her raised arms beckoned him and in an instant his head
was being embraced. Joyous kisses were sucking at his forehead, his eyes, nose, mouth – a warm, gladdened puppy
snuffled his face with an abundance of love. He thought,
Half of them perish at sea; she'll go mad – and pushed his
face into her hair. Perhaps, if it's an iron boat, not one of
those flimsy river barges . . . One wife dead, one mad.

He was near swooning as he knelt there at the edge of
the bed, stupefied by the sensation of lips on his skin, the
smell of her hair, his own response. Her slender, intelligent
hands were already reaching down his belly. He thought,
If I could die now, move through to the other plane and
not see her as she must become . . . how? Turned inwards,
with dull eyes?

Now he was sitting on the bed, untying his shoelaces,

standing to unbutton his shirt. Only half of them die at sea. Or from the pirates. He was smiling into her smiling eyes, saying with his, It'll be all right. I'll protect you, I'll protect that other part of you – them. She was unknotting her webbing belt – very French, her choice of dresses. She did everything with style. You survived. You hitched a ride on a bomber, somehow, at Tan Son Nhut during that shameful panic – the 'bugout', as the Americans called it – and jumped out at Bangkok with a thousand dollars in your hand. A gift, you said, 'from a screwball Southerner'. And your only piece of luggage that wretched fortune-telling book, a gift from Mama. The dress billows over your head and flies across the room, a collapsed parachute. 'War reparations, honey,' the American had said. You bought a ticket to Sydney and got a job – like that – teaching French. And played the flute in the school orchestra. You've worn a bra today, for mass. It's a lacy white thing, flying in a tall arc, missing the chair. Teaching French, and carrying placards in demonstrations on behalf of homosexual schoolteachers, in bare feet. If you could survive all that. The belt has left a red mark around your small, small waist. Afterwards, will you be mine again, ever? Three sons to look after. Won't you spend all your time with them? Making up to them for the four years you left them?

'Oooh, la,' Minou said, 'It's gone down.'

He stretched on his back on the bed. 'I'll come back.'

'*Of course.*'

She looked both composed and mischievous now, for this was her *métier*.

He lay passively, submitting to her skill, perhaps a gift rather than a skill, a gift of the body to communicate with another body, bypassing the mind, forming an alliance of the flesh to be presented to the mind as an invulnerable pact. Little pyramid breasts, too small for a bra. Smaller than my daughter's when she was eleven years old. I touched them

174

once, when she was sitting on my knee; I could see Hilary's hair stiffen on her head. She said 'Adrian! Elizabeth is growing up! You mustn't!' Elizabeth jumped off my knee and never sat on it again, nor held my hand when we crossed the street. And such polite, cold little kisses she gave me: 'Goodnight, Daddy' - rigid jab of lips on my cheek. And you, now, stoppering my mouth with your tongue that winds on mine, slowly, two bodies rolling together in a hot pool. Forget about the others. They're dead already. They're corpses rolling in the South China Sea. I can hold you up so easily. Lying on my back I could hold you at arm's length above me if I wanted to.

'You're my wife, Minou.' My woman-side. They're dead already. The sea is calm here now, but up north it's violent, *you* know. They're drowning every day. The letter didn't come.

But, of course, the letter had come.

Minou sat up and straightened her hair by flicking the backs of her hands through it, then offered to translate the letter. She looked even more beautiful now - rosy and tousled. It hurt him to look at her. I could never bring that depth to your eyes. Sometimes your face softens, and you laugh often, but there's always that reserve behind your irises. I used to think it was a trick of oriental features, or pigmentation.

Hobday folded his arms over his chest. It was tanned to a colour darker than Minou's but it was withered these days and he wondered, looking at the flaccid pleats of skin beneath a mist of hair, if sometimes he repulsed her, if she came to him unwillingly, moved only by a whore's self-discipline. The provincial military governor, the man she had first served, would be seventy by now had the Vietcong not stabbed him and thrown him under the durian tree. If that were true. If any of it were true. As if the details mattered! The crimes needed no elaboration - they were there, stored up behind her irises.

175

He looked at the ceiling, where transparent lizards stalked insect prey, tirelessly. They never seemed to sleep, and when frightened they self-amputated, dropping their tails. Perhaps their nervous systems were too primitive to need oblivion or to register the pain of dismemberment.

You're using your concubine's soft, patient voice.

Mama had received one letter in 1975 and knew Minou was in Australia, but then she had heard nothing more for three years. She and the boys had moved house many times; they were no longer in Cholon, and Quoc Quang, who was now almost fourteen, had been sent papers for military training. 'Letters from me started arriving again in 1978, saying I was going to Malaysia with my . . . husband. Mama wrote often to Malaysia, asking for money for a boat, but – well I didn't get them, did I? Then Quoc Quang made friends with a boy who has a relation working in the Australian mission in Hanoi, and this boy promised to ask his relation, who was a car-driver, to ask his boss to put the letter in the diplomatic bag. So Mama is praying that the boy has kept his promise and that the relation could be persuaded, and that the boss, who has a soft spot for his driver and has bought him a wrist-watch . . .

'And then she says that Uncle Tommy – that's not his name but the Americans called him Tommy – died a few months ago. His factory had been confiscated but he had been allowed to keep his house. Then Aunt Cam Binh fell ill. The government has made a law that ageing exploitative capitalists . . . oh, well, Aunt Cam Binh died too. But before she died she told Mama "ask the goddess for a boat". Mama suspected there was gold hidden somewhere in Aunt's house. They searched under the floor and took bricks out of the wall. Then she was desperate. She read the hexagrams and they said, "the wise man will think the unthinkable". And she took the hammer they'd been using to pull the nails out of the floor boards, and smashed the goddess. She was full

176

of gold! Fifty taels! Mama is praying that no ill luck comes because she smashed up the goddess, and has made a vow ... oh, la. That's not interesting for you. Quoc Quang is back in Ho Chi Minh City now and has arranged a boat which will leave sometime in February or March. An iron boat, which will take two hundred passengers. And there's a lavatory – Mama has a shy bottom, you know, but as she says, she will only be at sea three days.'

She lay back, dreaming, watching the transparent lizards stalking overhead. The windows were open to the hot peace of the afternoon. Traffic sounds did not reach this part of the house; the only noises were the low hum of an aircon-ditioner let into the wall below, in the guest suite, and an occasional croak of 'chick-chak' from the lizards. Clouds were banking, great folds of whipped egg-white; the storm was still a long way off. Hobday turned to Minou to hear the rest, but she was already asleep. Contented. Mama had not sold her; Mama *loved* her. Mama was now proving her love by risking death to join her. What else can a child of twelve whose mother sells her believe, except that it is done for her own good?

He took her in his arms to lift her limp body under the sheet and to move the wad of pillows from behind her so that she could lie flat. She did not stir.

I've lost you, he thought.

Miz Wilkes, as he called her with a smile in his eyes, chose brandy and ginger ale as her sundowner, but although it was an hour before the sun actually would set, any hopes of sitting out in the garden long enough to admire the sky's full display were threatened by the coming storm. Hobday took whisky as his evening drink; Minou would have a lime juice when she did come down.

Unable to sleep, he had crept out of the bed and spent the afternoon working on a dispatch to the Minister, warn-

177

ing him of the inevitability of a harder line by the Malaysian government, and the danger of 'a Palestinian situation' in the refugee camps. He had told Aunt to wake Minou at five-thirty, since Minou was possessed by the common South-East Asian superstition that to sleep through from daylight to darkness was to leave the body open to evil spirits. There was something solid to this fear. He had himself known the uneasy bump into consciousness and the suspicion of having been somehow cheated that came when one slept too late at the siesta in these sodden climates. Glancing up at the sky he wondered if, at five o'clock, it were not too dark already. The Wilkes girl was at him again now with a barrage of precisely worded questions, preventing him from going upstairs to wake Minou himself.

She had a sharp mind, Miz Judith Wilkes. The pleasure of verbal sparring with a buxom young woman – out here in the garden's soft greenish light, which sharpened up the luxuriousness of everything that grew so that the very grass seemed to be celebrating the vitality of its juice, where in the quietness their voices seemed like cords bonding them . . . The pleasure brought back Hilary. She'd had a sharp mind, too, and would debate with him on autumn evenings, after lectures. She'd lost it, of course. They all did, those clever university girls who married External Affairs men. There was the assumption of blinkered dedication for diplomatic wives in those days, dedication to husbands' careers, to children, national prestige, to anything but themselves. Satow's guide to diplomatic practice even stated it, he recalled – 'a wife is absorbed in her husband's role'. Hilary had ended like the others. Life-and-death melodramas over the servants and furniture shipments, that tone of friendly instruction she'd developed when speaking to any junior man's wife. And her resentment towards him! Because of a system that they had both at first so enthusiastically, so innocently, accepted as being proper and natural, like the laws of gravity. Resentment, hos-

178

tility. The children, pressed to feel awe for him, had become timid in his presence and later, cold. His closest friends were unwelcome in the house, turned away by lack of those necessary small gestures of admiration rather than by anything more definite, any insult. In the end she had acquired that battle-axe tone and spoke of 'my wives' – 'My wives will arrange the fete'. He'd cringed for her when he'd heard it but the reserve between them was by then too ancient to be breached. If cruelty were the greatest sin, perhaps ridiculousness was the worst misfortune.

They'd said: 'You're a fool if you marry this girl. Not a chance of being Secretary after that, twenty years of work down the drain, Hobday'; and 'Don't expect your friends to go on seeing you as if nothing has happened – people respect Hilary.' Socially reckless, but the most sober act of his life. He'd not believed, he'd refused to believe, that Minou would ever make contact with her family again. He had made a rational choice, a judgement on the needs of his spirit. When old Crabbe-Wallace had said, 'Good God, man, sex is not *that* important to you, surely?' he had come closest to releasing the secret. But his reply, 'The gymnastics of it? Not at all. But the symbolism . . .' had caused Crabbe-Wallace to cock an eyebrow, as briskly as a dog cocking its leg, and the secret had retreated back inside him.

The green light and the greenness of everything around glowed so strongly that Judith's white clothes were tinged, as if she were underwater. Even her face and her blonde hair looked green, he noticed. Like a drowned corpse.

Hobday stirred suddenly and Judith leant forward, eager for a reply which had been so long in coming. He said, speaking as he so often did, as if dictating a report, 'Some of the people of this region still have the Graeco-Hindu-Buddhist tradition of tolerance of belief. We are witnessing the final stages, after five millennia, of the defeat of tolerance by intolerance – by the Judeo-Christian-Islamic tradition to which

179

Communism is also heir. A direct result is the persecution of non-believers – capitalists – in Vietnam. I'm no longer a Christian; I suppose, like others in times of change, I've returned to the ancient gods, to concepts of Oneness. So, no, I cannot agree with you that the Thaipusam practices should be banned, any more than you can agree with the Church's dogmatic stand against abortion – a subject dear to your heart, I hear. We should recognize when our most intimate prejudices have been aroused, and know we are *re*acting to prejudice.'

'But there's a huge gap between tolerance and indifference. The Hindus appear . . .'

Hobday sighed. 'Is there a huge gap? It seems to me the tragedy of India that the gap is so small, a mere crack.'

'So if horror is a commonplace . . . ?'

'It will become more of a commonplace. A new war is coming. Its origins, I believe, were in 1969 when the Americans outraged a tenet of Islam by putting a man on the moon. In tweaking the Russian nose, the Americans startled the Islamic world awake and into self-defence. And now we are beginning to see some of the results. In the West, Islam will be pictured as the new, monolithic enemy. Inevitably, a new McCarthyist era will come, with all that that entails.'

'What do we do? What do you do?' Judith asked.

He smiled, gazing up at a tree whose leaves, in this strange light, were black-green. 'I get very tired. Then I go into my greenhouse. Would you like to see it?'

They went past the regimented stands of hardy mauve orchids, behind which were the swimming pool and badminton court, towards the far left-hand side of the garden. This was an unplanned area, growing wild with vines and banana palms on which hung dull green chandeliers of fruit. The palms and vines gave way to forest trees. Hobday took Judith's elbow to help her across the tangled ground.

Beyond the palms the light was permanently dimmed by

180

the large trees and the air was dank with leaf rot, the tropical smell of living-and-dying in unbroken balance. It was hotter and more clammy in here. Hobday saw kraits sometimes, a sudden flash of sulphur yellow which would disappear into the bedding of leaves. They were not as aggressive as cobras, and their fangs were not grooved for efficient injection, but their venom was more deadly, and he always moved slowly, placing each step deliberately into the decaying sponge. Previous high commissioners had laid baits of poisoned eggs, released mongooses and engaged snake charmers, to rid themselves of the kraits. But after success had been announced, the snakes always reappeared, seemingly invulnerable against anything short of total destruction of their territory – felling all the trees and concreting the ground. 'We must destroy this village to save it.' Oh, yes, he'd gone along with that logic, once.

He smiled at Judith, noticing – he still found it difficult to notice details of dress and so forth, except in Minou – that she was wearing open, high-heeled sandals, unsafe for this area.

'Not far now. There's an easier way round, from the front drive through the garages, but I thought you might like this wilder track.' It was not true: he himself had wanted to delay. He rarely invited people to see his lilies, and once the offer was made, always wished to retract it. Once he had become so agitated with a guest that he had pretended to have lost the key to the greenhouse, and had shooed the man away, saying 'They're not in flower, anyway. There is nothing much to see.'

'It's not a large greenhouse. I'm afraid you'll be disappointed if you were hoping for gorgeous orchids. My next-door neighbour, a Chinese chap, *he's* an orchid man. Perhaps I should take you next door?' He was fiddling with the lock.

'I didn't say anything about orchids,' Judith replied. She had a bold, quizzical look on her face.

181

'No, of course you didn't. Well, here we are. Nòthing much to see.'

The greenhouse, recently built in clear glass, had the raw look of any new building unsoftened by use. Shiny new gardening tools and packages of fertilizer lay on a bench in front of the door. Behind, stretching the length of the shed – about four metres – was a central aisle of cultivation boxes, each holding a young plant, fifteen centimetres tall, with spiky, radial leaves. At the end of the row of boxes were two large plants, apparently full-grown. At the apex of one was a single, magnificent bloom, a great scarlet and white trumpet. Judith gasped as she saw it for it dominated the greenhouse as a live tiger would dominate a drawing-room.

'The Lily of the Sultan Who is Navel of The Universe,' Hobday said. 'It used to be sacred to the rulers of the Majapahit Empire. I first saw it back in the fifties in a palace greenhouse in central Java. The colours, you know, the way they fit together on the petals . . . '

The configuration of each petal was extraordinary, Judith saw, like a gestalt drawing which, if the eyes relaxed on it, changed from a face in silhouette to something different as the white background became foreground. Each petal was differently patterned in scarlet and white and each one brought on this strange optical illusion of jumping backwards and forwards, red-on-white, white-on-red.

'In China it's known as the Yin-Yang flower and in Ceylon as the Buddha's Lily, or the Flower of the Unborn and the Born. The Japanese call it the Lily of Life.'

He was fidgeting with the soil around the plant's base, sinking his fingertips into it and rubbing the crumbs of earth between thumb and index finger as if he were testing silk. Having dragged her through the soggy patch of jungle, he seemed suddenly impatient with her presence, his eyes flinching away from her as he spoke.

'Does it have a Western name as well?'

182

'Hmmm? Oh yes.'

He was now, with a handkerchief, wiping dust specks from each spiky leaf. If I were interviewing you, Judith thought, I'd think you were telling lies. Politicians set up these distracted, fiddling routines when they're cornered.

'This is a male plant. That one without the flower is the female. They're like papaws – you need male and female. But only as primary stock. The next generations become ordinary hermaphrodites.'

Hobday continued fingering the shiny, sharp leaves; he had lapsed into silence again. The greenhouse had been growing darker. Glancing up through the roof Judith saw that the sky was about to splinter open. There was a piercing crack of thunder and lightning combined, which shook every pane of glass, then a thump. Her eyes winced shut. One huge rain drop had hit the roof above her upturned face. But still the cloud would not break – it was as if, momentarily, a weight had been lifted off their heads while the storm paused. In this moment of waiting Hobday said, 'It's known as *Lilium amoris*, the Lily of Love', and suddenly he grabbed her arm. 'We'll have to be quick!'

He was dragging her after him, slamming the door, then sprinting through the grass into the gloom of the patch of forest. The rain was belting on the leaves above as together they dashed past the first tree trunks into pitch dark. Then Hobday stopped and let her go. Judith could barely see his face, but she could sense his agitation. 'Your sandals,' he said. 'There are snakes here.'

He seemed unable to decide whether to go back or forward. Cool rivulets were running down her arms and neck. She hugged herself and ducked her head low as a second crash of thunder shook the ground and the tree trunks suddenly flamed white. 'We'll be struck if we stay here,' she shouted. The whole place was rocking. Hobday grabbed her wrist, shouted something, and, half-crouching, she was dragged after him through the rest of the jungle area, her feet sucked down in the foul-smelling decay. As she concentrated on keeping her balance a thought raced into her mind – that, in some obscure, obsessive way, Hobday identified himself – and Minou? – with his lilies.

Abruptly they were in the open again, running across the lawn to the lamp-lit patio into the shelter of which the servants had already moved the tables and chairs, and their half-finished drinks. Minou was standing there, her left arm making a triangle from shoulder to waist, and tapping her foot.

If I get into the camps it will be in the teeth of her opposition, Judith thought. I'll have to use Ralph Hamilton. Somehow.

18

They drank champagne during dinner, one bottle, then another. 'To Aunt Cam Binh!' Minou said, and 'To iron boats!'

Her display of irritation earlier, when they were wet through from the storm, had been a joke. She'd yelped with laughter as they'd splashed on to the terrace. The three of them sat together now at one end of the dining table which, extended fully, would seat thirty-two. The table's surface shone, the candles shone and Minou shone. Her hands reached out to fondle Hobday's face and to stroke Judith's fingertips.

'I was so surprised, this morning, when you told me you had children,' Judith said.

'Of course I've got children, la! How would it be possible for an Asian woman not to have children? We don't lock our bodies up.'

The servants stood around with the air of having been struck deaf to all speech, except commands. When Minou interrupted, in mid-sentence, a description of her home village in Song Be province to say, 'I want to play my flute. Where's my flute?,' one of the servants left the room immediately. He returned with it as another servant was handing round the *gula Malacca*.

Minou pushed her chair back from the table and hooked her right foot over her left knee. The flute was not the silver one Judith had seen before, but a small wooden pipe, a villager's instrument.

'Quack, quack,' Minou said. 'This is a song to call the ducks.'

Hobday, laying down his spoon beside the creamy pudding, had an air of intense, dreamy preoccupation. The flute's voice was softly burred; it sang one pastoral tune of tremulous, piercing tenderness, then another. The room was charmed by it, as if diners, servants, table, winking candles and silver had all been detached from the rest of the house and, encapsulated, had fallen back, into an infinitely good past. She played for maybe half an hour, until they were all half asleep and the candle flames, undisturbed, climbed straight. Then she sat with closed eyes like a cat absorbing sunshine, awake but shutting out everything except what she wanted to feel. She still held the flute to her lips but had ceased to breathe into it, caught up in the memory of some tune that made her smile. Hobday, Judith saw, was now watching Minou with an expression of patient gloom. The deaf servants stared into space; the room was returning to earth.

Minou dropped the flute from her mouth, cracking it hard against the satiny edge of the dining table. 'Shit! I've forgotten it,' she said. 'I wanted to play a song about crossing the Pearl River, and I can't think how it goes.' She gave a loud sniff, hitching up one nostril. 'You didn't know I was a musician, did you?' she said to Judith, with a vivid, tough grin.

The two white-jacketed statues turned back into servants and began clearing away the dessert plates.

'They' (she meant Judith and Hobday) 'will have coffee on the terrace,' Minou said to one of the men in her flat, peremptory tone.

Hobday seemed locked inside himself. He paced behind the women from the dining room, his chin sunk on his chest.

186

'Oh, Papa, you're like an old bear,' Minou said to him as they settled into cane armchairs. There was little softness in her tone. She turned from him with impatience and addressed herself to Judith: 'You and I will go to the Bellfield Camp at six-thirty tomorrow morning. It stinks, la, so the earlier we go the better. You can interview the camp leader. He speaks good English.'

'What about a pass for me to get in?'

Minou gave a tight smile that indicated her forebearance had been taxed beyond its limits. '*I'll* get you in, Judith Wilkes. Just relax.' She glanced around herself, as if the very floor tiles had become displeasing, then stood up. 'Well, I'm going to bed,' she said. 'I'll leave you two intellectuals to it.'

Hobday broke his silence. 'It's only ten o'clock and you slept three hours this afternoon.'

She bent over the back of his chair, lifting one leg behind her, a mocking pose. 'I know, Papa. I want to look into the *I Ching*. I've got lots of questions to ask it.' She kissed his ear and was off.

For Judith, Minou's departure brought the same relief as the breaking and draining out of a storm. She felt relaxed and sleepy. Ceiling fans churned the night air. She and Hobday sat intimately, in a pool of light from a silver table lamp.

'Another brandy?' Hobday said. He, too, seemed relieved that Minou had left. 'She's nervous, you know. She won't admit it, but until her family has landed, safe, she's going to be like this – changeable.' His eyes appealed to Judith to understand. There was a conspiracy of sympathy between them. Neither referred to another possibility, though it was there, humming in the air.

Judith told him about her divorce from Richard, a story which turned out to be long and rambling, and needing several more brandies to sustain it.

She began to cry quietly as she explained how she had

187

wanted to have David aborted, that he was a cuckoo, and that every time she had looked at him in his bassinet he had gazed back at her with reproach.

'All babies look reproachful,' Hobday said. He touched her hand for a moment.

She said, 'Thank you. Yes,' and knew it was not true, for David had lost his reproachful expression only when he had mastered an imitation of Richard's air of tolerant scorn for her.

'I couldn't bear to be alone with him. I went straight back to work when he was six weeks old. People thought I was brave. I'm really very conventional.'

Hobday's tone was soothing, but firm. 'You are wilfully tormenting yourself with these ideas. Stop.'

He felt no urge to confide to her his own years of self-torment. She was too young, too confused, incapable of understanding. 'You've come here to do a job,' he said. 'Do it and deal with the other problems when you get home.'

'Yes. I'm being ridiculous.'

She was none too steady on her feet; Hobday went with her to the guest suite, checked the airconditioning and set the alarm clock for 5.45. She kept saying 'Please don't bother', not knowing his pleasure in these small, feminine gestures of caring, which he passed off now as a host's good manners.

At the door he turned; she was sitting on the bed, her head cocked to one side. 'Well, goodnight, Judith,' he said. He felt old and tired and at odds with himself. But as he mounted the stairs to join Minou he thought, What do I care about that twitchy young woman and her common-place problems?

Judith knew three things immediately when she woke up. That she had slept like a stone; that she would die if she did not have a drink of water; that she was still drunk.

188

There was a thermos jug of iced water on the bedside table, but its miserly quarter of a litre was not enough. She bumped into the bedroom doorway as she was moving through it. Navigation of the ocean of white-tiled floor with its reefs of armchairs and table lamps needed caution. It was sickeningly hot in the main reception room now that the ceiling fans were off and the curtains closed. The heat and the dangerous armchairs made progress slow. Walking with feet laid completely flat to the ground seemed the most prudent course.

After a while she had crossed the heaving sea and entered a clothes closet, which smelt of naphthalene and mice. Judith thought she might just lie down quietly for a little while with the clothes and the mice. But then she saw there was another door – that was surely the kitchen. It was an immensely large kitchen; armies of small ghosts were drawn up in the glass-fronted shelves. They were probably wineglasses, but they looked like ghosts. There were two stoves and more than two refrigerators humming to each other self-importantly. The refrigerators might be the local commissars. Judith thought she would have to run to get past them to the little sink, far away at the end of the kitchen, where a tap dripped sweetly. One of the refrigerators gave her a whack on the hip as she slunk in front of it. And, then, there she was, expanding and contracting, standing at the sink, drowning in nectar.

On the third glass its taste changed to chlorinated water. The refrigerators didn't try any tricks on the way back. She got tired half way across the white sea and sat down in an armchair. She supposed it was about 3 am.

The noise that woke her, maybe a minute, maybe half an hour later, snapped her head from her neck with a twist and put it back on again the right way round. It was a sound from Bedlam and it came from directly above.

Judith returned quickly to the guest suite. With the door

shut and the airconditioner drumming she could not hear what was happening upstairs, where Minou was being pursued by devils. And Hobday. There had been two sets of feet galloping across the floor upstairs. Hobday's yell of 'Stop it! Stop it!' did not sound equal to saving her.

'Sleep well?' Minou asked. She was inhaling the steam from a cup of jasmine tea. They were at breakfast. It was pre-dawn and under the electric lights in the shadowy room Judith felt puffy and larval. She nodded.

'And you?'

'Always, la.'

The Black and White put in front of Judith a plate with two eggs, fried in rancid-smelling butter, then stood back with her hands on her hips watching, as a child might stand back to watch with delight when it has lit the fuse to a large firecracker. Judith stared at the rubbery white and orange things – the texture of squid, she knew without even prodding them. The Black and White cackled.

'You drink wine too much. Ha-ha,' she said.

She had given Minou a bowl of fresh, peeled fruit and a lacy little pancake over which she poured, drop by drop – alert for the order to stop – a citrus syrup.

'I don't know how you can eat eggs for breakfast,' Minou said.

Judith had not asked for eggs. Perhaps the appalling noises in the night had been another of Minou's jokes? She looked, now, like an advertisement for something wholesome or beautifying – muesli, breath freshener? Her face was painted-on carefully and her eyeliner toned accurately with her green skinny-legged trousers. The cap with Hermes wings was lying where she had tossed it on to the sideboard.

'Hurry up,' Minou said. Her tone nevertheless suggested that she would indulge all of Judith's eccentricities, despite inconvenience to herself. 'Now remember: you're my assistant. You're working the film projector. If they ask about your tape-recorder, say that you're recording the children's singing. Look like a High Commission hausfrau, la!'

Film cans of *Mickey Mouse, Donald Duck's Birthday* and *Goofy Goes Fox Hunting*, plus *Perth – Gateway to the West* were stacked on the front seat of the Citroen. They were using Minou's car today. The projector and *I Can Speak English* books were already in the boot, Bala said. The morning air was a water-colour haze through which the jungle trees in gardens on the other side of the road loomed silently, like friendly ships encountered at sea. A kingfisher swept forward from them and lassoed the Residence front garden in its flight before landing on a frangipani tree near the car. The blue of its wings almost hurt the eyes. Judith stared at it.

'You're as bad as Adrian, la,' Minou said. 'He's always looking out for that silly bird.'

Minou spent the drive – through the forest suburb, past commercial areas of boarded-up Chinese shophouses and huge blocks of government flats sluttish with washing lines – chatting to Bala. When he had exhausted the saga of his son's first tooth, she lapsed into silence.

For the third time Judith checked her cassette recorder. 'You'll introduce me to the camp leader, won't you?' she asked.

Minou grunted.

The Citroen was now climbing one of the hills that cropped up in the city, a shabby oasis of small trees and vines. The road was winding and surfaced with grey-white sand, barely wide enough for two cars to pass. Since the morning was still cool they had the car windows wound down, instead of using the airconditioner.

Judith sniffed. 'God, what's that?' A smell, not of decay but of concentrated, living filth, had entered the car. Around there was nothing to be seen but sandy road and bright green vines.

191

'That is 705 new Australian immigrants waiting for a Qantas flight to take them to the promised land,' Minou said. 'You should smell Bidong, la.' She glanced at Judith's tape-recorder. 'A nice little story for your nice little newspaper. My mother and boys will be going to Bidong. Or Cherating. The Malays have cut down all the trees at Cherating and wired in the beach so that the children can't swim. They can sit all day in the sun and look at the water, which is just six metres away, on the other side of the wire. It was too much trouble for the Malaysian government to use another few metres of wire. They said that if they did the communist secret agents – you know, the boat people are all communist agents – would swim away and start a revolution. So instead they give the children sunstroke.' She snapped on her larrikin grin.

A tree-denuded area of ground had come into view and a high fence of cyclone and barbed wire. Behind it there were shelters made from packing cases and sheets of galvanized iron. Newly washed rags of clothing were spread out to dry on the drunken houses. A few children had hooked their fingers through the diamonds of wire. As they caught sight of the car they shouted.

The main gate – two metres of barbed-wire overhang – traffic boom and police post now appeared. Rushing towards it were scores of barefooted children. Judith saw a collective smile of worn-down milk teeth and over-large, square secondary teeth that stretched from face to face. Malay police with pistols in white holsters shouted at them to get back, but the kids were reckless with excitement, calling 'Minou! Minou!' and hooking themselves on to the wire. A policeman grabbed a boy and pulled him from the gate, as one might pull a cat off an expensive curtain. He tossed the child to the ground.

The gate was opened; the boom raised. Bala opened the boot and took out the projector. A cheer went up from the

192

children, who had been knocked over and trodden on as the gate was opened. Several scuffled for the honour of carrying the equipment. The police looked bored but businesslike. Only one, an older man, was smiling.

'Here goes,' Judith thought. Minou was already out of the car, sauntering over the naked earth towards the police. She had not looked back.

Judith caught up with her as she reached the police box beside the gate. The children swarmed around both of them, their wonderstruck, black-bean eyes glistening. A greasy exercise book was opened for signing; Minou disengaged her hand from the paw of a little girl and wrote. She looked up at the young policeman who was standing inside the box, jerked her head at Judith and said something that Judith did not hear. The cop blinked. As Judith stepped forward to sign the book he snapped it shut. Minou was already moving off, borne away like a cork in water by the laughing children. Judith looked after her but she was ten metres off, walled in by bodies and noise.

The stench of the camp was overpowering now. A group of teenage children had hung back beside Judith and watched her inquisitively. 'I'm Lady Hobday's assistant,' she said. 'I'm working the projector.'

The policeman smiled slowly; in his line of business he had heard everything. 'You are an Australian journalist,' he said. 'Lady Hobday gave you a lift here in her motorcar.'

Judith laughed; the policeman laughed.

It was the old policeman who finally gave in, spreading his hands palm upwards, in that supplicant, helpless way that Kanan had, and giving a self-deprecating grin for his weakness. What could one do? The problem was too great, his outstretched palms had assigned responsibility to Allah. He had seen, in the set of Judith's mouth, that she was prepared to argue with him all morning to get her way. The young

193

policemen stood back in a circle, their arms crossed over their chests.

'White women are as hard as Chinese,' one murmured to another. 'Chinese don't respect anything but money. White people don't respect any laws.'

'They stole our country.'

'They imported the dirty Chinese to rob us.'

'They kick us around.'

'No respect.'

When old Rashid bin Ali, the sergeant, gave in, they all smiled at Judith and one offered to find the camp leader for her. All the children had disappeared, sucked up by Minou's magic like leaves to a whirlwind. Only adults and older adolescents were still around – women in black pyjama trousers and floral blouses were squatting in groups, chatting, or washing clothes in filthy water. Most of the males were as inert as caged beasts: they lay stupefied on the refugee-issue sleeping mats of red-and-white or blue-and-white cotton. Some of them had their eyes shut; others stared at the rice-bag ceilings they had rigged up for shelter. Two young men naked to the waist and with black cotton bands knotted across their foreheads were standing at the camp kitchen, chopping up chickens – heads, wingtips, feet. Only the beaks and toenails were deemed unfit to eat. They had already shredded a two-hundred-litre drumful of cabbage. The chickens had been too long out of refrigeration and were beginning to rot. Judith gagged as she approached. The smell of the camp was shit, piss and high flesh.

'It is wonderful here,' the camp leader said. He mouthed the words carefully, slowly. 'After Bidong it is wonderful.' Dressed in shorts and refugee-issue rubber thongs, he was instantly identifiable as a business executive – soft belly, spectacles, those bland businessman's hands with which he gestured to the office-rice-store-film room, the open-air kitchen, the latrine pits, the sign boards above the wood-iron-and-ricebag rows of shelters. The signs said K1067 and L235.

'They are the boat registration numbers. We are organized according to the boats we came in.' He had been the manager of the biggest scrap-metal contractor in South-East Asia, he said. 'I bought the scrap metal from the war – aeroplanes, tanks, any metal things, even spent bullets, and we sorted it and sold it to Singapore, Hong Kong. On May Day, 1975, I was called in and all my possessions were taken away by the State and I was required to stay on, without pay, managing the business for them. You see, I know how to do it well. I know everything about scrap metal, how to manage a big business. I tried to flee three times, but failed twice. That cost most of my money. On the third time we got a thirteen-metre boat, with ninety-six people on board, just a four-day trip it was. Then two months in Bidong. I've been in Bellfield three months, waiting for my wife who's still in Bidong.' He had been speaking quietly; his voice was now trapped down inside him, as a man's voice would be if confessing to a crime. 'My wife, you see, has some problem with her chest and she can't pass the medical for Australia.' He stared at the ground. 'It's only one lung.'

'Is she getting treatment on Bidong?'

He smiled apologetically. 'There are no medicines. There's no refrigeration on Bidong – no electricity – so there's no point in taking medicines there. They would only get ruined.'

'How long will you wait for her?' Judith asked.

He gestured with his soft hands. 'You see, her baby died on Bidong. If I leave Malaysia she will lose contact. This man here . . .'

A Chinese or Vietnamese – it was difficult to tell the difference – was approaching them. Everyone, even Minou, admitted that few could distinguish by appearance Hoa

195

from non-Hoa. The man was wearing an ill-fitting woollen suit and carrying a cardboard briefcase. A woman in black pyjamas trailed behind him in a daze.

The man beamed at Judith. 'G'day, Aussie,' he said. He had his hand out. 'I'm from Newcastle – y'know Newcastle? I work in the injineering shop for BHP. Y'know it?' He turned to the woman and swept her forward: she looked drugged. 'Seven years! I got a scholarship to study injineering in Sydney seven years ago. Left her with the kids for a year and, y'know, the war . . . She had to move, I moved to Newcastle. Seven years! And I found her this morning. Spent all my money looking for her. Been to the Philippines, Hong Kong, Singapore. Probably lost m'job, now.' He roared with laughter. Judith and the camp leader laughed; the woman smiled, uncomprehendingly. 'Just think. She coulda got down to Aussieland, maybe gone to Newcastle even, and we might never've met. Passed each other in the street. Tsk.'

'That would have been crook,' Judith said.

'Real crook,' he agreed. For a moment he was dumbfounded by misery, but amazement reasserted itself quickly. 'Y'should see the kids now,' he confided to Judith. 'Grown! Y'wouldn't believe it.'

The camp leader gave a little cough of distress and the man and his impassive wife moved off towards the junk-heap shelters.

'Do you think I will find work in Australia?' the camp leader asked. Behind his spectacles his eyes pleaded; he was apologizing for bothering her.

'Unemployment is high.'

'I have been told. Before I left Ho Chi Minh City I taught myself to cook. I learnt to cook twenty different menus, so maybe . . .'

'Vietnamese food is certainly becoming known in Australia. There are two Vietnamese restaurants in Canberra.'

196

'Really? Do you yourself like it? I will cook for you. I will come to your house. I will show you how I can cook.' His soft hands coaxed at the air to get her to believe in him.

From a wooden building nearby there had been shouts of children's laughter. This was now replaced by singing. 'Lady Hobday – we call her The Angel. She comes almost every day she is in Kuala Lumpur. In Bidong she sleeps on the ground like everyone else, uses the same – you know, the latrines there. There are thirty thousand people and only two latrines.

Judith nodded stiffly. She thought, Ralph said he'll be back from Bidong this afternoon. I'll ask him, as a favour, to get me on to the island. If he says no, I've had it.

'And she is not even . . . well, she is of mixed race,' the camp leader added.

'Yes. Most unfortunate,' Judith replied primly. She had been wondering, since Minou double-crossed her at the gate, where she would stay when she at once moved out of the Residence which, inevitably, she must now do. Perhaps Minou would let her walk back to town, as well, down that ankle-breaking sandy road. 'Shall we?' she said to the camp leader, thinking again, Here goes.

Judith squeezed past the sacks of rice – big tight bellies lurching against each other – that littered the corridor leading to the film room. Outside the sun had already burned off the early haze and had been strong enough to make Judith sweat lightly. The corridor, with its sharp smell of jute-sacks, was uncomfortably hot; the air in the film room must have been 43 °C. Scores of children were sitting on the floor, singing. It felt to Judith as if the air in there was pure carbon dioxide and that she would pass out. She breathed deeply, preparing herself to outface Minou, to say to her, Thanks for the lift. I'm walking back to town, now.

Minou was seated on the floor near the doorway, leading the singing. As she saw Judith she gave a shout and flung

197

up her arms. The song stopped; hundreds of amazed black eyes stared.

'Judith! Hi! Come in.' She beckoned, urging Judith to squat down beside her. Then, in a rapid quacking, she addressed her audience. The children cheered and clapped.

'What did you tell them?' Judith asked. She had remained standing.

'That you are my beautiful Australian friend, my sister from Australia.'

On the drive back into town Minou prattled incessantly. At one stage she scratched her scalp, examined the underside of her scarlet-varnished nails and said, 'Oh, look. A louse.' She cracked its body and flicked the tiny broken corpse on to the carpet of the Citroen. 'I'll go through your hair tonight. It's easy to see them in blonde hair.'

'Terrific,' Judith said, pulling a face.

Minou looked put out. 'These camps are very clean and healthy. There's a bit of TB at Bidong. But no plague.'

'*Plague?*'

'Yes, la, *plague*. Do you think plague has vanished from the earth just because you little Australians don't have it? I used to have injections against it – bi-i-g needles.'

They rode in silence, Judith feeling inept and bourgeois, remembering that she had seen references to bubonic plague in Vietnam. Presumably the badly crowded camps in Thailand had it. She was startled by Minou's breaking of the silence.

'Do you ever wonder why you are alive?' Minou asked.

'No.'

'I mean, why your life has been spared and somebody else's hasn't?'

The Citroen had drawn up outside the office block where Judith was to interview the Malay Tunkus she'd met at Jamie's party. 'I do,' Minou said. 'I think about it often.

198

How come I was one of the lucky ones to get out, in April '75, when thousands of others failed?'

Judith had gathered up her tape-recorder and notebook and was edging along the seat towards the car door, which Bala had already opened. 'I know the answer,' Minou continued lazily. 'I have a purpose. A good purpose.' She glanced down at Judith's equipment. '*You* have a function. You overcome other people's wills, for your job. But it is just a function. You haven't got a good purpose.'

Judith replied, 'I earn my keep.'

This time, when Minou looked at her, it was with genuine scorn. 'So does a cow.'

'Bye,' she added, and turned her head away to look out the other window, across the road, where a white-turbaned man had all sorts of exotic junk laid out on a cloth on the pavement and was waving a brass cobra at a couple of young Australian tourists, dressed as if for bushwalking – with knapsacks, zinc-creamed noses and shorts. People were staring at their hairy legs; only coolies wore shorts in the street.

19

She stood there, a cackling gnome, with one stubby hand on the brass knob of the Residence front door, bare feet planted wide, each brown toe separated from its neighbour like small stones spaced regularly in a line. Her black satin trousers were creased sharp, her white cotton jacket with curly frog fasteners was starched. And she laughed at Judith. Her belly jerked up and down beneath the stiff clothing.

'India man,' she said. And 'clicket'.

It took Judith a while to get from her a proper account of what had happened while she had been at Bellfield and later interviewing the Tunkus. It seemed part of the amah's policy of bullying everyone except Minou to deliver messages at first in code. The old biddy was a master of power games – half a century or more of service to the white misfits, petty tyrants and dreamers whom colonies attracted, had taught her every trick in the servant's trade of reversing the official order of superiority. At length it became clear that Kanan had telephoned the Residence, inviting Judith to lunch at The Dog that day at 1 pm. After lunch there would be a friendly cricket match between a visiting West Indian team and a scratched-up side of players from The Dog; Judith was further invited to stay on and watch the game, which would end with failing light, at about 5 pm.

She felt slightly sick; she had not thought of Kanan all morning and now, suddenly . . . 'I'll write the royals story while I'm watching the game,' she said unnecessarily to the amah, who received this information without a blink. 'Please get me a taxi.'

The amah waddled out on to the front porch and shouted 'taxi' at a Malay gardener who was clipping the hedge in slow motion. Judith went flying through to her suite, straight to the mirror. Her face, thank God, no longer looked like slightly warmed putty, as it had at six o'clock that morning. She had only ten minutes to repair it if she were to reach the Club by one.

When the taxi was halfway along Jalan Ampang she realized she had forgotten her notebook and felt for Kanan a surge of resentment for making her rush. The clock on the pink Moorish building on the other side of the *padang* struck one as her taxi went clatter-bang, and stopped. She tipped the driver too much and hurried up the front steps. A lot of men were seated at the long polished bar, others were strolling towards what she supposed was the dining-room. There were Sikhs, Tamils, Chinese, Tunku Jamie, who lifted a beer glass to her, the West Indians, and a few limp-looking British Foreign Office types. Kanan was not in sight.

He arrived twenty minutes later, at the moment when Judith thought her anxiety and humiliation – the waiters had brought her a fresh lime juice and had exchanged looks when she had tried to pay – would explode in irrational action. That she would smash her glass. Or slap Kanan's face.

He came towards her with his palms pressed together, touching his fingertips to his forehead and saying, 'Sorry, sorry, humble apologies', and she felt her legs had turned to those of a new-born foal. He had had to visit somebody in hospital on the way to the club. Of course, she understood. She had been enjoying the view and the beautiful blue day. And thinking.

In the dining-room, which had been modernized to look like any other dining-room, he said, 'But you're eating nothing.' He gazed at her with consternation, as if she were an important piece of machinery that had unexpectedly broken down. He himself had wolfed an assortment of vegetarian curries and had looked with interest at the crème caramel a Sikh was toying with at the neighbouring table.

Judith, who had talked about Bellfield and abuse of privilege by the royals, was thinking that his hair was too long – he had a blue-black mane – but that it suited him. It was the unstylishly long hair of a man whose self-confidence placed him above fashion, a man who suited himself. She frowned, trying to recall something from the jumble of images she had of Kanan, but they had melted together into an inscrutable mass. It was all just there, a shiny orb in her forehead, with his name written on it, as incomprehensible and fascinating as the rings around Saturn.

'Actually, I'm nervous,' she said, and blushed.

His eyes were limpid with sympathy.

Ralph Hamilton had the wry, satisfied smile of a man who has enjoyed himself illicitly. He had sauntered towards Judith, who was seated on a cane chair on the club verandah and was checking through her morning's notes. She'd gone back to the Residence to get them, now that Kanan was only a small white figure on the bright green *padang*, fielding at deep square leg.

An Oxbridge voice said, 'Oh, the bugger! He's dropped it!' Judith looked round to see a languid young Sikh in a pink turban flapping his hands together in a slow clap. Behind him Ralph was approaching her.

Ralph dropped his hands on to her shoulders, still under the influence of the sexual arousal, now an amorphous sensuality, created by Lan. There was a shiver of muscles, the involuntary movement of rejection that runs along the flank of a horse when a saddle is heaved on its back. Ralph squeezed the tremor down, then lifted his hands.

'What a suntan!' Judith said.

'Bidong's not too bad for some things. I just got back. Haven't been home yet.' He squinted across the field towards Kanan. 'You're the guest of Dr Midnight, eh?'

He was so pleased to realize that Kanan, after all his chastity bullshit, had made a play for Judith which she'd accepted, that he felt a genuine current of pleasure in seeing her sitting there. Kanan's piece of fluff. Her presence was, he felt, a personal achievement for him. His body was easy, too – not a twinge since Saturday. This, with the other physical pleasure – Lan had been half-spavined from it he'd noted proudly when he'd waved her goodbye on the wharf that morning – had created a mood of benevolence in him.

'I hope he's been looking after you. Let me get you another drink.'

'Just lime. I'm still working.'

The clock on the Moorish building said 4.45; the sky, which had been cloudless all afternoon, was now a lilac-grey haze.

'I'll have lime too,' Ralph said. 'We'll have to start drinking properly when they come off, though. Look at the bloody Chinaman!' He went to the verandah rail, made his hands into a megaphone and roared 'It's cricket, not baseball, you Chinese nit!'

The Sikh drawled, 'Johnny has given away ten runs this over. Isn't it?'

Judith found she loved it all – loved sitting there among the pot plants and the Edwardian white cane furniture, identified as Kanan's guest, drawn in to his mysterious life. The difficulty of cajoling or threatening Ralph into helping her get in to Bidong had been illusory, she now realized. He was her buddy. They were all buddies on this verandah.

She asked him about Bidong directly, with confidence in his answer. It was all arranged by the time Kanan came bounding up the steps, his forehead nuzzled to the temple of a West Indian whose arm draped around Kanan's neck. She and Ralph would leave on mid-morning Thursday, by car. That left two and a half days for more interviews in KL. The timing could not have been better.

'I'll now have one of those things called a *stengah*,' she said, and was arrested and edified by the coquettish choice of her words, and the tone of her own voice.

Kanan was two metres away, talking to the West Indians, but he was looking at her over their shoulders, his Tutankhamen eyes bright with exertion and admiration. Those black, leggy men in their cream shirts and trousers smudged on the groin where they had wiped the cricket ball, were pawing each other tenderly, making Judith want to pluck Kanan away from them. She felt locked in a battle of wills with them. Then Kanan slapped a man's shoulder and broke free saying 'I must wash up', and Judith leant back, placated. She took a long swig of the whisky soda and smiled at Ralph who raised his glass, grinning.

The little bats had been out on their evening forage and had been swallowed by the darkness of the sky by the time Kanan, smelling like a flower, returned and dropped into a chair beside Judith.

What had happened next that night? She could not be certain, even at this point, half an hour after the Residence front door had swung heavily and clicked, shutting out the sweet night with its sickle of moon and Kanan, who had leant up against the white-washed porch saying, 'I can't go home. To tell you frankly, I can't walk.'

Judith lay open-eyed in the dark, hearing above the noise of the airconditioner words which, when spoken, had knitted the night together with the perfection of a final, central piece in a thousand-shape jigsaw and which now, recalled in the bed of the Australian Residence guest suite, stood out from their context like gems laid on velvet. There had been one

204

bad moment, an instant like biting into a fruit when the teeth and tongue meet rottenness – but it was only a small blemish. It had been late by then and they were all pretty drunk. KL was a drinking and whoring town. As Ralph had said: 'The colonial tradition bedded in the Asian tradition.' The Chinese made money to spend it on food, drink and women; the Malays made money to spend it on cars and women. The Indians? Kanan had thrown up his hands. 'Everything goes on dowry! A daughter is a financial disaster.' Ralph had laughed: 'And treated as such.' There had been silence, Kanan brooding. Then, to Judith, 'You see, daughters are abandoned. Sometimes.' 'Tell her about the city rubbish dumps.' Kanan had been earnest. 'No, no. That is an exaggeration, Ralph. It happens rarely these days, and the babies are usually of mixed race.'

That had not been it. That conversation had been early in the night, at Bangles. The three of them had eaten there, scooping up curry sauce with spongy wads of nan. Ralph and Judith were the only Caucasians in a bright, mirror-walled room of Indians – Punjabi women in trousers and head-shawls; Hindu women as vivid and shrill as birds; thin men arguing noisily; fat, sombre merchants whose eyes were set in circles of charcoal-coloured skin. A youth had detached himself from a group engaged in some family celebration to approach their table. He had touched his fingertips to his forehead in front of Kanan. 'I've passed you,' Kanan had said and the boy had returned to his relations, walking backwards and bobbing his head. 'Bloody guru,' Ralph had said to Judith. 'You should see him giving his Patterns-of-Culture lecture. Which acting school did you attend, Kanan?' There had been a lot of play between the two men, sharpening the thrill of the more elaborate game of feigned disinterest, of formality, of serious discussion between Kanan and Judith, which went on, secretly, like the steady burning of a fuse to explosives.

205

After Bangles, it had been 'somewhere nice for Irish coffee'. The Garden Lounge of the Regent – soft light, plush furnishings, a Filipino combo playing Harry Belafonte songs. Young Malays had strolled past carrying themselves with the elegance of movement which develops in bodies nurtured in fresh air, and accustomed to mats on wooden floors for beds. They wore platform shoes and gold chains on their wrists and ordered cocktails which came in large glasses with slabs of pineapple balanced on the rims.

Kanan had sat beside Judith and had talked across her to Ralph until Ralph had announced, 'A piss, old son. Must have a piss.' and had stumbled out of the rich, imprisoning seat. Judith's thigh had again grown hot from Kanan's pressed against hers as it had to be so he could talk to Ralph. She had known he would touch her before he did. But the shock of it, after all.

Like someone holding a pear, deciding on which surface to bite, he had turned her chin and with slow deliberation had sunk his tongue into her mouth. After a few seconds she had opened her eyes and seen his, wide open all along. With the same leisurely action he had withdrawn from her and had stared down through the glass of the table top, at his feet. He had swayed his head. He'd been becoming more Malaysian as the night went on, forgetting words, breaking his sentences with 'la!' and 'isn't it?' and, more often, 'to tell you frankly'. Then he was suddenly abashed, speechless, at *her* mercy – the novelty of this was an exquisite sensation. 'To tell you frankly, I desire you,' he'd said and made a disconsolate gesture, still staring through the table top on to which they'd spilt peanut salt and had marked with the wet circles of glasses of the beer that had followed the Irish coffees. He'd turned his head to look up at her: 'You see, my aunt lives with me. She's very . . . How can we . . . ?' Her voice had been steady: 'Why don't you come to the East Coast next weekend?' 'Four days! It's so long.' Her tone, to conceal the giddying sense of power, had been reasonable: 'I can't invite you to the Residence.' He'd nodded. 'The East Coast, then', and his smile, like a strip of white neon surging to full strength, had switched on.

Ralph's eyes had avoided theirs when he returned. 'Listen, old son – the Brass Rail. We need a game of darts and one ... final ... beer.' Had they gone by taxi? Judith couldn't remember at what point they'd dispensed with Kanan's car. 'This is a dive, but Zaridah is O.K.,' Ralph had said as they pushed through into the low-lying smoke and dark of the Brass Rail. It was deserted except for a Malay woman, maybe twenty-five, maybe forty, and some manic Malay boys. They had sounded as if they were on speed, they were shouting and talking so excitedly. There were bogus English-pub stalls covered in fake leather. Ralph had pulled the Malay woman down beside him on the narrow bench and balanced a beer glass on his forehead to impress her.

Judith, visiting the lavatory, had been driven back by the reek of vomit. When she had returned Ralph and the woman were playing darts; Kanan was almost invisible in the gloom of the stall. He had kissed her again. Peeping at him she had seen him glance up for a moment and had realized that Ralph was standing behind her, watching them. She had tried to pull back but Kanan had held her to him, pressing the nape of her neck with his hand. When he'd released her she'd turned immediately and seen Ralph leaning against the woman, one hand cupping her breast. Kanan had not even looked at the Malay. 'Let's go, Ralph.' It had been so calm and so brutal – the woman was just a whore, she could be picked up or abandoned at whim, by Ralph, by Kanan, by anyone. Standing under the lights outside the bar, seeing her own skin pallid and naked under their glare, the portent of that dismissal had struck her. This was the real Asia: infant girls abandoned on rubbish dumps; women murdered for losing their virginity; wives divorced by the repetition of three words; villagers stoning to death helpless people because they were Chinese. No mercy here for the weak. You'd be kissed in public whether you were embarrassed or not. Kissed, killed – it was a matter of degree only, the source was identical, disregard for the unimportant. Playing cricket was important, and being tolerant, being an unpollutable Hindu, a life-tenure academic.

Ralph had found some last-minute diversion inside the bar and she and Kanan were alone together on the pavement. She had stepped back from him.

Then Ralph had come bursting out of the doors, yelling, 'I'm a swing-wing', and had zoomed in circles around the pavement, making them laugh. Kanan had encircled her – soft, talcy whiff of violets as he'd raised his arms – holding her cheek against his. Ralph was off, dancing on the roadway, giving airport landing signals for a taxi.

'I think your husband has been cruel to you. I will be gentle,' he'd said.

They'd moved out of the light's ambit, their faces no longer peeled naked by its glare. Her indignation had sunk back into the place she thought of as river-bottom mud, her foul, subconscious mind.

They'd gone on to the Coliseum – 1930s, soda fountains, toasted sardine sandwiches, frothed-up lime juice served in tall, scratch-bleared glasses. Then dancing at the Tin Mine, among Chinese dollies and young executives jumping and bumping, not sweating a drop. Then home, with the sickle moon riding above the jungle trees.

Judith fingered her belly through the thin blanket. The menarche for this month was just over – in four days she would still be safe.

20

Ralph poked his foot at the cat that was tucked in, asleep, on the rug that looked like a stained-glass window, inside his front door. The cat awoke and made its back into a dromedary's blinking apprehensively at him. Kanan picked it up and said, 'Kitty, kitty'. They had just dropped Judith off, a thousand metres away at the Residence. Kanan had decided to sleep the rest of the night at the Hamiltons.

'It's got fleas,' Ralph said. He gave Kanan a penetrating, distrustful stare. There was nothing they could not say to each other, in theory, but the very tenderness between them created special taboos, as with lovers who will grieve inwardly for a partner's shortcomings rather than try to challenge them.

'The modest Indian householder. The man of chastity,' Ralph said.

Kanan scratched the cat's chin; it responded with ecstatic stretching and purring. 'I hadn't seen Judith then.'

'Oh, that's it! You usen't to mind if they had faces like arseholes. I remember in an economics tutorial one day you said, "By definition, all women are attractive." It was a bloody marvellous concept.' Ralph didn't add the rest of it, the presumption 'attractive, so long as they adore me', which each one did, until Kanan dumped her and found a new one to wash his clothes and write up his lecture notes. Ralph continued, 'A marvellous concept - it encouraged me with Sancha.' He gave a guffaw, which turned into a coughing fit – Ralph smoked too much – and flicked him forward.

Kanan noticed but decided not to comment. He made kissing sounds to the cat, saying between them, 'Sancha . . . is . . . nice'. For him, the fact that Sancha was rich indicated that she had accumulated good karma.

Ralph's spasm passed, leaving his face like crumpled brown paper. He was trying to recall the thread of conversation. 'Anyway, what about you and Judith?'

Kanan had a look of sheepish pride for the confession he was about to make: 'You see, she knows nothing. She is stiff and tense. She's like a virgin.'

Ralph's shout bounced around the stone-floored room. 'Of course! Only Indians know how to live. All wisdom arose in Mother India. India can teach the West how to live, including how to fuck.'

'We did write a book about it,' Kanan said to the cat. He was not in the least disturbed by Ralph's teasing. He knew his own attitude of mind was proper, and therefore his actions were proper.

'Mild-mannered Dr Kanan Subramaniam reveals himself as Super Screw to enlighten . . . Oh, yes, the guru comes down from his mountain top.'

Kanan nodded amiably. 'I will help her, isn't it? That is an act of charity.'

Ralph grasped his friend by the back of the neck and shook him gently. 'Well, good luck, you narcissistic bastard. I'm going to bed.' He mounted the stairs, singing 'Lloyd George Knew My Father', wishing that Kanan would be a bit less holy about fucking Judith, the way he used to be in the good old days. Not that he and Lan would ever want to be involved in one of Kanan's group scenes. The idea made Ralph recoil, the very thought that any other man had seen her naked. Her husband had, but he was a swine who had beaten her. Regularly.

210

People thought it must be sordid – so crowded, so dirty. They knew nothing. It was like a dream world, up there on Bidong, with her.

The black-and-yellow long-distance Mercedes taxi spattered the gravel of the Residence driveway as it pulled up. Judith, perspiring in the shade of the porch, ducked her head and saw that she would be the fifth passenger. An uncomfortably crowded trip, and without airconditioning.

The driver, a Malay in his fifties with a chimp face of dynamic ugliness and good humour, opened the boot for her one overnight bag – maximum luggage, Ralph had warned. Ralph had followed him round to the back of the taxi.

'Have you spoken to Minou today?' he asked.

Judith had barely seen the Hobdays since the trip to Bell-field. She had been working, either out on interviews or in her suite typing. In the evenings they had been at official receptions and dinner parties. One lunchtime in the foyer she had run into Minou, dressed as neatly as an airhostess, wearing a little pill-box hat. 'French Ambassador's wife's luncheon,' she had said and dashed out to her Citroen, shouting back, 'I hope the servants are looking after you. I've got to give a speech.'

'She's flown up to Trengganu. She's bought a kerosene fridge for Bidong – to store penicillin, and stuff. She wants to take it out on the boat with us tomorrow morning,' Ralph said.

'Hell! Did you tell her I'll be there?'

'No. Look, I can get you on to the boat. But she can have you off-loaded. You'll have to play that hand yourself.'

He jerked his head towards the passengers in the car, then touched his forefinger to his lips. The introductions were first-name only. 'Judith's going to talk to the head of the UN in Trengganu, and get some local colour', Ralph

211

explained to the fellow passengers. None of them – two Australian immigration officials and a young Malay government official – seemed interested.

The official asked a few questions in English, in a tone of *noblesse oblige*, then returned to his mother-tongue discussion with the cab driver, who chuckled and wheezed. The Malay had the excessively neat clothes of all bureaucrats in recently de-colonized countries; in comparison to him the Australians, dressed in shorts and sandals, looked as offensive as over-flowing garbage bins in a florist's shop. One of them was exceptionally tall. He seemed worn out from the heat already, although he was only in his late twenties and the trip had just begun.

He said, 'I sleep every five days. Get rotten and go to sleep.' He was returning, he explained to Judith, to Mersing camp where he worked in four-day stretches, sixteen hours a day, interviewing, selecting, rejecting. He spoke a Chinese dialect and Vietnamese. Learnt where? Judith wondered, and looked at him more closely. He had the blunted, hostile eyes of a man who has seen too much, too young.

The presence of the Malay made conversation difficult.

'What do you eat at Mersing?' Judith asked.

He shrugged. 'Your stomach shrinks,' After a silence he added, 'I like raw fish.' The Malay turned round and flicked his eyelids with disgust.

The car was passing abandoned rubber estates, the trees elongated and struggling against a choking undergrowth of vines. At Gombak a police jungle unit blocked the road: guerrillas had fired some rockets there that week. The Australians fell silent. This group of Chinese sympathizers and admirers (Who, in Australia dared not admire China these days? Or scorn Islam?) were being held up at a police check because of a decades-long war fought by Chinese, men who only saw daylight when they emerged to murder policemen or steal provisions. The Malay smiled and chatted to the cops. They were waved through and began to climb into the Genting Highlands, where the air became cool and milky soft. There were fish-farms in the villages below, but few signs of habitation. Apart from the rectangles of water reflecting the sky, fields of rice and cassava, and the smooth black road – built by the USA, a road made for army trucks – there was only jungle. It was extraordinarily green and quiet. And oppressive. It stopped their desultory chat with its weight. Even the two Malays were affected by it and fell silent. Judith thought again how unequal she, or any of them, was to coming to terms with this environment.

Planters had gone quietly mad from the oppression of these ancient trees; the Malays themselves had invented a vast demonology, and magic rituals for mollifying demons, to help them cope with it. This was the proper domain of tigers and tapirs and seladang, the forest bulls which would trample incautious hunters to death. One had killed a chief of police; its beautiful head, with horns two and a half metres across, was now mounted on the wall of the police mess, and had been drawn, proudly, to Judith's attention at lunch the day before. It was a merciless environment. The thought raised something hazy in her mind, and she frowned, grasping for it then giving up.

'If you put lime juice on it you don't get scurvy,' the giant remarked, still brooding on his dietary fetish. 'People think you don't get scurvy if you eat chillies, because they've got a lot of vitamin C. But chillies go straight through you. And you get scurvy all right. Gums bleed. That's the start of it.'

'Does the interviewing get you down?' Judith asked. The Malay had gone to sleep, the way they could, just anywhere.

He considered this for some time. 'Nup. Used to. When you'd give somebody the card "acceptable for Australia subject to medical" and they'd cry and kiss your hand. One time that would upset me. But you get used to it. The ones you reject – they don't show anything. Just bow and walk away.'

'You never know what they're thinking,' the other man, all blond and muscly like a footballer, put in.

'What can they say? You're sentencing them to death,' Judith said.

Nobody responded.

Ralph, whose suntan had turned yellow in the course of his days in KL and who looked to Judith as mean-tempered again as when she had first met him, raised his eyebrows high, like a fading actress at a risqué joke.

The giant and the footballer, dragging boxes of immigration papers and rucksacks pregnant with bottles of whisky, got out at the Kuantan taxi station. Their departure, the extra room, but above all the changed landscape lifted the feeling of reticent gloom that had filled the car. They had travelled through the thumping green heart of the country and were now on the East Coast. The road ran through coconut groves of squat young trees with yellow fronds shading clusters of orange fruit the size of human heads. Through the trees, across white stretches of beach, they could see from time to time, a smooth, celadon glaze stretching to the horizon – the lovely, treacherous South China Sea. This afternoon it was as still as a painting. There were Malay kampongs here and there, clusters of wooden shacks with corrugated-iron roofs crumbling with rust.

The government official turned to Judith and said, smiling blandly, 'You'll never see Chinese living in houses as poor as those.'

The cabbie wheezed and laughed and regaled them in English on the subject of how much rent he had to pay for his cab to its Chinese owner. He had two wives and six children to support. 'We can't eat,' he said, grinning at the monstrous joke life had played on him. 'And the big men tell us this is the richest country in ASEAN.' His hands flew off the wheel, that same, helpless gesture. But more derisive.

214

The government man seemed to take this last remark as a personal affront, and changed the subject. He pointed out to Judith a stretch of lustrous water where, two weeks earlier, a senior bureaucrat and his wife had drowned. 'They say the undercurrent is so strong at ebb tide that it feels like hands grabbing you by the ankles. The village people say it is the hands of the Goddess of the Deep. Unless you know the area, it is suicide to swim here.' He appeared satisfied that he had re-established his authority with this information and fell silent.

The road veered inland again, through an area of violation. Whole hillsides had been slaughter-hewn and left with the greying corpses of trees, apparently not worth drawing to the timbermills, among the stumps of better quality trees. Passing the mills the air was fragrant with camphorwood scent. Occasionally there were more poor Malay villages, unpainted houses built on stilts with a few bougainvillea vines straggling out of kerosene tins, some goats and chickens, and naked babies carried on the hips of older sisters who wore the discarded dresses of grown women. Then there was jungle again; then hillsides covered with what appeared to be an invention of science fiction – monstrous green hairy spiders. A million of them, nesting leg to leg over the hillsides. 'Palm oil estate,' the Malay said approvingly.

One hillcrest away a brilliant red dot appeared. The cabbie squinted at it and muttered in Arabic. The government man, too, was agitated.

'Pull over! Pull over, man!' Ralph said.

The red bullet was coming straight for them. Ralph and Judith cringed involuntarily as the noise from it increased to a crescendo. Small rocks tattooed against the side of their car, which the driver had managed to swerve to a stop in the long grass beside the road. They all turned to stare at the red Lamborghini which had blasted past. For a number plate it had a gold crown.

'One of your Sultans going for a spin?' Judith said.

The official looked sulky; he and the driver fell into a spirited discussion in Malay which, from his ironic gesticulations, the cabbie seemed to be winning.

Ralph took the opportunity to lean to Judith's ear and whisper, 'Have you ever seen someone stoned to death?' He smiled at her horribly.

'Of course not,' she replied crossly.

'Maybe you'll have a chance to.' The road had retouched the coast and they were driving past a grove of tall, voluptuous palms. Ralph looked out to the sparkling sea. 'This is ideal weather for boats to land,' he said aloud. 'There'll be a few coming in if it stays as calm as this.'

The Malay nodded, his jaws tight. Judith thought of Minou's toast 'To iron boats!' and the screaming she had heard in the night. 'Where's the turtle beach?' she asked.

Ralph nodded towards the ribbon of white sand where a few ramshackle palm-leaf shelters were built close to the line of coconut trees. 'Right here,' he said. There was some low, seaside scrub between the road and the palm trees. Ralph squinted at it. 'Did you see a car in there?' he muttered to Judith.

She had not. Ralph tapped the cabbie on the shoulder. 'Just stop and go back for a minute, please. I thought I saw something back there.'

They returned the few hundred metres, Ralph and Judith bent forward, staring out the window. 'Nope. Must have been a mistake,' Ralph said. He and Judith glanced at each other. Both of them had seen the rear mudguard and some of the central panelling of Minou's Citroen concealed in the scrub.

When they stopped a while later to buy some bananas at a road stall Ralph muttered quickly, 'She must have sent the car and the driver up, while she flew. Jesus Christ, that was the beach where they stoned a whole boatload in January. The ones who weren't dead they threw back to drown.'

The government man was walking towards them, offering bananas.

'Thank you *very* much,' Judith said, surprising herself by the false, ingratiating tone in her voice – the ease with which she had been unnerved, not by this man but by what he represented. If she, an outsider was unnerved, how much more easily were those who lived here, who were pushed up against the furnace of Malay resentment and its violent manifestations? People like Kanan. She felt, for a moment, as if a grave had opened.

The man was smiling at her, nonplussed by her enthusiasm for bananas. 'That's my pleasure. Please. You are a guest in my country. Please enjoy yourself,' he said.

As Kuala Lumpur was Chinese, Kuala Trengganu was Malay and therefore, Islamic. The town, as shabby as an armchair with its stuffing coming out, had grown out of a fishing village built on the entrance of the Trengganu River. It was so flat that from one side of town you could see the uneven white domes of mosques on the other. There was a roundabout on the main road encircling a statue in tin of a leatherback turtle. The turtle was less than symmetrical and its paint was peeling. The government man said, 'Nobody knows where these animals live, but they build their nests in only three places in the world – Costa Rica, Surinam, and Trengganu.' His tone indicated that this was a victory for the Malaysian government, against some other government. Thailand's, perhaps.

The taxi lurched into traffic and Judith had the discomforting impression of being half-naked: there was not a bare female arm, head or calf among any of the women and girls who were strolling, slip-slop on plastic sandals, along the pavements. Her short-sleeved shirt and knee-length skirt suddenly seemed immodest. On shops the signs were in Arabic script and their colours were muted; the exuberant red-and-gold signs of KL, with their huge optimistic ideograms, were hundreds of kilometres away, and several centuries. Every restaurant they passed advertised its purity for Moslems with a *halal* sign; enamel bowls of greasy curries were displayed in their windows, the cynosure of flies. The government man got out at one. In the fasting month the religious police patrolled the streets with truncheons, Ralph said, as soon as the man was out of earshot.

The late afternoon heat was like a buzz in the air; it had sucked up from the river mud, the fishing fleet, the markets and the flat dusty streets in which goats rummaged through garbage, the smell of old fish, and it breathed this over their heads.

On the ceiling of Judith's room in the Pantai Motel there was an arrow indicating the direction of Mecca. The room was cool and green-furnished – what else, but the holy colour in an Islamic town? – and overlooked the sea. And other things.

'This is where it all began,' Ralph said. He had joined her on her balcony to watch the day expire in a lilac-grained change of lighting which united the sea and sky. There was a breeze now which carried both the sea and the scent of frangipani from the gardens below. Judith thought, In two days Kanan and I will be together on this balcony, and felt for a moment that she would jump on to the railing and dance.

Down in the garden a large, black iron boat had been run up the beach to the grass and was secured there by steel hawsers. It was one of the early arrivals, back in 1978, before the flotilla had become an armada. The hotel had bought it to convert it into a mini-bar, but it had been there months and no amusing redecoration was as yet in progress. The idea had become rather tasteless in the interim.

Behind this boat the beach was littered with skeletons of other, less substantial craft, the flat-bottomed river boats that became floating coffins when the seas got rough, or when the pirates off the coast of Thailand gave chase in their swift, well-armed trawlers. Some of the ribs were charred: the refugees had learned quickly that it was safer to burn their boats than to face being pushed out to sea again.

'I saw that one come in,' Ralph said. He indicated a monster's ribcage. 'They'd been attacked six times by pirates and were all half-mad. The first group of pirates had been in a hurry and had cut the women's earlobes off to get their earrings. In later attacks, when the Thais found nothing to pillage, they simply raped and drowned a few more. The boat would have been pushed off, but they were so crazy they scared the tripes out of the villagers, who thought they were *jin* and went for their lives. I couldn't accept any of them – brains scrambled. They had sunstroke, too.'

'What'll happen to them?'

Ralph shrugged. 'The Swiss might take them eventually – Switzerland accepts only physically handicapped refugees, which might be stretched to include mentally handicapped.' Since they had arrived the aura of hidden rage that had enveloped him had dissipated. He was now openly irritated, and more human. He had cocked an eyebrow, watching a man in a sarong who, directly in front of them, was squatted down on the beach. The man stood up holding his sarong gingerly and went to the water's edge. A stubby snake lay curled in the sand behind him. The man splashed water on his bottom with a cupped hand, and strolled away.

'That's an efficient discouragement for walking along the beach at night in the moonlight, past their village,' Ralph said. He turned to Judith, '. . . if that's what you were thinking of doing.'

'Did Kanan tell you he's coming up?'

Ralph put on an unnaturally noncommittal expression. 'He indicated . . . something.'

Judith felt again an irrational surge of liking for him. It increased later that night.

219

'We'll have a decent meal before we go shopping,' Ralph said. 'It will be our last good feed for a while.'

When they handed in their room keys at the desk they asked again about Lady Hobday. Her driver had returned to the hotel (he was staying in the servants' quarters), bringing word that she wanted her room kept for several days, but that she might not be sleeping in it that night. 'She must be staying in Kuantan,' Ralph said loudly. Earlier a group of Special Branch men had been drinking in the Turtle Bar, just along from the reception desk. The walls had ears in Trengganu, Ralph had muttered.

When he and Judith moved away from the desk he said, 'Jesus, I'd feel happier if she had the syce with her on the beach tonight. She sounded more hysterical than usual when I spoke to her on the phone this morning. Silly bitch. Oh, sorry.'

The town's apartheid came into focus at dinner. It was necessary to search for a Chinese restaurant of any type and none could be described as superior or attractive; they were, rather, apologetic. Foods forbidden by The Book were not allowed to sully the town's market, Ralph explained, and the ingredients for Chinese cooking were sold in a street of narrow shops in the Chinese ghetto. In KL whole barbecued pigs hung on hooks just a few metres from the noisome goat and cow carcasses in the Malay butcher stalls and you could buy a snake or a tortoise to stew, right next to a Muslim stall of fish-with-scales. They found a place lit with neon lights and with a dirty tiled floor and ate their way through an indifferent assortment of unclean meats – crabs, pork and cockles. 'Too many chillies in the *halal* joints. My gut, you know,' Ralph explained.

Then they went shopping. Like most men, Ralph was an incompetent shopper, Judith noticed immediately. He went into a daze as he stood, too large for the alleys designed for women and small women at that, gazing at the supermarket shelves. They had to take all the food they would eat in three days on Bidong, he said.

'Tell me what the cooking facilities are and I'll know what to buy,' Judith said, but Ralph continued shuffling from one foot to another, picking up then replacing tins of camp pie and of lychees. The display was a hodgepodge of imports.

'You've done this twenty times. What do you normally take?' she asked at last. The supermarket was hot and had a pervasive smell of dirt and mildew. A Malay was thinning out the grime on the floor with a charcoal-coloured rag and a bucket of black water.

'Normally, I just buy luxuries,' he said. 'Fresh fruit, toiletries, Coke, cigarettes. I live on rice and noodles, like the rest of them, out there. I just take . . .' he dropped his head and she saw the look of someone discovered in a shameful but tenderly held vice, 'black-market stuff.' There was that pause during which people assess what damage they had done to themselves by a confession. 'I was hoping you might take some stuff for me. Women's stuff.' He had steered Judith to within a few metres of the cosmetic section, apparently unconsciously, but now he turned deliberately towards the glass cases of face creams, lipsticks, powder compacts and nail polishes. The brands were Shiseido, Revlon and Max Factor. A Chinese shopgirl was waiting, alert and with an inner glow from the intuition that she was about to make a sale.

Judith murmured, 'You said the police may search us when we arrive.'

He replied, speaking into his chest. 'Yes, but there's a system. I've secured one of the cops.'

'If anything goes wrong, you've got diplomatic privilege. I haven't. I can be arrested.'

His lips barely moved. 'You won't have to carry it. Just buy the stuff. It looks suspicious if I buy that junk.' He pulled at his earlobe and stared straight at her forehead. Judith

221

could feel the shopgirl's curiosity about this domestic dis-agreement boring into her back.

'What, then?' she muttered.

'Everything. One of everything. Get that Japanese stuff – it's the right colour.' Aloud he said, 'Get whatever you like, then, Sweetie-pie,' with a good imitation of a husband abandoning the effort to reason with his wife. He spent two hundred Malaysian dollars on the fripperies she chose.

When they emerged into the hot dirty street Judith felt as if she were breathing again, suddenly, and that oxygen had rushed to her brain, making her light-headed. 'I hope she's worth it, whoever she is.'

'She is. Thanks.' He glanced around at the Malay boys who were lounging on the steps of the supermarket, laughing and chatting, but never for a moment – you saw, if you had the nerve to pause and observe them – missing one move-ment that you made. Their bodies were always relaxed but alert, and you could feel them watching you with the backs of their heads. 'You must assume up here that any unusual behaviour gets reported to Special Branch,' Ralph said.

Maybe this was true; she had no way of knowing.

He dropped his head again and Judith suddenly under-stood, with a spasm of pain for him, that his fears were a fantasy, that the cloak-and-dagger nonsense over the cos-metics for his girlfriend was a deliberate self-deception, an attempt by him to feel at risk for her. He was proving, in this make-believe, how much he loved her, trying punily to live up to her courage. Judith marvelled at him, then abruptly her sympathy changed to envy. Men like him had love affairs all the time, whereas she, only once, with Ben, had experienced that incandescent excitement. And had been forced to disown it ever since. She sighed, then remem-bered: in two days Kanan would be here.

'Come on, comrade. Let's have a drink,' she said.

There was only one table left in the Turtle Bar when they

arrived back at the motel. The crowd was pulled in there
by a Tamil singer who accompanied himself on an organ.
His voice was as rich as a cello. He sang American love songs
to a room full of men: Judith and the barmaids were the
only females present. The Special Branch group, who had
been drinking all evening, were now very jolly.

'Out to Bidong in the morning?' a couple of them called
to Ralph and pulled faces.

'There's a new police chief,' a big Sikh in a white turban
said, and wagged his finger at Ralph.

'What does that mean?' Judith asked.

Ralph crouched over his beer. 'Probably . . .' he rubbed
his thumb and forefinger together rapidly. He was distracted
by his own thoughts, hunched up and debating with himself.
He said abruptly, 'You know, I'm going to leave Sancha.
As soon as I get Lan to Australia. I'm going to resign. We
won't have a red cent, but . . .'

She listened to an outpouring that was like a breached
dam, interrupting only to ask, 'Have you told Kanan?', to
which he nodded. 'He disapproves.' 'And Sancha?' Ralph
shook his head. 'She's guessed.'

In her room later she thought of the similarity of his reckless course and Hobday's: anger, then love of an intensity
great enough to drive both of them to social crimes. Hobday
had been enraged by the war, as he'd told her; Ralph, by
its aftermath. His hard and penetrating grey eyes had looked
straight into hers as he'd said, 'I can't bear it any more. I
can't bear the human suffering. I usen't to be a softie. I've
punched in heads myself, oh, well, years ago. But now, when
I see people in pain . . . I get so *angry*.' Each had been gripped
by that anger you saw in week-old babies – rage at impo-
tence. And each had transformed it into the second tyranny,
love. Perhaps that was it: you had to experience the first
before you could feel the second: Mars and Venus, Hobday
had said. And Siva – destruction and sexuality, all-in-one.

223

She thought of Kanan again, who appeared never to have been angry in his life. They'd talked of Kanan down there in the bar.

'Kanan thinks I'm sick because I'm collecting bad karma in the camps,' Ralph had said. 'He says that the untouchables are untouchable because they mix with death. They're the butchers and animal-skinners. He says that the work I'm doing means I am breaking caste, and for that you go to hell and are reborn as a leper. Or something.'

They had both felt tormented, sensing in the exotic web of language a thread of truth, the fact that Ralph's job was brutalizing. 'The bugger is so modern in some ways. But he lives by the *Bhagavad-Gita*, you know.'

'Whatever *that* means,' Judith had replied and they'd both laughed with relief at breaking the spell, and had gone on to talk of the little restaurant that Ralph and Lan would open – she'd cook, he'd serve.

'I'm only infatuated with Kanan,' Judith told herself now, lying in bed beneath the arrow that pointed to Mecca. 'Whatever *that* means.'

21

The wharf was on the southern bank of the Trengganu River, the town side, a few hundred metres from the market, so it was not surprising that banana leaves, coconut husks and other vegetable refuse from the markets floated nearby. Minou wrinkled her nose at the floating rubbish, indicating, in particular, that *her* sensory organs were highly sensitive and, in general, that she was still in a difficult mood. The coolies, four of them groaning and shouting contradictory orders at each other while they dislodged the refrigerator from the back of the truck, had dropped it rather heavily on the wharf and this had caused Minou's first flare-up. Her fastidious nose-screwing now signalled that other people might feel the rough edge of her tongue.

She, Ralph and Judith stood in the shade of a small shed at the shore end of the wharf, which was made of grey wood with splinters like darning needles. Across the slack water of the estuary, on the north bank about a kilometre away, was a large fishing village, its ramshackle thatched huts partly hidden by hundreds of small boats, as disordered and poverty-stricken as the dwellings in front of which they were moored. There was the sea smell, the market smell – predominantly dried fish – the smell of richly polluted mud, the stink of the goats wandering around picking at garbage, and the sharp reek of hot coconut oil coming from a stall just across the road where a Malay boy was frying *roti chanai*.

Ralph, Judith and Minou had breakfasted there, at seven o'clock, when their boat was already half an hour late. Silent men had watched them eat; some wore *haji* skull-caps. They sat with their gnarled feet pulled up on the benches, dragging smoke past teeth that had brown grooves of accumulated tar. They had responded to smiles with a nod, turning their heads sideways, like ravens. Judith had felt the exposed skin on her arms creeping. Not that any of the men had looked at it, rather the reverse: they had averted their eyes from her bare arms. Minou was wearing a long-sleeved shirt and a scarf over her head, like all the other women.

'For Christ's sake don't touch anything with your left hand,' Ralph had muttered. They had eaten rice out of banana leaves and crisps produced from glass jars opaque with dirt. Whining Arabic music filled the stall, muffling the monosyllabic comments the Malays had made to each other about the foreigners.

'If that boatman doesn't turn up in ten minutes ... ' Minou now said. She poked the toe of her navy espadrille at the hessian around the refrigerator. 'I'm going to hire a different boat.' She looked at Judith. 'There might not be room for you.' She gave one of her crocodile smiles. 'Tough titty,' she added and turned to speak sharply in Malay to a peasant woman who was fingering the refrigerator. The woman pulled her hand away and looked at Minou with sullen eyes.

'You slept badly?' Judith said lightly.

Minou replied 'Ouf!' at the inanity of the question. 'And *where* are the Yankees?' she demanded from Ralph, staring at him as if the Americans – immigration officials who regularly shared the Bidong boat with Australians – were his responsibility and he had mislaid them.

Then the boat arrived, a fishing trawler pitched high at stem and stern, and the whole process of shouting, groaning, and screaming from Minou began again when it seemed the

226

coolies would drop the refrigerator in the water, or crash it into the trawler's cabin.

By the time it was tied down on its side on the afterdeck and all the other gear had been loaded and stowed in the shade of the narrow cabin, the Americans had turned up. They sauntered along from the markets carrying braces of live chickens tied by the feet, which they tossed on the deck, and pineapples still on their stalks, which they put in the shade, and copies of *Time* and *Newsweek* and the morning newspapers, which they handed out with that easy American confidence that any gift of theirs will be welcome. Everyone was now smiling. Even the coolies managed grunts of pleasure as Minou passed around banknotes. The three Americans called Judith 'Ma'am', assumed she was another immigration officer, announced they had hangovers, and stretched out on the deck with towels over their faces.

'Goodbye, world,' one said as the trawler pulled out from the wharf.

At the stern of the boat there was a platform of slats extending a metre past the trawler's waterline.

'Come and sit here,' Minou called to Judith. She giggled. 'If we have to do pee-pee, we do it here, through the slats. I have got champion aim, la. When the sea is rough . . . ouf! Ralph,' she raised her voice from its little-girl whisper, 'have we got life-jackets?'

'We won't need them today,' he replied.

Minou frowned, still in a high state of nerves. She was dabbing Judith's nose with sun-block and smiling on-and-off brightly. Her quick, cute smiles were more pathetic than irritating. She kept on glancing towards the breakwater at the mouth of the estuary. 'It was calm early in the morning, but it always is. Do you think . . . ?'

The sea on the other side of the breakwater was the marvellous celadon green Judith had seen already, but it was now humping in waves more than a metre high, some of them creaming at their crests and bursting against the rock wall.

'That's the sandbank,' Minou said. She stared towards the heaving water, then swiftly looked away again.

'Bobby', Ralph jerked his head at one of the prone Americans, 'was swept overboard there a few weeks ago.' His old, angry smile was back. He and Minou looked at each other, sharing some frightful secret knowledge.

'Are you going to be seasick?' Judith asked.

Minou's face had turned yellow and she was shivering. She opened her lips to speak then snatched back the breath into her throat. They were just nosing through the gap in the breakwater. Suddenly the trawler's bow jerked upwards and spray broke on to the deck. The Americans woke up, saying 'Shoot!' Then there was pandemonium as two more waves broke on the bows and the chickens, squawking, began floating along the deck and the pineapples and a case of Coke came tumbling out of the cabin.

'Get inboard!' Ralph shouted. Minou and Judith barked their shins as they scrambled for'ard, cringing from the whip of salt water. Through the glass at the back of the cabin they could see the boatman struggling to keep the trawler's bow to wind as he negotiated the channel through the sandbank. There was a soundless *whack!* The boat shuddered and they were all knocked sprawling. One brace of fowls rose in the air and fell, helpless with their tied legs, into the dumping water. They floated, a fluffed ball of white feathers, a giant daisy, for less than a second then, as Judith stared after them, disappeared underwater. She turned to Minou, who had grabbed her hands, and the look in her eyes made Judith's scalp tingle.

'Can you hear them? Can you? I can *see* them,' Minou said.

It all lasted less than two minutes, then they were clear of the bank and the fowls were ten metres away, lolling on the wave crests, small now with their wet feathers, and dying. Minou had rolled herself into a ball, her forehead pressed on to her bent knees.

'It's all right now,' Judith said.

Minou's whole torso jumped when Judith touched her shoulder. She continued cowering, curled up against the world. Ralph beckoned Judith away and they lurched for'ard to the bows, their ears buffeted by the wind. They had to crouch in the shelter of the gunwale to talk. 'She always hates that sandbank, but I've never seen her so bad before,' he said. 'That's the famous sandbank.'

'What . . . ?'

'A few months ago a big boat arrived in rough weather and foundered on that bank. Two hundred people were drowned. The bodies floated ashore into the estuary and along the beaches for days and they were all chewed by fish and shrimps. The people started saying, "The fish has fed on human flesh", and nobody would buy fish. The bottom fell out of the fish market, which is the economic benchmark here, and the fishermen and their families were starving. The boat people were blamed. They'd been tolerated up till then, but it was war after that. The villagers started pushing them out to sea, and stoning them when they resisted. Mad rumours went round.' He turned to look aft, the wind licking his silky hair into his eyes: Minou had not followed them. 'They believe in ghosts. So does she. She told me once that she can hear the people crying for help every time she crosses the sandbank.' He gave one of his nasty, cheek-crack smiles. 'Or she *says* she believes in ghosts.'

The water had changed from the green of the coastal shallows to the sapphire of deep sea. The sky was kilometres high with a diaphanous white mist across it, but still showing blue. They might have been off on a picnic.

And when Judith and Ralph went aft, they found Minou and the Americans playing five-card stud; Minou had won six cans of Coke, and was crowing. The Americans kept up an argot patter – 'A deuce', 'A big lady', 'Oh, a puppy foot! She's leading in puppy feet'. But after an hour or so the monotony of the trip, the blinding dance of the little suns on the surface of the sea and the hot salt air made them droop into silence.

It was almost noon when Pulau Bidong came into view. On the empty, flashing sea its appearance seemed an event which revealed for an instant the mysterious force of creation; it looked as if some giant goddess had turned lazily on her back and exposed one sumptuous breast above the waters. The island had been, of course, a submarine volcano. At the breast's peak there was a tiny indent now softened and swollen with jungle, once the ditch of a crater.

'You'll smell it soon,' Ralph said.

They were all staring towards the island, as people stare towards their houses after a trip away, cut off from news, suddenly anxious about fires and burglaries and the garden.

'I hope the new police boss is O.K.,' Ralph said.

'He might not let me land.' Judith muttered, caught up in the general atmosphere of apprehension.

'He can get knotted.' Ralph was fussing with the gear. 'You're my new assistant, and that's that. I've taken enough shit from the cops out here.'

A crescent of white beach came into view, littered with the skeletons of boats. Behind it there was a building project, the sort of thing that might have been made by a subnormal child it was so obsessive and disordered, a town of toy-sized houses for thirty thousand people, made out of bits of stick and the blue-and-white ersatz hessian of plastic rice-bags. The shanty town occupied the area of flat ground beyond the sand; at its back the mountain rose up sheer. There was a rocky promontory on the southern edge of the beach and on it perched some galvanized iron sheds. The Buddhist temple and the churches, Ralph said.

They were about five hundred metres offshore when the smell of Bidong heaved up at them in a rush, as if the trapdoor to a dungeon had been wrenched open. It was a filthy acrid odour, containing only two elements – woodsmoke and excrement. As the boat drew nearer Judith could see that the beach was fouled.

'The children do that,' Minou said. 'They refuse to use the latrines.'

Hundreds, maybe thousands, of children and a few adults had gathered on a jetty still being built and too short for the trawler, in the shallow water, to reach it.

The water, from a distance, was the colour of lapis and turquoises but changed to a pellucid light green when you looked straight down into it, in the shallows. Through it Judith could see a submarine architecture of destruction – dead coral and sunken boats – on the seabed below.

A sampan was being poled out to the trawler, which had dropped anchor. Minou waved to the throng on the jetty and pointed to the refrigerator. A cheer went up. Ralph was scanning the crowd.

'Can't see Lan,' he said. 'Listen, Minou, you're going to be an hour getting that fridge ashore and installed. Judith and I will go on ahead.' His impatience had given an irritable tone to his voice; he was now scanning the beach.

From the sampan they had to clamber on to petrol drums, then on to the jetty. Hundreds of brown hands were yearning to help them up; Judith suddenly knew what it was to be a beloved member of a royal family. They cheered when she scrambled from one petrol drum to a closer one and cheered more loudly when, panting, she let them lever her up the rail. Then, there she was, standing up – hooray! – an idol, a living fetish object towering above them.

Ralph got up next and it all happened again. 'O.K., O.K., kids. Let's get on with it.' They parted in front of him.

'There've been a few changes,' Ralph said, as Judith

231

caught up with him. About two hundred children had followed them; the others had waited to help the Americans and to watch Minou. He nodded towards the beach. 'Cleaned up the black market. The stalls used to be there.'

The police station was a few hundred metres from the beach, to the north, in a coconut grove. The children halted at the roped-off area which marked the grounds of the station. Police with shotguns leaned against the trunks of coconut palms. They were all young, all Malay. They looked unimpressed by the arrival of visitors. One held out the registration book without greeting. As agreed, Judith let Ralph sign first, then scribbled in her name under his. In the column marked 'purpose of visit' he had written 'official'. She put ditto signs, and handed the book back with a smile. The policeman did not respond.

'Mr Hamilton,' he said, 'our new sergeant would like to speak with you.'

A shadow fled across Ralph's face. 'Fine,' he said.

Judith said, 'It's very hot, isn't it?'

The policeman looked at her with unconcealed hostility. 'This is the tropics. It is always hot.'

A smiling middle-aged man with his shirt unbuttoned at the neck emerged from the wooden station. He had the unnatural casualness and *bonhomie* of a man superior to his milieu, holding all the cards. 'Mr Hamilton!' His arms were outstretched in greeting and his fine teeth bit on an ivory cigarette holder. He turned to Judith, 'And Mrs Wilkes? A new officer? Delighted, delighted ... please.' He was shepherding them forward into the police station. Mind the step. A calm trip? Frightfully hot. Lady Hobday has the kerosene refrigerator? Excellent. Most welcome.

At the rough wooden table, a shrug – 'our local carpenters' – he sat and looked at them, beaming, as if by some trick he had produced them himself out of the air, and wished to contemplate his handiwork in silence. He smiled more at Ralph than at Judith. 'Of course, you'd like some tea,' he said.

Judith thought, For Christ's sake sit still, Ralph.

'Love some,' Ralph said. His voice was flat.

The sergeant smiled and nodded. He had really *hoped* they would want tea; from a corner a young policeman rose and went out through a back door, obedient to his boss's glance. Judith thought, I mustn't sound like a journalist, but if I don't start questioning him in a minute, he'll start questioning me, and I'll slip up. Maybe he knows already. I had to give in my passport at the hotel. If Special Branch has checked the guest book there they could have sent a radio message. Do they have radio contact with the mainland? She'd forgotten to ask Ralph. I have illegally entered a prison camp and made a false written statement. Bellfield was different. This is a proper maximum-security gaol.

The sergeant, however, had other things on his mind. For this relaxing noontide, at least, he was not a law enforcement officer at all but more the manager of a charming rural estate. He chatted about a new well that had been sunk, the water pump, and the three babies recently delivered by Saigon's foremost brain surgeon – a neighbourhood character, they were given to understand. Then, to Judith, 'We have more medical specialists on this island than there are in the whole of the State of Trengganu.' Smiling and sipping his glass of tea, boasting mildly.

Ralph said, 'I see you've cleaned up the black market.'

The sergeant put down his glass with precision. For a moment his expression became sombre, then, as if recalling his duty to guests, he smiled again. 'You see, Mr Hamilton, there have been some embarrassments.'

Ralph's face clenched. 'What sort?'

He waved the ivory holder in the air, pre-empting the development of alarm. 'Nothing for *you* to worry about, Mr Hamilton. My problem . . . discipline, la.'

233

It was another fifteen minutes before they could escape. Out in the coconut grove again Ralph said, 'I've *got* to find Lan.' His eyes were violent, Judith thought.

The presence of the hundreds of children, who had carried the gear from the jetty and had waited by the roped-off yard of the police station, was suddenly burdensome. Ralph ordered them away with yaps of Vietnamese. He and Judith – alone except for a small band of five-year-olds who stared at Judith as if she were a pink elephant – plunged into the lanes of the shanty town. The heat and the stench were dizzying. They moved between houses made out of bits of bamboo and sacking where people lay listlessly, eyes open, looking at nothing. Judith had a sensation of *déjà vu* that jolted physically, like the sting from a faulty electric plug. The pets shop again, but here the tiny cages held humans. And from that she knew something else. Eventually, some of these people would be eaten, too – they would be thrown into the sea.

Lan was not in her house. Her neighbour stared at the ground when Ralph questioned her. He seemed to Judith to be asking 'What's happened?' What's happened?' The woman shook her head, then pointed in the direction of the promontory.

'The temple,' Ralph said, and set out almost at a run.

An old man stood in the doorway of the corrugated-iron shed, his arms folded over his white singlet. Past his shoulder they could see inside to the red-and-gold altar table, shrine, image, paper flowers and silk hangings suspended from nails in the metal walls. Something in his manner, his total calm and sweetness, prevented any argument. Ralph could not enter the temple. Yes, Lan was there but she would not come out. She did not wish to speak to him.

Flaps of skin drooped over the outer corners of the monk's eyes, closing off the whites and giving him the look of an old, patient monkey.

Ralph stood with bent head, silenced. Then he looked up to snap some question at the monk, who nodded.

'Police?' Ralph said in English.

The monk nodded again.

Ralph was off, running now, back along the promontory to the steep track that led down to the beach. He was already halfway along the beach, towards the police station, while Judith was still slipping down the track, hanging on to the coconut trunk that had been laid there to give people a hand-hold. Kids and adults had begun chasing after Ralph, distracted from the marvel of the refrigerator which just now was being carried ashore across the coral and was landed, *wah!* with a cheer, a metre up the beach. Suddenly the whole beach was a crowd of running, yelling people making for the police station.

Judith looked around for Minou or one of the Americans but they were not in sight. The crowd in the coconut grove was immense now. She hurried along the beach and stood at the back of the gathering, trying to peer over shoulders and heads. The throng was thirty-deep, spilling from the grove to the unshaded beach. They were whispering to each other, weaving their heads like seals, trying to see, too. Then there was a whistle blast, and another. Judith saw a police-man's hand wave them back and she almost fell as the crowd, with a centrifugal spasm, jerked away from its nucleus.

'What's happening?' she asked a boy, who shook his head to indicate he could not speak her language. She asked another and another. People were beginning to move off. The police were blasting their whistles repeatedly and she now could see their faces, torn open with shouting at the crowd. 'What's happened?'

A teenage boy – she realized abruptly that they were nearly all men on this island; the ratio of men to women was about seven to one – said 'Hit. Hit policeman.'

A Vietnamese – or Chinese – man, was addressing the

crowd now, jabbing his hands at the sky. He must have been one of the camp leaders for he'd been pulled out of the crowd by the police. Unwillingly the crowd obeyed him, turned and slip-slopped through the dirty sand, trailing their hands against the coconut trunks, back to the boredom of their cages.

The police had drawn together in a group in front of the station. All of them were smoking and several of them, as they spoke, cast glances towards the room from which, half an hour ago, Judith and Ralph had emerged.

'May I go in?' Judith asked.

One of them nodded and averted his head.

Minou and Bobby, the American, were inside already. So were two refugee doctors. Ralph had been laid on the table from which they had drunk tea. One doctor was taking his pulse; the other, with movements as light as a humming bird's, was fluttering his fingers over Ralph's exposed abdomen. Below the navel there was a red bruise the shape of an axe-head – no, it was the butt of a shotgun, Judith realized – while the surrounding skin was putty-coloured. Ralph's eyes were closed and a light sweat covered him. The only noise in the room was his panting and the murmurs of the doctors to each other. As Judith moved to stand beside Minou a cold hand felt for hers. The air was so tight it seemed to be squeezing their temples.

The examining doctor looked up.

'She might know,' Minou said.

Everyone – the police sergeant was there, too – turned to Judith.

'Did this man have abdominal pain?' the doctor asked.

'He's got colitis.'

The doctors exchanged nods that were gravely satisfied. The senior man announced, 'Ulcerative colitis. His bowel has been ruptured by the blow he received. He now has peritonitis. He must receive treatment immediately.'

236

Shoulders heaved. They were all, suddenly, taking deep breaths, as though this were good news. And of course, it was. Their fears had been released, the paralysis had changed into a command for action. Treatment immediately: it was three hours by open boat to the mainland, but mentally they had leapt over that.

Minou announced, 'We'll get the stretcher', and took Bobby off with her.

Ralph, abruptly, had become a problem rather than a person, and they moved away from him without bothering to glance back. A new feeling asserted itself in the room: an air of accusation emanated from the police sergeant and from the young Malay officer seated on a chair in the corner. Deepest reproach welled up in his brown eyes and from his swollen, broken lips. He winced as the junior doctor gingerly raised that part of his upper lip which was not purple, exposing the broken front tooth and bloodied gums. The police sergeant stood by, avuncular and protective, gazing balefully at Judith. She turned away.

The senior doctor was still with Ralph, turning his limp right hand as if it were an interesting piece of driftwood he had found. 'He also has a broken hand,' he said.

She looked at him pleadingly and he followed her out on to the verandah.

'He could die in the next couple of hours. Or he can make a complete recovery, with proper draining and antibiotics. A woman here, last week . . . ' The authority left his voice. 'You see, we have no drugs. Not even alcohol to use as an anaesthetic and disinfectant. I could have operated on her with a fishing knife, but not without some alcohol.' That note of apology again. 'Madam, if we could only have Oxo cubes. For the babies – the one to four-year-olds. They are not getting enough protein, their mothers are not strong enough to breast-feed them long. Just some Oxo cubes. It would stop their diarrhoea, which is the beginning of their

237

malnutrition. The adults and older children are all right. But the one to four-year-olds.'

'Yes. Oh, I'll try. I'll get you some.'

'One case of Oxo cubes per week. Please.'

She pulled out her notebook and wrote it down. A policeman from the knot muttering and smoking together began to stroll towards them. The doctor continued blandly, 'Mr Hamilton will become delirious. Give him small sips of water.' The policeman paused and strolled away again. Judith wrote down at the doctor's dictation the name and address of somebody living in Melbourne and promised to contact him or her, with news that their uncle was on Bidong and hoped to be accepted for the USA, but that he could not contact them – letters were difficult.

'Keep Mr Hamilton as cool as you can. Bathe him,' the doctor continued. 'There is a man here with a serious eye complaint. He will lose his vision. Do you think he could . . .?'

It was Minou who wheedled permission from the police sergeant to take on the boat with them the man, whose eyes were too disgusting to look at, and a girl whose foot was black and swollen up like a hoof.

'Hospital ship, la,' she said to the sergeant. And 'Don't be made of stone, la'. Two policemen accompanied them, as guards; the man whom Ralph had punched and a second man. They boarded the trawler first and withdrew immediately to the skipper's cabin, leaving Judith and Minou to oversee the placing of Ralph in the shade of the other stern-facing cabin. And it was Minou who thought of the oil company's helicopter, used to transport staff to and from the drilling rig, and persuaded the police sergeant to send a radio message to the mainland about it.

It was almost dusk as the boat lurched through the shallows outside the breakwater. The yellow lights from the town and the fishing village opposite it disappeared behind the stones, then sprang back again, brighter and more

238

friendly. Then suddenly they were safe. The estuary was deeply peaceful, its slack water turning from brown to glittering black in the lilac-coloured light.

When, several hundred metres from the wharf, they saw the crowd gathered along the waterfront and above their heads the white rotor, Judith in effect went to sleep. She walked and talked for the next couple of hours but it was not until nine o'clock that night, dining alone with Hobday in the Residence, that she woke up again. Even at the University Hospital, where Sancha, martyred but game, had been waiting and had demanded details from Judith, she had been asleep while she talked.

'But *why* did he hit the policeman?' Sancha had demanded.

'Because they shaved somebody's head,' Judith had replied wearily. Sancha had snorted.

'I imagine it was his *petite amie*.' Grim satisfaction had inflated her like yeast in dough. She had stalked out of the hospital lobby with Judith, mowing down with a glance the stares of the curious, dull herd waiting in casualty. Hobday had sent his limousine to the hospital to çollect Judith. They had halted beside it, Sancha saying 'He only married me for my money. We'll see about *that* in future.'

From the car window Judith had asked, 'You'll turn the tables on him?'

It had been weird to see a smile from Sancha not given in obedience to social convention but springing from internal pleasure. 'I hope so, Judith. I hope so,' she'd replied.

Judith had forced her eyes to stay open during the ride from the hospital to the Residence. When she closed them the images and noises of the aeon that she and Minou had spent on that perfect, hot blue sea, with Ralph raving at the sky and arching his back as if the point of a knife were forcing him to, all came back, imprinted on the inner surface of her eyelids. The helicopter ride did, too. That had been

239

exciting for a few minutes, as she had looked down and seen Minou and the crowd growing smaller, the womens' headscarves blowing off in the rotor's gale. Then a dull composure had set in: Ralph would die before they got him to KL and into hospital and she would be sitting alone with a corpse, while the pilots chatted and joked and concentrated on their instrument panel.

She had so accustomed herself to this idea that when Ralph had startled into life again, talking nonsense, she'd not felt relieved but angry that he was still alive, and she'd told him to shut up.

22

'She's got the other two into hospital in Kuala Trengganu,' Hobday said. An expression of pride softened his face. 'It wasn't easy, apparently. They don't like admitting the boat people. The hospital is small, there's the problem of who will pay for their treatment, and security . . .' He looked at Judith challengingly, an eyebrow asking, Could *you* do as well as Minou?

'She was amazing on the boat,' Judith said. 'Ralph was conscious for a while and she just kept talking to him quietly, telling him that Lan, his girlfriend, would be all right, that it was only a problem of losing face. She ran up to the temple and spoke to Lan before we left Bidong. The police had shaved Lan's head only last night. She'd been running a card game, using the money she'd made out of black market-eering as her bank. Minou says she's a real crook.'

'I'll see to it that she doesn't get to Australia.' He studied the emu-and-kangaroo crest on his wine-glass. 'You'll keep that to yourself, of course? Young Hamilton is going to be in no condition for disappointments for some weeks. If he survives tonight.' He glanced at his watch. 'The senior medical officer told me that by midnight they should have some news of his condition. Could you join me in a second bottle?'

They sat in silence as the servant uncorked and poured more wine. The table stretched metres away into the dark. With only two places and the candles set at one end, they felt oppressed by space and huddled close to the orange flames and to each other. The servants, as usual, were distant while technically present.

Judith said, 'Lan wanted to open a restaurant in Australia. She was probably trying to raise capital for it through the card game.' Hobday's sad, bent head made her defence trail off, discouraged. It shamed him that this careerist young woman had, for the moment at least, a moral authority, a greater compassion than he. It was based on ignorance, of course: she did not know that Lan had shot her husband.

'You have become soft-hearted, Judith,' he said. His tone suggested irony. 'That first morning I met you, you put it to me that Australia was accepting a lot of undesirable riff-raff – blackmarketeers and hookers, you said.'

'I was only trying to get a quote out of you.'

He smiled, tolerant of her single-mindedness: that interview had been a background briefing only and she had known it. But now she was making it clear that what he had told her would appear in print – perhaps, to keep some faith, attributed to 'a senior official'. It fascinated him that she apparently had no idea that her ruthlessness could work against her. It was as if there were a gap in her head. Probably, he thought, the gap left in her life when the more foolish teachings of her Church had become vulnerable to her common sense and she had rejected everything, good and bad, finding nothing with which to replace it except her women's dogma. So that a hot sense of injustice and resentment against the powerful now served her for morality. For the weak – women, children, animals, the poor and so forth – she was probably capable even of heroism, but towards those whom she defined as powerful she was without conscience or tolerance. Or even the consideration owed by one life to another, good manners. How she'd boasted to him of the slathering in print she would give the decadent Malay princes who had been her hosts. And that outburst, 'Muslim

242

men are so blinded by sexism that they don't know when a woman is beating them in an argument. They listen to you indulgently, as though you were performing a trick, like playing the piano cross-handed. I *loathe* Muslim men.' There had been a pause, the sort of emptiness that follows a statement which has been a half-truth.

She disliked all men, he guessed, and not for the reasons that she acknowledged – unjustifiable male power – but from the deeper, inchoate perception of injury, the suppression of her male side. In very primitive peoples the men and women were alike; you could not distinguish from their faces, their hands, feet and limbs which was male, which was female. But in the course of civilization a dichotomy occurred so that a Caucasian, like her, looked not only of a different sex, but a different race from the male. The soft, hairless skin and small hands and feet. Women's very bone structure and skin texture had altered through centuries of selective breeding and conditioning. In court cultures, where most effort had been spent on breeding a distinct female type, the ladies looked a different species from the males. He had met Javanese and Vietnamese imperial courtesans who were not recognizably human, they were so fastidiously made. You feared to touch them, like gardenia petals. And, of course, in time, they threw weakling sons. Women subconsciously understood their breeding-out of maleness, in each generation. Freud called it penis envy. People hate people who have what they envy.

Civilized women's faces were such mysteries, he thought, looking at hers. A civilized man's face, even at her age, was already a record of behaviour and experience, but a woman's life could be hidden behind her face. Was it because all of them were forced at some age to an awareness of the importance of their appearance and used their faces constantly, like television sets projecting messages that were not truthful but were simply signals, that they had, by an unconscious

243

but calculating process, decided that camouflage would be to their advantage? As she is doing now with that fraudulent submissiveness, that big-eyed look of anticipation, waiting to hear me speak, pretending to be afraid that I'm going to rebuke her. And that other thing they do, painting out their faces in a way that focuses attention only on their eyes and mouth – these, too, made theatrical, unreal in colour and size – so that really you are mesmerized and see nothing. Minou looks just a child, boy or girl, unpainted. And this one?

'I enjoy looking at you,' Hobday said.

Later Judith cajoled, 'Do we have to move outside?'

The servant was swaying from foot to foot, waiting for them to follow the proper course and take their coffee and liqueurs on the terrace where he had already lit the mosquito coils and put out an ashtray for Hobday's cigar.

'Certainly not. We'll have it in here.' He gestured to the servant whose face registered a look of enforced obedience to a wrongful act. When the man returned with the trolley of coffee things Hobday said, 'We'll serve ourselves, Ahmad. You may go, and so may the others. I'll shut the windows.'

Judith spilt some of her second glass of cointreau on her hand and licked it off. Hobday grinned. It was such a childish gesture, the sort of thing Minou would do, anywhere, at the Palace. But there was a difference. Minou made those gaffes to shock, consciously; they were symbols of aggression. But this one usually had that aware restraint in all her movements that girls develop, oh, around ten or eleven years old, and just now, licking her hand, she had simply had a moment of forgetfulness. She was a boozer and carried her drink well, considering how much of it she took, whereas Minou would be drunk and uncontrollable on three glasses of wine. She was tipsy now, all the tension of the day gone, relaxed, idly fingering things, the candles. He wondered. Her new gestures looked unconscious, too. When Minou did that at a dinner party, ran her fingers gently down a candle, it was a game between them, and so was the effort to continue one's conversation without allowing one's expression to change or one's eyes to linger on her fingers.

'What's amusing?' Judith said. There was a bridling tone to the question.

It was now or not at all, though he did not have time to think that clearly, the knowledge came swifter than reason. There was the merest tremor of resistance from her, the tiny leap the body gives when the cells rebel against invasion and the will crushes their objections. Her lips were small, like Hilary's. She felt both familiar and strange, for Minou's mouth was Asian and much bigger than his own.

When they stood up Hobday said, 'Let's take the bottle. Let's take two bottles. I'll stick with the brandy.' She had a look of fright and excitement and her eyes were so bright she could have been on the verge of tears. He licked a finger and thumb and pinched out a candle. When he kissed her again a luxurious dizziness flowed between them.

And then, there was a sickening jolt. It was as if he'd seen the water in a vase of flowers begin to rock, and the furniture move – the appalling, freakish surprise an earth tremor causes.

Her face, her body, her very hair was tensed.

Hobday stepped back. 'What's wrong?' His hand was reaching for the other candle. 'What's wrong?'

'I'd prefer you not to do that,' she whispered.

Hobday felt the silence stinging in his ears. 'Of course, my dear. Do forgive me ... You looked so ... appealing. Please.' They'd moved a metre apart from each other. 'I'm so sorry. I misunderstood.'

Her voice came back. 'Oh, look, it's all right. I'm sorry too.'

They stood there in the sumptuous gloom, then began saying things like, 'Well, let's go and sit down' and 'I wouldn't mind another drink, actually.'

245

The reception room seemed to be watching them as they trod carefully across it - suddenly its floor rugs were a camouflaged trap of weals and furrows to trip their feet. 'Careful,' Hobday said. All its chairs looked occupied. 'Well, here?' Hobday suggested. They sat on a linen-covered settee, with the edge of their bottoms.

He had lipstick on his mouth. Judith concentrated on his forehead.

'You know, I have a theory,' Hobday began, then had to stop. It was so hard, after these years of practised reticence, to speak up. He reached for the cognac and poured some into his glass. Perhaps the truth he believed he had discovered was not the pearl, but merely its core of irritating grit, and its nacre was of his own, slow making? People acquired theories from a chance remark or out of the air, like germs, and embedded them in their beings. Over the years they collected material to enclose the inflammation so that in time it swelled and hardened from an idea to a fact, a truth. You could observe the process in politics and foreign policy, in any social change. The whole of a war - Vietnam, for instance - could grow from a prick of irritation to a huge, mesmerizing lump about which millions of people knew *the truth*: 'We must destroy that village to save it.'

'I believe we are all hermaphrodites,' he said to Judith.

She nodded politely. It was an idea enjoying currency these days, yet he had brought it out with the conviction that people reserve for their most profound superstitions.

He went on quickly, 'You see, when I first met Minou I realized she was my other half. It's like the lilies I showed you - they are half-male, half-female. The male has only white flowers; the female only red, then they cross-fertilize and become patterned. In Java, where I first saw them, the word for man is "half a woman" and for woman "half a man". They know that our souls are broken in two and that we must, if we are ever to find completeness, discover . . .'

246

Judith was alert, frowning with attentiveness. 'I've read that theory.'

He was off the settee with an exaggerated display of energy. 'Now where is that damned thing? I know!' He went striding off towards her suite. Judith rose, hesitated, then trailed after him, wondering, What the hell now?

There were bookshelves filling one wall of her bedroom, beside the desk. He stood with his hands on his hips, leaning backwards as he scanned the titles. A shirt tail had somehow come adrift from inside his trousers.

'Here we are!' he announced. He had pulled out a paperback with a white cover, bordered in brown, and was leafing through it impatiently. Judith sat down on her bed.

Without his spectacles, he had to hold the book at arm's length to read. 'Listen. "Each of us then is the mere broken tally of a man ... and each of us is perpetually in search of his corresponding tally ... The reason is that this was our primitive condition when we were wholes, and love is simply the name for the desire and pursuit of the whole".'

'Aristophanes' speech at The Symposium,' Judith said. She had been able to read the title on the cover, and had plucked Aristophanes out of the honeycomb of memory. (Richard had made her drop philosophy and take economics, she also recalled.)

Hobday was incredulous, even disappointed. 'That concept has been the lodestar of my life,' he said sombrely, and abruptly sat down in an armchair.

The suite's airconditioning had been running for some hours and the room was deliciously cool and antiseptic. Hobday slouched brooding over his book and after a few minutes Judith said brightly, 'I'll fetch your drink. Don't move.'

She brought the glasses in from the main room and excused herself: she was bursting to have a pee.

Minou had re-decorated the guest bathroom, making it

into a fun parlour of mirrors and voguish *objets* – including some antique Chinese bowls of the type other people displayed in their drawing rooms on little rosewood stands. Judith ran the taps loudly as she was urinating, not from modesty, but to conceal her giggling. Bugger Charles Darwin and the descent of man. She remembered the whole theory now, how humans had once had four arms and legs, were rounded, and moved about by cartwheeling. She had a vision of Hobday and Minou, glued back to back, cartwheeling around the reception room. This woman-man, this pushmi-pullyu, got Australia into the Vietnam war! In the looking glass twenty of her laughed.

Then, as she sobered herself, the question that had been a flickering suspicion, like the fear that a shark is beneath your keel, swerved up and revealed itself: what will happen with Kanan?

When she emerged from the bathroom she was irritated to find that Hobday, relaxed now, and with his legs stretched out, was anxious to go on talking about the desire and pursuit of the whole. She perched on the bed.

After a while he asked reproachfully, 'Am I boring you?'

'Not at all. I'm fascinated. But I've been worrying about Ralph. It's past midnight. We should ring the hospital.'

The old creature was standing there in the dark. Perhaps she had been there for some time, listening to the voices from the guest suite, or perhaps she had just arrived on those silent, square feet of hers.

'Good evening, Aunt,' Hobday said.

'Master.' There was no acknowledgment for Judith. It might as well have been Minou herself standing near the downstairs telephone, catching them together coming out of Judith's room. They had, both of them, jumped backwards when they had first seen her, but it was only after she had moved off towards the kitchen that their eyes had met. Hobday's were round and alarmed.

'You leave windows open, Master. Oily man come,' Aunt called without looking back.

They stared at her, then saw she had a cleaver in her hand.

'Oh Lord!' Hobday said. He muttered to Judith, 'I'll find out in the morning. I hope she hasn't . . . Oh Lord!' He was suddenly aware of his untucked shirt.

The news that Ralph was in a satisfactory condition, could not receive visitors and would be in hospital for another two or three weeks, was not just an anti-climax; it was a maddening distraction now to their central concern.

'I'd better say goodnight,' Judith muttered.

He nodded vigorously. Judith did not have time to remind him that she probably would not see him in the morning, that she was getting a lift back to Trengganu in the helicopter at eight o'clock and would be leaving the house at 7.15. He had turned and was stalking off across the reception area towards the stairs. As the sound of his footsteps faded Judith heard the Black and White muttering horribly from some dark corner of the room.

'Shit,' she said aloud. She thought she should summon the servant to tell her to turn down the bed, to *prove* their innocence, but when she called, 'Aunt, Aunt,' there was no reply.

23

A hornbill slid along above the valley in front of them and the Malay pilots, authentic fly-boys, chased it for a kilometre or so until it swerved down into the jungle canopy and they shouted '*Wah!*' and turned round to watch Judith with great, white grins.

'Tigers down there,' one said. 'Plenty.'

Some of the jungle rivers were as dark as black coffee, flashes of water winking up at them like eyes here and there from places where the streams widened and the overhanging trees were parted.

'Yellow men live in there,' the co-pilot said and they both laughed, lords of the air and of the land below. 'Eating monkey food.' Roars of laughter.

'Now China won't help them any more. Won't send them any more rifles.' Chuckles for this, then, 'China is a conservative power these days. Russia at her front door, Vietnam at her back, India looking in the window. There's no time to export revolution now. The yellow men hide in our jungle, eating berries.'

At the coast they flew out to sea for a few kilometres, stared down at the million suns dancing there, and hovered above a grey leaf: just a fishing trawler.

'They', meaning the boat people, 'try to land on our rig,' the co-pilot said.

'What happens to them?' Judith asked.

'It's company policy to give them food and water.' He turned to the other man and their glances interlocked.

But for all that they were good-natured men, well-paid and well-fed and tolerant because of it. As the co-pilot helped Judith out of the helicopter and they stood on the tarmac with their hair turned crazy from the air currents of the dying rotor he said, guarded and slightly off-hand, 'Tonight, would you like. . .?'

'I'm going out tonight,' she said. He looked her up and down furtively, and nodded. It was extraordinary, she thought. Two propositions in twelve hours. A friend had once told her, 'Women are the real controllers of sexuality. If a woman is having an affair and is sexually aroused, every man in sight senses it and finds her attractive.'

Kanan would be arriving at lunchtime, by taxi. All her plans - to spend the night on Bidong, to return by boat to the mainland that morning, writing up her notes on the way - had been thrown out by Ralph's illness. And there was the other thing right now: how to look Minou in the eye? In three days Minou would be back in KL and Aunt would be telling her, 'Master in bedroom with girl. Kiss kiss.' She'd make those disgusting gurgling sounds in her throat, describing the lipstick on Hobday's mouth. And then? Perhaps one of those confrontations *à trois*, with Judith and Hobday explaining that *nothing* had happened. Minou would never believe them. Lady Hobday she'd be - as dignified and enraged as she had been at the funeral, a thousand-times born, a thousand-times wronged.

'Ooh, la, you look as if you've been up all night,' she said as Judith arrived after a bravely steady walk across the tarmac to the Citroen. One quick look at Judith's hair. 'Have a shower and I'll blow-dry it for you when we get back to the hotel. With your beau coming' (Judith had told her about Kanan in the heat-craze of the trip from Bidong with Ralph) 'you don't want to look as if . . .'

251

'As if?'

Minou grinned. Perhaps she knew already; perhaps Hobday had told her over the telephone. There was no shade; the car had been parked in the sun and the heat inside it was buzzing, like a swarm of bees – that swarm she had seen before. Judith closed her eyes, stunned by a premonition.

'I spoke to the hydrographic survey people this morning,' Minou was saying. 'You can use their telex machine to send a story to Sydney. The office will be open all weekend.'

'Thanks.' Judith had to struggle with the feeling that she and Minou were enemies again. 'I haven't written the bloody thing yet,' she added, compelled to be forthcoming, appealing for sympathy in this show of frankness, a play-act that had nothing frank about it. The special attentiveness of people who are lying and who dislike each other. On the boat yesterday it had been so different. Judith had said, 'It's as if I'm having blackouts. I'll be concentrating on something when suddenly I'll think, "Has David got enough clean shirts for the week? Has Richard remembered to buy mandarins for their lunch boxes?" I feel like an insect, which looks as if it's doing things *it* wants to do, collecting food and building a web out of spit, but all the time there is this undercurrent of anxiety; it's not thinking of itself at all, it's considering its eggs and how to preserve them. Everything women – mothers – do is affected by that nagging responsibility to house, children . . .' she'd sighed. 'I think about how, if I bring off this job up here, I can become bureau chief. Then I can choose my own hours and I'll be able to look after the kids properly, on my own. I've known for years I'd have to split from Richard. And then I tell myself that's nonsense. I want to do this job well because I'm ambitious. I love it when people say, "Judith Wilkes? The journalist?" All that motherly, female-instinct stuff is probably just conditioning from the nuns, and my family and . . .' She had

252

gestured out to sea, as if society had stood there. 'I'll just never *know*. I'll never bloody well *know*.' Minou had pushed her forehead into Judith's shoulder, as a dog will comfort its owner with a caress.

And now it had all been swept away by that idiotic experiment with Hobday, that moment of vulnerability.

'Actually, I wish Kanan weren't coming. I've got so much work to do,' Judith said.

Minou kept her eyes on the road ahead; there were a lot of bicycles and goats and chickens wandering around. 'Cold feet?' Her tone was derisive.

'Of course not,' Judith replied sharply. They let the matter drop.

When, at twelve-thirty he walked into the motel lobby, his shoes making exploding noises on the tiles, his head turning from side to side with that vague, superior air he had and when, on seeing her his face lit up with easy confidence, Judith knew she was terrified. He claimed her, with that look of delight.

The motel restaurant, like its rooms, was decorated in shades of green ranging from the virulent emerald of the matchboxes, with their illustrations of a white leatherback turtle, to the dark bluish-green of the fabric on the seats of cane dining chairs and upholstered benches, and the murky green of the carpet. Kanan had put on – from a clairvoyant vanity? – white clothing so that he dazzled in this cool, dark room. Judith, in a blue batik dress, and Minou, in denim overalls with a gold spanner brooch pinned on the bib, were visually swallowed by the colours of the furniture. But Kanan shone.

He looks like a gorgeous white heron with a couple of brown quail, Judith thought. The idea took the edge off her nervousness and she was able at last to look at him and grin, which he interpreted, she guessed, as eagerness. They began talking of Ralph, and Bidong and the police chief – Minou

253

and Judith animated, entertaining him. His amiable, reserved manner tended to make those around him seem like garrulous clowns. The more one talked, the deeper his silence, the more enigmatic his thoughts, the more beautiful the composure of his features – and the more ominous one's feeling that he, alone, was in control. He'd made no remark when Judith had told him that the room she'd booked for him was next door to her own. Perhaps he would expect her to go there with him after lunch! She should not have grinned at him.

Judith looked down through the glass of the tabletop at his long legs stretched straight and crossed at the ankles, and her eye darted from his knees to his crotch. It told her nothing about him. She felt reassured by the ordinariness of the white cloth, with its spokes of creases radiating from the centrepoint across his thighs and upwards, towards his hip-bones, just like any other pair of trousers. But then, when she looked up, she found he had been watching her and that his face with its scrolled lips and nostrils was full of contentment.

Minou said, 'I'm going to the beach when we've finished lunch.' She poked a rubbery square of bean-curd with her spoon. 'I feel so fed up, after yesterday, and this morning.' What had happened this morning? Her expression was almost tearful. This was a new act, Judith guessed, a variation of Minou's 'I-can-see-ghosts' role which she played so effectively on the boat, crossing the sandbank. Yet it was as impossible to ignore her demand for their care as it was to ignore the smell of fire in a house.

'Why? What's wrong?' Judith felt genuinely alarmed by those trembling lips. Even Kanan was leaning forward, attentive.

Minou gave a sigh that exhaled world-weariness. 'You see, Mama and the boys are coming. At this moment they are at sea.'

She had their full attention now and she knew it. She went on rapidly, hot with the burden of her emotions, projecting them around the lunch-table, netting her audience so that suddenly they were not thinking about what she was saying but were being gathered in to her, willingly. Her glance flicked from Kanan's to Judith's face and back again. 'Look, they will come to the turtle beach – the boat captain is experienced, he's done ten runs already to Malaysia, I heard on Bidong yesterday. And that beach is the best one for larger boats. It has the deepest water close to shore. That's why the turtles like it, no? But this is the problem. I went there this morning and yesterday morning, at dawn. And this morning I was just standing near the coconut trees when . . .' She lent to Kanan and tapped his shoulder with her index finger. 'Special Branch. Nice Mr Hussein from Special Branch came up behind me. "Lady Hobday," he said, "you are coming very often to this beach. Are you expecting some friends?" He looked back over his shoulder at the village. Then he said, "It is my duty to tell you that the people in that village have sworn that no more refugees will land here. There are police in the area, but . . . I advise you to leave this beach. Please do not return to it." And he watched me until I got in the car and drove off.'

She looked from one to the other, her eyes saying, I'm desperate.

'I must go back there this afternoon.'

Kanan dropped his chin on his chest.

Minou added, 'I know they are coming. Today. I can feel it.' The coins she had thrown that morning had made the hexagram Heaven, the Creative Force, and Water, The Abysmal: conflict. But this had changed to Breakthrough. Water, the abysmal element, had been very strong: it had ruled in Breakthrough. The Book was never wrong. It had told her, 'Do not alienate inferior persons, for they become useful.' She'd acted on that already: Bala, whom she'd sent

255

off for the day, had a young Indian friend who was a night-watchman and who needed money. It had not cost much, the thing she'd got Bala to get for her, from the nightwatch-man. 'You must help me to trick Mr Hussein,' Minou said. 'You see, Malays are hot-tempered, but they cool down quickly. If you give them a surprise, something unexpected, they forget they are angry.'

They sat there, their voices stolen. Then Judith said, 'You think if the three of us . . .?'

'Yes. Yes. If the three of us go we are just making a picnic. Swimming . . .'

'You cannot swim from that beach, it's too dangerous, isn't it?' Kanan said.

'O.K., la. Building sandcastles. Looking for shells.'

'Sunbaking,' Judith put in, then blushed. Kanan? Sun-baking? He was almost black.

'If you wish to sunbake,' Kanan said, and smiled indul-gently.

'Shadebaking' Judith corrected herself. It was an apology to him, to his race, and by making it she felt her resistance to him drop away. His admiring look hugged her to him like an encircling arm.

'Yes. I'd love to lie there on the beach with you. There are some palm-leaf shelters.'

And the beach would be deserted at this time of day. In front of the village the fishermen would be mending their nets or painting the boats with pitch, and the women would be drying shrimps, spreading them with hands splayed into fans, over mats laid out on the sand. But otherwise they would be alone on kilometres of cream-coloured sand. And Minou. She could amuse herself somehow.

'So you'll come?' Minou faced one, then the other, pulling from them an agreement to something unstated, something greater. They nodded, ensnared by their own desires into her tangle. They wanted to caress each other, not to outrage

256

proprieties, of course, but to lie together in the shade with the light breeze off the sea on their half-naked bodies, to prepare themselves for tonight. To achieve that they were conceding something, making a promise to Minou the nature of which was still obscure to them.

'I'll show you something when we get there,' Minou said. The abrupt tone of confidence in her voice made Judith uneasy. For one second she thought, Minou's got a gun. If the villagers make trouble she's going to shoot at them. Then she realized that was ridiculous; it was the pilots' chatter about rifles that had dragged up the idea to the surface of her mind.

Minou drove past the roadside scrub and parked the car in the discoloured sand at the top of the beach where the coconut palms, stately and voluptuous as beauty queens, cast down a pale-grey shade, like X-rays, from their distant plumes. It was high tide. The sea was motionless, then it gave a sigh and stretched a few more centimetres up the sand and collapsed, exhausted. There was nobody about for half a kilometre. Off to the north, in front of the village, a few people were wandering around the beached boats and the spread nets and the racks of fish that, split open to dry, had turned opaque and yellow like chamois leather and were already as stiff as boards. It was siesta time, full tide of heat and quietness.

Minou said, 'Now I'll show you.' She opened the Citroen's boot with the pride of a girl opening for the dazzlement of friends the box containing her engagement ring.

At first Judith could not make it out, this flabby orange thing. Then she saw the oars and the air pump. There were silvery coils of rope, a grappling iron, a whistle.

'And flares. The flares come with it,' Minou said.

'Where did you get it?' Judith demanded.

'I just got it, la. It will hold twelve people. Will we inflate it now? It only takes a minute to inflate. I did it in the hotel

257

room last night and it blew up so quickly that it knocked over a stupid table lamp. The manager is going to charge me ninety bucks, the crook, for smashing it. I told him I was skipping and my rope caught on the lampshade. Then I couldn't deflate it – I had to jump on it for twenty minutes. I kept thinking nice Mr Hussein will come to the door and say "Lady Hobday, why are you filling your room with a rubber dinghy? I advise you . . .".' She made his hand and head movements.

Kanan was examining the stencilled markings on the dinghy's flabby walls.

'This is from the Navy,' he said.

Minou nodded smugly.

'Possession of such things by civilians . . .' Kanan said. He was actually frowning; Judith had never seen him frown. 'Minou,' he continued, 'you have diplomatic immunity, you can disregard our legal system if you wish. But Judith and I . . .' His hands flew apart, helpless and and appealing to her to understand.

'O.K., O.K.,' Minou said. 'We'll leave it here until we need it.' She smirked. 'I suppose you two want to go for a walk. I'll just hang around here.'

When Judith and Kanan reached the beach proper he said, 'I can go to gaol as an accessory to theft for that.' He looked into her face, wanting her support. Judith felt it flow from her in a rush and suddenly his hand was lacing hers. They had halted, he had turned her shoulders and his huge eyes were steady mirrors above hers. Then he moved back.

'*Khalwat*,' he said.

'We can get into trouble for almost anything this afternoon,' Judith murmured. The local newspapers in the past few days had been full of stories about the offence of *khalwat*, close proximity between the sexes. Vigilante groups were on the lookout for couples committing this crime against Islamic decency.

Kanan shrugged. 'This is a police state.' It was nothing more than an observation from him.

'Bloody Minou!' Judith said. 'Getting that thing stolen.' She walked along, kicking up sand that was as soft as talc. 'But you've got to admire her flair,' she added.

Kanan looked amused. His lips parting in mild derision seemed to indicate that for him flair, virtuosity, prowess, whatever she liked to call it, involved not vision and reckless-ness, but skill, restraint, training, self-awareness, controlled and absolute concentration. She realized abruptly that he was a true conservative.

The palm-leaf shelters constructed by the villagers for turtle-watching tourists became dilapidated between seasons, and since there were still three months to go before the first of the giants would come labouring up the beach by moonlight, nobody had yet felt the need to start repairing them. The rattan mats which served as walls were torn or missing, and the palm-frond roofing had come adrift. Dried branches hung listlessly from the roof edges, creaking and hissing in the breeze. Fifty metres from the car and still a long way from the village they came upon a shelter in good order, walled on three sides with new rattan, a lair from which they could view the sea, concealed, except from some-one standing directly in front of them. As they spotted it, they forgot Minou and her stolen dinghy.

They padded into its dark, rustling shade as unhesitat-ingly as a hunting pair pad to their cave to enjoy the kill. In silence. And in silence lay on their towels, then turned to drink each other up, eyes, skin, hair. It was another world, a dream-life in here, enclosed, sealed in. There was nothing else, neither sun nor sea, no heat or cold, only the warmth of mouth-on-mouth, the flow of energy between their eyes and the flow of each others' warm breath. His pad of tongue and the slippery-sweet membranes of his mouth welded with and became her own, seeming as if touched for the first time.

259

That straight pipe of flesh that pressed against her was burning, calmly, as her own small, stiff rod burned calmly. She wanted more than anything to take him in her mouth and knew that she would, later, in the night-time. Strong, dizzying scent came from his hair and clothes.

She felt as languid as one does part-waking from a dream and falling back into sleep. She dropped away from him on to her back on the sand, knowing that somehow in the minutes or hours that had passed with no sense of passing, her mind had been unlocked, that he had enraptured her, as the truly beautiful can do. You see a great painting or a famous view and suddenly everything is washed away, you have no name nor country; your mind has stopped.

She knew that tonight, with him – he was becoming 'him' again – it would be all right.

Within a few seconds she was asleep, her hand resting on the stretched fabric of his trousers. Kanan observed her slow regular breathing, then lifted her arm stealthily, looking at the oatmeal colour of her skin against his. Never mind what the Aryans said. Frankly, his colour was more beautiful, he thought – navy blue, like the Lord Krishna's when he was young, playing with the milkmaids.

The tide had turned and, ebbing now, flung lacy cloths of bubble on the sand then snatched them back to expose grooves on the beach as sharp and ordered as the ridges down the turtles' backs. When they came, those great, gravid females it was at midnight, out of mountainous seas, and they laboured harder than any woman in birth. He'd stood beside one as she panted and sighed and then dug for hours, flinging sand in the air with hind limbs that could strike off a human leg with one flick.

Kanan could see the boat now; it was a kilometre or so offshore, a high-sided rust-red thing without flags. A Malay child from the village was standing at the water's edge, one foot drawn up and pressed against his knee, the way such children stood when they were uncertain.

When the turtle had dug her nest and laid the eggs – coming out in a stream as if from a tap at full turn – the Malays would wait until she had finished, covered the nest, smoothed the sand, disguised what she had done there, turned and begun her journey back towards the sea. Then they dug out the eggs and took them home, to eat or to sell. Some were saved, of course – there were laws about it now. But the turtle did not know that, any more than she knew that plunder was taking place, that her huge efforts were being undone even before she had completed the cycle and returned to the sea. The tourists were always outraged, on her behalf. Kanan smiled, recalling the English people who had pleaded with the villagers, then lamented ... If only they had felt what he had as the eggs were stolen – that in such a sequence you saw the awesome playfulness of The One, who had invented both turtles and men.

It was a most poetic sight, that moment when the huge beast re-entered her element. He had watched one – how big? almost three metres long? four hundred kilos in weight – lumber down to the wet sand and lie there, her chin sunk on the beach with fatigue. Dead, she'd seemed. A wave had broken over her head and she'd stirred forward about a metre. Then a moonlit cliff of water had reared and she'd lifted up, spread those great wings and flown, weightless, perfect, up and away into darkness. His guest, Kanan recalled, a professor of colonial history from an English university, had said, still angry about the eggs, 'Well, that's that. How much should I tip him?' A village youth had attached himself to them, acting as guide for the night. He'd made a sour face at the ten dollar note the Englishman had handed him with a curt nod. The English had so many ways of showing their anger.

Perhaps it was the same young man who had now joined the little boy, and was staring too towards the incoming boat. It was approaching slowly, the water was deep out there but the sandbanks began abruptly. The two were talking to each other, then the younger turned and ran, his brown legs working as if they were pistons.

Kanan could see the passengers now, massed like insects on the deck. There were hundreds of them.

'Judith,' he said. He spoke quietly; it was not good to wake somebody abruptly. 'Judith.'

She opened her eyes and smiled at him.

'Minou's boat has come.'

She was still smiling and blinking. Then she said, 'Oh, Jesus,' and sat up.

The boat was rolling gently in a light swell, motoring at no more than one knot. People in the bows were peering overboard, checking the depth and the possibility of anchorage. The older boy turned and fled north towards the village, and then Minou came into sight running, sinking into the mushy sand close to the sea. She was dragging the orange dinghy, half-inflated. Then she stumbled and went sprawling.

Judith was aware of flying down the beach, grabbing Minou and wrenching her up out of the glueing sand.

'I couldn't get it through the coconut trees,' Minou gasped. 'It's so heavy. I had to deflate it again.' They heaved the dinghy back from the verge. It was unbelievably heavy, but it became lighter when their leg muscles could brace against hard, dry sand. The dinghy panted with them, a sickly breath of rubber exhaling from a hole in its side.

'Quick, get the bung in,' Judith said.

'Minou's hands were trembling like an old, sick woman's as she jabbed the black plug of rubber at the hole. 'Oars! I couldn't carry the oars.'

As Judith skimmed up the beach towards the car she felt

herself observed by an elegant white-clad figure. She was half-way back, with the oars, when she realized she had forgotten the air pump and, veering towards the shelter, yelled 'Get the pump!' to Kanan.

Minou had pulled the dinghy a few metres further along the beach until it was almost directly opposite the boat. The orange sides were flaccid, you could sink a fist into them. Judith looked back and saw Kanan disappearing among the coconut trees. 'He's getting the pump. We'll have to wait.'

Minou sat down abruptly and closed her eyes – she seemed momentarily to have gone to sleep. Then she opened them wide. 'You mustn't come with me,' she said.

'Why not? Oh, God, where is he?'

Minou had not heard, 'You mustn't come,' she repeated. She was gazing along the beach past Judith's shoulder. Judith scrambled up and dashed back to the coconut grove.

Kanan was leaning against the car with his arms crossed, admiring the view.

'What are you doing! Where's the pump?' Judith shouted.

'Don't be silly. Just look,' he replied amiably, gazing in the direction of the sea. There were about fifty men, marching in a body, coming from the village.

'We must help her!'

'Why?'. he said in that same, even tone.

Why! She could not believe what he was saying. She turned to flee from him but as she did he stretched forward with that easy cricketer's grace and caught her arm, as if fielding a ball.

'Stay here. You don't want to get killed. Maybe she does.'

Judith shook her arm violently to break his grip, then realized she could not. He was even taller than Richard, and had twice her physical strength. But there was a time, once, when she'd wanted to save her own life. She looked up at him, appalled. He smiled, then let her go, and she stood

263

there beside him looking at the dirty sand. He draped his arm over her shoulder and stroked her cheek.

'Don't look so sad. She is doing what she wants to do. Just watch.'

'She'll make it without the pump.' Judith said.

Minou had launched the floppy dinghy and was rowing towards the boat; the village men had halted, and were milling around now, uncertain of their next move. Minou's rowing was clumsy, hampered by the lack of tension in the dinghy's sides but she was moving fast enough, carried towards the boat by the current as much as her own efforts.

Judith and Kanan moved out of the shade of the coconut trees, half-way down the beach. Some of the fishermen turned and were, Judith guessed, glaring at her. A movement of Kanan's torso as he squinted against the glare of the sea made her aware that he was enjoying watching this ritual unfold.

'Why wouldn't you bring the pump?' she asked. Minou was within twenty metres of the boat now; they could hear people yelling greetings to her, high bird-like calls drifting across the water.

Kanan's expression was both pained and amused. 'It is not my function, or duty. I am a teacher, isn't it? I don't pretend to be a hero. If you try to be that which you are not . . .' He shrugged.

The look she gave him hurt, she thought, for he added, 'The warrior must be brave, the peasant must look after his cow. They are not my people on that boat.' He was silenced by her inattention.

Minou had stood up in the dinghy, which rocked in the swell. Her arms were stretched upwards, gymnast-style, for balance or because she was waving, and then she seemed to rise in the air, there was a white explosion, and she was gone. An invisible hand guided the empty dinghy past the boat and to the north-east, out to sea.

'She jumped,' Judith said.

'Yes. That, I think, was her intention.'

Some of the men from the boat had dived overboard to rescue her and were struggling in the water. The current must have been extraordinarily strong, for three heads bobbed along together moving rapidly, but Minou was already fifty metres away. She was wearing those damned-fool overalls, Judith remembered. Once down, twice. It was as if the sky had halted. But there was no third time, as the stories had it, and Minou disappeared completely after the second break for air.

Kanan fell the pull, the irresistible inward drag as the wave sucked back to itself that which was its own, and the great wheel turned over, spinning individual consciousness, that woman, up and back into the eternal revolving force.

'That is known as Satyagraha,' he murmured to Judith.

Her look was uncomprehending.

'Watch,' he said. 'Watch what she has done. See what the fishermen do now.'

The men on the beach broke loose from each other, their communal purpose abandoned; some squatted down and pulled packets of cigarettes from the waist knots of their sarongs and offered them around. They laid their parangs and lengths of pipe and other weapons on the beach and started chatting.

'You see,' Kanan said. 'They are satisfied now. They will go back to the village and say "The rich Chinese woman is dead; her ghost will keep the others away from us". Or something like that. In a while some of them might make a shrine for her. You know, near here there is a shrine to a mermaid whom the fishermen captured about a century ago. She died. If you talk to these people they will tell you stories of their grandfathers who heard the mermaid speak, and who described how beautiful she was. There are always fresh flowers on her grave. And further north, at The Beach of Passionate Love . . .'

265

'Oh, shut up, Kanan,' Judith said.

She sat down abruptly on the dry squeaky sand and began critically examining her toe-nails, prising away the grit lodged beneath them with a splinter of palm leaf. Her head felt as huge and empty as the inside of a balloon. There was nothing in the world of any interest or importance, except these sand grains wedged between the rounded pads of flesh and her toe-nails. Cleaning them out was fascinating. They dropped, particle by particle, from those huge hard carapaces covering the pink globes of flesh. As she watched, saw her feet become as big as a giant's, she saw, too, a long way off, approaching her eyes from behind as it were, a scene, a set-piece . . . she and Richard laughing and running together in bleached summer grass and then another, of tigers, playing with something they had caught, tossing it and leaping after it, in delight. She'd had the dream again, last night. The animals had not turned on one another at the end of their play. The male tiger had broken off the sport and had walked away, slowly, insolently, into the shadows. The female had stared after him, then had cringed down and curled inwards upon herself. The bars of a cage had formed around her, and tightened. Presently she had become a solitary python, coils pinched cruelly by the wire.

'She did it deliberately. She threw herself in,' Judith said, but it came out only as a croaking whisper and Kanan, who saw her lips move, did not hear.

The enormous empty space inside Judith's head began diminishing swiftly until her skull felt its normal size again. But she was cold now, and shivery, and spasms of nausea contracted her chest. She thought, Minou couldn't stand the frustration any more. She decided that her people weren't on that boat, that her purpose had been brought to nothing, that she'd have to live alone, playing Hobday's baby-doll. I don't even have that despair to grieve over. I just earn my keep, a function without a purpose.

266

Kanan squatted in front of her and stared at her forehead until she looked up. 'Judith,' he said quietly, 'your mind has been shocked, isn't it? It is better if you stand up and walk about slowly.'

She was chalky-white, the horrible colour of women who have smeared wet rice-powder on their faces. He moved his hand from right to left in front of her face and she looked at it, unblinking.

Kanan took her elbow, saying, 'Come, you must try to stand up.' She was a dead weight, but unresisting, and he got her to her feet and was steadying her when suddenly her face flooded with colour and she wrenched herself away from him, her eyes vivid. 'Get your hands off me! Stop pushing me around, Kanan!'

She noticed that he had the supercilious look of a camel in that lofty head of his.

Then Mr Hussein arrived and introduced himself.

There was Mr Hussein and any number of policemen. They strode along waving their arms at the villagers as if they were straying chickens, shooing them back to where they belonged. The adults moved off with surly looks, but the children danced around yelling and darting out of reach when a policeman lunged at them.

Judith put her hands on her hips and glared at Kanan. 'I will never forgive you for not bringing the pump,' she said quietly.

'The pump was irrelevant,' he replied, and returned her look with an expression of mild indifference.

Judith snorted and kicked at the sand. 'Well, I now don't care what you do. I've got to do *my* duty.' She sighed heavily. 'This is a bloody good story. I'll have to speak to Hobday. Where's the nearest telephone?' She noted his shrug of ignorance and distaste. 'Oh, of course you wouldn't know. I'll find out from Hussein.'

Mr Hussein, however, had other ideas, and since he also

267

had twenty-five policemen at his command, whom he had already ordered to board the boat and arrest the captain, it was necessary to stay on the beach.

24

The sky had taken on the lilac haze of dusk. Up at the village men were launching the few boats they had left for the night's fishing. The village headman had already made an official complaint about the police's commandeering of the other boats, now motoring back and forth, transporting the refugees to shore, where they were made to sit in rows on the beach while officials from the Kuala Trengganu UN refugee office wrote up their blue cards.

Soldiers had arrived in trucks and were felling the coconut trees so that they could drive on to the beach and load up the boat people for Cherating. The village headman had made an official complaint about the destruction of the trees, the second time arriving importantly, on his bicycle, with a white business shirt over his singlet. Mr Hussein wrote out his complaint in a shorthand notebook while the headman squinted suspiciously at the Roman script.

Judith walked between the rows of people asking in English and poor French, 'Does anyone know Minou, the woman who drowned?' Their faces were closed. They shook their heads at her. Either they did not know Minou or did not understand Judith's question or did not care to talk. Ralph had said they were always like this when they first landed: 'Until they work out what's going to do them most good they're all deaf and dumb, figuring out the situation.'

One teenage girl pointed wordlessly towards the rust-coloured boat. Maybe Minou's family was on board still. How would you know? Mr Hussein had discovered from the captain, who was sitting apart from his cargo and smoking two-handed because his wrists were still manacled, that there were 416 passengers, including a day-old baby and excluding an old man who had jumped overboard near Thailand.

Nobody prevented Judith from interviewing the captain, who was a crew-cut Hong Kong Chinese, recklessly boastful now that his game was up. In five months he had collected, he told her, six thousand taels of gold and four hundred thousand dollars in cash. American dollars, not Hong Kong. He made sure she got that right. Who were his principals? Who owned the boat or boats? Who organized the trade? What co-operation did he have from Ho Chi Minh City officials? He raised praying hands to his mouth and took a drag on his cigarette: he could not understand any of these questions.

Did he think he was trading in human misery? He could not understand that either, apparently, and gazed past her shoulder, out to sea, with that still, reflective sailor's look. Then he said, 'My job. Your job', and jabbed at her scrappy palmful of notes with a cage of fingers. As she stood up he leant back, flinging one curious glance at her from head to foot. 'You and me the same. We make money from peoples,' he said and laughed, grating his handcuffs in the direction of the refugees.

Judith looked at her watch. If they drove like hell in the Citroen she would have half an hour in Kuala Trengganu to telex her story before the paper was put to bed at ten o'clock, Sydney time. 'They'll have to remake the front page,' she said to Kanan, who had gone to sit in the shade. He nodded incuriously, bored.

'Poor old Hobday, I don't suppose the police have told him yet,' she mused.

Kanan watched irritation move across her face and the

270

small, disdainful jerk of her shoulders as she chucked off the
unpleasant thought with the movement a dog would make
to dislodge a fly. 'But they will, soon. Hussein's a fantastic
operator. He'll arrange that.' She added, 'Sydney will have
to handle the KL end – Hobday – themselves, by phone.'

Kanan did not bother to nod for this irrelevant piece of
information.

Earlier, when he had asked Mr Hussein some pleasant
questions about his family and so forth Judith had said to
him, 'Kanan, *I'll* do the interviewing.' He'd noticed then
that she had crescents of sweat under her armpits and beads
of it on her upper lip. The crescents were the size of half-
moons now and her face looked as if she'd rubbed it with
melted ghee. The *Mahabharata* said, 'A wise man will avoid
the contaminating society of women as he would the touch
of bodies infected with vermin'.

Judith realized he was still sulking when they reached the
car and he refused her request that he should drive, so that
she could write her story on the way. Pleats formed between
her eyebrows. 'Look, I'm sorry I yelled at you earlier. I was
really pissed off with you for refusing to help. It seemed cow-
ardly.'

'It *seemed*,' Kanan replied. She was surprised to discover
that he was capable of anger: his voice was now scornful.
'I explained to you at the time. But you prefer to rush
around. All you Westerners rush, rush. *Satyagraha* – you say
"self-sacrifice" – is a very noble act. You would have inter-
fered and maybe prevented her doing the noble thing she
had decided upon. Western people know nothing about sacrifice. Even to fast for one week or to be chaste is impossible
for you. You have no control over yourselves.'

Judith's breath hissed in. 'I see. That's your last word on
the subject, is it?' and she thought, I'm fed to the neck with
this Hindu claptrap. In the back of her mind the outline
of an idea had begun to shimmer. Sacrifice?

271

It was ten o'clock, local time, when she told the hotel switchboard to put through no more calls.

Sydney had gone mad with the story – it was being syndicated everywhere – and TV crews were already booked on the first flights out of Australia to Malaysia. The cream on the top, the item that Judith had just telephoned through (having confirmed with the local refugee officials), was that Lady Hobday's family was not on board the boat.

'Not, repeat not,' Judith told Bill, who was in the composing room, 'IN MY PYJAMAS! I hate pyjamas!' he roared at her, as though she had invented them.

It was Bill, suffering, 'but still thinking, dear, still thinking,' who had also roared, 'You can't say in so many words that she suicided! There must be a coroner's inquiry. You'll be in contempt of court. Do they have courts up there? Well, you silly bitch, you can be charged with contempt. Now, Lady Hobday, wife of brilliant, senior blah-blah, *fell* in the drink and drowned, while trying to rescue her children – who were not on board. Anyway, our readers wouldn't understand that someone could feel strongly enough about their kids to commit suicide for them. They kick 'em out of home when they don't get jobs, don't they? This is Australia, dear. We'll spill to page three. Tomorrow send us three thousand words on the whole boat people scene – "The Last Casualties of the Vietnam War", eh? Now, back to page one: Beautiful, young ... How do you want to describe Lady Hobday?'

'Beautiful, young will do,' Judith said.

At intervals hotel staff members had arrived at her door with message slips that representatives from *Time*, *Newsweek*, NBC, *The Far Eastern Economic Review* were waiting on the line. Bill had cleared it for her to give brief – a maximum of two minutes – radio and TV interviews and was arranging credits, syndication and copyrights at his end. The ABC man in KL had promised to ring back when he had something on Hobday, who was still 'unavailable for comment'. Two Malay policemen had turned up and had sat smoking and chatting in a corner of the room prepared, it seemed, to wait all night for her to leave the telephone and go with them to the station to sign her statement, as Kanan had already done, they told her. But after an hour they had departed.

She struggled off the bed and along to Kanan's room. There was no response to her tapping on his door. 'Sulk, then,' she muttered. She stood back from the door, possessed abruptly by a vision of herself kicking it in. The image snapped out. As it did, something else happened. She shouted, 'I hate you!' and dashed back and slammed her own room shut.

She felt pleased with herself now that she had got *that* sorted out and lay down on the bed to compose, in language of quintessential subtlety and venom, her views of a man whose arrogance was such that he would stand by while a human being destroyed herself, whose ethics were so impoverished that the basic social concept, I *am* my brother's keeper, was, to him . . .

Several hours later she woke up, still wearing her blue batik dress and cold from the airconditioning, and fumbled her way under the bedspread and blanket.

Kanan had been awake when Judith knocked on his door and had heard her shout at him from the corridor, as one hears with disinterest the common noises of daily life – traffic passing, or starlings scolding at each other or the transparent, lilac lizards calling 'chic-chak' to their mates on another part of the ceiling. He had bathed carefully on returning from the police station and had dressed in the navy silk *kurta* which Mariam had given him last Deepavali, and he, too, was lying on his hotel bed, thinking. His thoughts moved on and around the changes to his modern history course that he would have to make next semester so that the course would reflect the growing solidarity of ASEAN

273

in the light of the military threat from Vietnam. Mr Hussein, who had come to sit under a coconut tree with him for a while, had mentioned that China seemed to have invaded northern Vietnam that morning, but that reports were still ambiguous.

'China may be our saviour,' Mr Hussein had remarked.

'Things change,' Kanan had agreed. And they had smiled at each other for the unspoken – that there were some things which never changed, long term, and that China was one of them.

'The Dragon Emperor used to call it' (Kanan referred to China's invasion of Vietnam) '"a dose of frightfulness". Now Chairman Hua Guofeng says "teaching them a lesson".'

And so they had chatted nicely, and Kanan showed Mr Hussein a coloured photograph of baby Indra at which Mr Hussein's pupils expanded, admiring her buttermilk skin.

Kanan noted Judith's remote knocking and shouting, and felt sorry for her.

Hobday was in his glasshouse at a time when the light made everything green; two more great buds had formed, their tips pointed like the tips of certain cigars before a flame has been held to them. One, this evening, showed a shaving of scarlet where a petal would first unfold. There had been no sunlight on the plants now for several hours and the air in the glass shed was becoming heavy from their carbon dioxide exhalations. It was, of course, still extremely hot. There would be a storm later.

He heard the double stamp of police boots, then saw them, a metre or so from the door and for a moment he felt the perfect stillness of the air, the equilibrium of things living and things dying, and the silence. Then, as they tapped on the glass – it was not necessary, he could see them, he had turned and was coming towards them – there was flamenco stamping inside his head. One policeman had a white plaited

274

cord running from his belt, over his shoulder; Hobday thought his eyes would burst out of their sockets as he looked at it, as if the whiteness was plucking the eyeballs from his head. They said something, 'Excellency, it is with profound regret . . .' His head was bursting open in showers of red and white. They saw his hand cling to his neck, behind the ear, and heard him say 'I have a headache. A very bad headache.'

'May we escort you?' one asked. Hobday nodded.

In the event they had to carry him, holding him upright between them, each with an arm of his strained tight against their chests, for as Hobday said, several times, 'It's very dark. I'm afraid I can't see.' And then, when they got him inside the house where the lamps were already lit, he moaned, 'Oh, the light. The light.' and screwed up his eyes. A servant had made the spontaneous cry of distress; it flushed the others, seven of them, from the back rooms of the house, so they came running like game pursued. They rushed to open the guest bedroom door and watched, making strange clucks and grunts, as the policemen laid him down in the dark.

He felt darkness as a palpable presence, like the warm breast of a woman pressed against his temple, then felt her body stretching against him right down his left side. She was big, this woman, as tall as he was. His skin, even those areas of it where he had never before been conscious of the pleasure of touch – his calves, his waist and hips – glowed exquisitely from the warmth of life. As she nestled there, a comfort and a delight to his flank, he fell asleep.

It was a long time later, he knew, when he awoke and remembered that he had had a pain in his head that had been both visual and auditory, a stamping of Spanish dancers' feet in the chamber of his skull. There was no pain left now, though his vision was somehow still affected – the guest bedroom looked odd, lopsided.

Odder still was the fact that old Aunt was sitting beside him on the bed, holding upright an arm, somebody's arm, and with her fingers as strong as steel springs, was massaging it. He could see her doing it and wondered where she had found this arm – it belonged to a man, it had hairs on it, and a gold signet ring on the hand's little finger, a ring his father used to wear. Then he realized what had happened to him, that he'd been cut in two, and this manifestation of all that he had so passionately believed, coming as it had in such unexpected form, made him attempt to laugh out loud.

Aunt dropped the man's arm and patted at his face with a handkerchief, then left the room so that he was allowed to contemplate in privacy the experience of loss of half of his body.

She returned after a while with a Sikh. Hobday had met the fellow at his own cocktail parties and recalled that he was notable for something – cricket? hockey? He was apparently a doctor, too, for he peered with a lighted magnifying glass into the backs of Hobday's eyes. He did it with as little regard for the living flesh as an art dealer, minutely examining a painting, would think of the atoms that spun inside the paint to make the colour rose, or black. It didn't matter to Hobday. He didn't care that the doctor treated him like this, he was merely interested that it should be so.

After some moments of professional absorption it seemed to occur to the doctor that Hobday was organic, even human, for he smiled down at him. 'You must rest,' he said. 'Please, Excellency, do not attempt to speak. We cannot understand you. It is not such a bad stroke that you have had. In a few weeks . . . '

He moved back from the bed and his smile changed to an expression of false cheerfulness. 'Excellency, it will make you jolly to learn that the King intends to honour you as Tan Sri. My cousin has a Malay friend who works in the Palace.'

He had already said too much; had, in a good cause,

broken a secret, as adults will reveal the nature of a Christmas present a week too early, to calm a child. He ended limply, 'It will be announced soon in the newspapers.'

So, I am respectable again, the Malaysians will make me a Lord. No doubt the Australian government will give me something too, in the Queen's Birthday honours. And when I get home there will be invitations to Government House once more. Hilary and Minou will be pleased. They're both vulnerable to snobbery. Each in her own way is susceptible to offers of group belonging, group admiration, to that sensation which people so often confuse with the words 'loved' and 'loving'.

He'd had that frailty, too, although he'd denied it often enough, even to himself. But it had been there always. Delight in belonging to the virile elite, delight in being remarked upon enviously – or even with disapproval – as a man who could demand the body of a girl his daughter's age. Little Elizabeth. Cold kisses. What power he had felt in owning Minou! The tricks she'd do for him, eager as a circus poodle, while he held the whip.

Love, he'd called it. The desire and pursuit. The idea of it now presented itself to him as he lay still as a gaudy silken bundle. A package of sorts, wrapped in metres and metres of aged silk. In the middle, he knew, was the mystery that had always evaded him, and all he had to do now was quietly, steadily unwrap it. His fingers moved voluptuously. But the mystery was very small and thickly imprisoned, and with only one arm he soon felt too tired to continue.

25

Richard, whose experience in asserting his will upon telephonists was so well developed that it could be called an art, woke Judith at seven – eleven o'clock Canberra time, as he told her. He had wasted two hours of the morning already in trying to find out where she was.

Yes, David had recovered. It was a very mild case of the mumps and Sebastian had not been infected. And how was she? On the morning radio news programme she had sounded tired, Richard thought. She would be glad to know that there was an excellent front-page display of her story on Lady Hobday's drowning.

'Did she really chuck herself in the drink to create a diversion, so that the villagers on shore wouldn't attack the refugees?' His tone was incredulous.

'I didn't say that in so many words, did I?' Judith replied insolently.

Richard refused to take offence. 'You implied it pretty strongly,' he said, and laughed. 'It coloured the piece no end, too, as you no doubt meant it to.'

I'm the one who knows why Minou killed herself, Judith thought. And that's enough for her and me.

Richard was racing on about how he'd arranged already for a question about the boat people scandal in the House, when it resumed sitting next week. The brouhaha would continue for at least a fortnight, he thought. But to more immediate matters.

Had she, he inquired – this reasonable and concerned old friend – had she realized that, the Malaysian legal system being based on the British, it would require that she give evidence before a coroner? And that she must therefore be circumspect in any statements she might make on local radio and television concerning the drowning of Lady H? The police hadn't warned her that the matter was now *sub judice*? Christ Almighty! He'd look up the relevant section immediately.

And as she waited, hearing Richard say, 'Gloria, my sweet, the *red* file, r-e-d,' she could visualize his face, his small eyes closed in forebearance, a smile of patience playing on his lips. She thought, I *know* you. I know the smell of your breath, distinct from any other, when you've been drinking beer, and how the rasp of your beard hurts my face if you want sex in the morning and how, lying there, I feel like a piece of raw schnitzel being hammered with a mallet.

Richard had the lawyer's trick of being able to maintain a desultory conversation while he was running his eye over a document, and muttered, while he was doing it now, 'Here we are. How did you get on with Minette, by the way?'

I loved her, Judith thought. 'Quite well,' she replied.

'Was she useful. Before she went for her swim?'

'Oh, yes.' She showed me what my life is, how futile. She had the sudden courage of despair – and I've got none. I'll just go on. She knew what a cheat her life was, and theirs too – those exiles who've got no hope. What good is a new home, a new country, when you are ripped out of your real setting, *déracinée*? 'A comfortable existence.' She'd said it with such hopelessness.

'She illuminated the situation for me,' Judith said.

'You came across well, on radio. Sounded *caring* – that's

the current word. There's a lot of what passes for uneasy conscience here, I think.'

Judith thought, For a while. The only people who really care are the ones who bond with the refugees, people like Ralph and Minou. For the rest of us, they're just a passing disturbance. 'They'll get over it.'

'Quite so. Meanwhile, do you think you could debate Australia's miserly refugee policy with the Minister for Immigration? On TV?'

'I think so. But I'm interested to hear that you now find the policy *miserly*, Richard. What about jobs for Aussies first?'

There was a break on their line for a few moments, their words becoming distorted. Both stopped talking. Then Richard said, 'By the way, I've won pre-selection'.

'Richard!'

He laughed modestly. 'Come 1983 I'll be Minister for . . . oh, I could take Immigration. Or Housing. One of the junior portfolios to start with.'

'No!' Suddenly she was not in an Asian hotel room with an arrow on its ceiling pointing to Mecca, but back there in the thick of it. Jesus! She could write the policy herself. 'No! Take Women's Affairs! And Aborigines! Think how much good you could do for . . . '

The line tangled again, then Richard's voice abruptly boomed, 'The boys are *very* fond of Mrs Jenkins. Our housekeeper. I've converted the end bedroom and the study into an apartment for her. She's a *splendid* cook. Of course, I'll be applying for you to contribute to her salary, as your share of the children's maintenance.'

'Is that so?' Judith said.

'Well, of course, Judith. You don't imagine that I'm ignorant of the Family Law Act, do you? It will be all perfectly civilized.'

'How *dare* you get a housekeeper and give her my study!'

280

She was shouting, but it was into a vacuum. At its perimeter an Australian telephone operator asked, 'Do you wish to extend, sir?' Evidently he did not, for after a while a voice broke in saying, 'Kuala Trengganu? Your Canberra party has disconnected. I have a call from Sydney for you.'

'Put it through,' Judith ordered. The handpiece gave out fizzes and clicks. She stared hard into its whorls of little holes, thinking, *At last.* Battle has been declared. The kids! *And* the house ... He thinks he's going to get the kids *and* the house. '*Come* on,' she said to the telephone.

She felt that surge of well-being which arrives, from the blue, after a long illness.

The Coroner's Court was housed, along with other courts of petty sessions, in a complex of government office buildings on a hill on the outskirts of Kuala Lumpur. The road there ran through an abandoned rubber estate where the trees had grown lanky and were choked with undergrowth. The inquest was to begin at 10 am and would be brief, Judith had been told. Minou's body had not been found, in spite of a three-day search and a reward offered to the villagers of the East Coast. Now, five days later, the predations of fish, shrimps, octopus (Turtles? Some, Judith knew, fed not on seagrass but on flesh), made the thought of her recovery unbearable.

Especially for Hobday, the person most capable of identifying her. He was already saying a few words, apparently, and in another month would be strong enough to be flown home. They'd told him, at last, that Minou was dead and he'd had no relapse.

Judith sighed, looking out of the window of Sancha's pale-blue Mercedes as it climbed the road through the pitiless fecundity of the passing landscape. When the trees died the undergrowth and vines luxuriated, while the force that drove both in everlasting competition remained indifferent as to

281

which side triumphed. The life force itself was the only thing that mattered . . . Judith had been talking to Kanan again; they had avoided speaking of Minou, except once, when he had said, as if it explained everything, 'She had descendants'. They had run into each other constantly in the past week – at Sancha's, where Judith was now staying; at the hospital, visiting Ralph; at The Dog, where Judith and Sancha went for a sundowner during 'crisis hour' (the time when the servants fed the Hamilton children) and where they were entertained lavishly by a hilarious young businessman called Johnny Kok.

She and Kanan had become reconciled. She supposed that was the word for the feeling of regret and shame glossed over with off-hand familiarities and strained chat that people used when they had been sexually infatuated without the benefit of companionship first, and then had ruptured the sexual bond. He was intelligent, she'd discovered, but he employed that infuriating paradoxical logic of the East which, after a while, brought any conversation with him to embarrassed silence. He could, for instance, make a lucid case for acknowledging classical Hindu thought as the precursor of recent discoveries in radio astronomy: the expanding universe which, in due course, would contract to infinitesimal smallness once more, then re-expand. Brahma, Vishnu, then Siva dancing the cosmos to atoms.

'It may be a brilliant insight, but you *can't* base your life on it. It's not practical,' she'd objected, and he'd smiled wistfully. She'd missed the point, he thought, and was doomed to drift along like a rudderless boat, moved by the currents, which she would call 'the realities'. Perhaps in another life she would have more wisdom.

Wordlessly, they agreed upon one point: they had had a lucky escape from each other.

The Coroner's Court was a chilled room in a wood-and-fibro barracks-style building. Its wooden verandah was

282

crowded with Indian litigants. They stopped arguing to stare at the unexpected sight of white women intruding here.

A fat Sikh in a maroon turban barred their way. 'Madam, I know you. Where are we meeting before, please?'

'You've seen me on television,' she replied. She'd become used to the question in the last few days.

The Sikh laughed, as if he had outwitted her, and wagged a finger. 'One autograph, please.' She signed the tatty piece of paper he produced – it looked like his driving licence – and he turned to beam victoriously at another Sikh, obviously his legal opponent.

She was in the witness box ten minutes.

The Coroner, a tired, drawn-looking Indian, asked her only to confirm her statement to the Kuala Trengganu police. When she was through she sat with Sancha on the benches at the back of the court to hear Dr Kanan Subramaniam's evidence. The tall black man who stepped into the box was a stranger to her – good-looking, even beautiful, with his magnificent eyes and his blue-black mane of perfumed hair, but somehow he had changed. He no longer looked as if he had just stepped down to earth in an envelope of starlight.

'Let's piss off,' Judith muttered to Sancha. Mr Hussein had assured Judith that accidental drowning was the only possible finding, that there was not enough evidence to support a verdict of suicide. She gave Kanan a friendly wave as she left the court with a bow to the Coroner. The bow was a reflex action that surprised and amused her as she did it – it was more than ten years since she had worked as a law court reporter. Sancha did not know that she was meant to bow towards the Bench. The Coroner gave her a dirty look as she passed him, languid but upright.

There had been five airconditioners going full-blast in the courtroom; outside it was repulsively hot and humid.

283

Litigious Indians were still crowding the duck-boards, giving off odours of curry, tuberose and BO.

'I'll be glad to get on that plane this afternoon,' Judith said with feeling.

Sancha sighed. 'Half your luck.'

It would be another fortnight before the Hamilton family returned to Australia where, after convalescence, Ralph would join 'one of Daddy's companies'. Sancha was not certain which one, or in what capacity. Ralph was jolly lucky that Daddy had been so understanding – jobs didn't grow on trees, these days. There would be no charges of impropriety against Ralph. His resignation from the Department of Immigration had been accepted, on the spot, as soon as he signed the papers delivered to him in hospital. Already the Hamilton front doorstep was littered with the sandals of dour Malays who squatted by the hour in the Hamilton living room, stitching rattan matting around the rolled-up, gorgeous rugs and the rosewood tables and cabinets. They would disappear from work at noon and sunset when, very faintly, you could hear the muezzins calling from the small mosques you rarely saw in KL but knew about because of this far-away, high-pitched singing. 'Have you noticed the times when Muslims pray?' Kanan had asked Judith and when she'd shaken her head had said, 'The prayer hours mark the passages of the sun.' 'So it's sunworship?' she'd asked and he had shrugged: 'It seems like that.'

Sancha and Judith strolled back to the powder-blue Mercedes. Sancha turned on its airconditioning and they sat for several minutes looking out over the lush green city, waiting for the cold blast to dry their perspiration. Then they fastened their seat-belts and as their heads bent together, hands searching for the locking devices, Sancha murmured, 'How can I ever have self-respect again?' and they both knew that her real question was, 'How can I ever respect Ralph again?'

For women of their age and upbringing, a husband had to be a superior, a provider and protector, or he was nothing at all. They were too conditioned in the ways of male dominance to tolerate equality. Off his pedestal of masculinity, he became not an equal but an object of scorn. Like Kanan, when he would not help save Minou. Like Richard, when he was a pompous nobody and *she* was the centre of attention. It was irrational, but no less real for that.

'Ralph will do well in business – he's *very* clever,' Judith said. It was the sort of excuse she had made to herself for Richard: 'Richard is an inspired cook. We'd be living on chops and tinned pineapple if it weren't for him,' and 'I can't control the children – they only listen to Richard.' She had encouraged him to bully her, but then had fought back, tooth and nail. *That* was a paradox. It was too hot to think. And dwelling on it disturbed the alert calm, the well-being, that had overtaken her after Richard's telephone call to Trengganu, when the war had really begun. Mrs Jenkins, indeed! Judith had created an uproar of urgency in the Tuggeranong Primary School by telephoning David there. Mrs Jenkins pretended not to be angry, when she was, David said. And she wouldn't let him and Sebastian watch *Doctor Who*. 'Is she nicer than me?' Judith had asked and he'd replied, 'Aw, Mum. She's really old and ugly – forty years old.' Her blood had thumped with gratitude to him.

'Yes, he *is* clever,' Sancha was saying. 'And he can pick up languages just like that. Johnny says Ralph's Cantonese is better than his.'

There was an hour's delay at Singapore airport. Chinese shopgirls, infinitely patient, helped Judith choose computerized models of R2-D2, C-3PO, Luke Skywalker, Darth Vader, Princess Leia Organa – the whole team. In a Dior shop she saw a pair of evening sandals, watermelon pink, with a ribbon of gold for heels. The price was so outrageous it was almost funny. She bought them.

'One needs an occasional self-indulgence,' the English matron alongside Judith at the counter confided.

Then, in the transit lounge, Judith saw Minou. She was standing in profile with a group of Chinese men and women, wearing her battlejacket and the black forage cap with green Hermes wings.

Someone opened a door and Judith saw the hot breeze that blew in sweep away the glittering shops and the people. They vanished, and she was standing on the threshold of the world, a vast plain of grassland. In the far distance a figure was walking – strolling – towards her; a figure as flat as a piece of plywood.

Then the door was shut. Minou turned round and faced Judith. She was a full-blood Chinese, probably local. The wings on the hat were blue, not green.

Judith huffed out a breath and thought, That *could* have been one of your vile practical jokes. To pretend to drown, then turn up in Singapore.

And what if it really had been Minou, alive?

With an effort of mind as prodigious as the effort of body she had made when she had flung the Indian off her in the car, she flung the idea from her. It went spinning away, out into some black space from which it would never return.

On the plane a hostess came undulating down the aisle towards her. The pilot would be happy if Ms Wilkes would join him in the cockpit soon after take-off. 'The view is better from up there, of course,' the hostess said. Then, 'I saw you on television during my break in Perth. Isn't it awful, really, about those boat people? I mean, it makes you think . . .'

'Oh, yes,' Judith said. 'The tragedy is that it's such a vast problem. There has to be a meeting between heads of state – ours, Vietnam's, China's.' The hostess assumed a mesmerized look of incomprehension.

286

Judith decided to save her fire-power for the Jumbo captain. She had noticed, as she had boarded, before moving down to the economy section, that there seemed to be quite a few empty seats in first class. But she would allow the pilot his half an hour with a celebrity before she dropped her hint.